The Legendary Tauran'creima

Star Beings of the Universe

By
Johnny Littlejohn Jr.

Printed in the United States of America

Library of Congress Control Number: 2020907229
ISBN: Softcover   978-1-64908-127-8
         Hardback   978-1-64908-340-1
         eBook   978-1-64908-126-1

Republished by: PageTurner Press and Media LLC
Publication Date: 09/16/2020

To order copies of this book, contact:

PageTurner Press and Media
Phone: 1-888-447-9651
order@pageturner.us
www.pageturner.us

The Legend Among
a Mythical Race

For eons, across the cosmos, there has been speculation of a star unlike any other, a star very unique. Yet, countless beings do not believe in such things.

However, all those disbeliefs are put to rest when strange events start occurring. A mysterious character emerges, its intentions cryptic.

Yet, something about this individual gradually eases the tension among those doubtful, as the powerful light about the entity makes its motive, its purpose, known to all.

Author Biography

Johnny T. Littlejohn Jr. resides in the state of Maryland, where he has lived most of his life. He decided to write to the nations to coax enlightenment to them through fantasy.

He imagines that by doing so, many communities will notice that they have the capacity to observe pass what they always assume to see – reading between the lines – so to speak.

Inspiration is one of his keywords in defining that growth always starts in the bounds of the spirit, not the exterior, resulting in the notion that the general public can surpass their primitive ways of thinking if they merely cease their materialistic and asinine ways of living.

He does not desire a perfect world. However, he deems humanity can be in a much better condition if mankind only transcend.

Johnny has always been a daydreamer, a visionary. He believes that there is more to life than what the populace presumes.

He does not live a generic existence. He finds it utterly bothersome. He creates various ways to keep his life very creative while exceeding the corrupt physical world, which he feels he accomplished a long time ago.

Johnny has always been fiercely independent. He chooses to do tasks alone versus with a group. He perceives that his willpower, passion, wisdom, and countless talents will get what he wants completed the way he deems suitable.

Johnny has pledged celibacy. He vows to never lose his virginity to anyone. He deems worldly matters troublesome. He is accustomed to his spiritual, isolated lifestyle. He prefers to do what he wants in a matchless fashion.

Johnny wishes to leave his stories – The Legendary Tauran'creima – for the people that will learn the true meaning behind the series and perhaps incorporate it into their lives somehow. He wants to have a lasting impression on them whenever he passes on.

He is a firm believer in that if you do not stand for something intensely positive, fuse it into your soul, and apply it in your everyday activities, then you will most certainly yield to anything unworthy.

Johnny has made exercise a regular part of his life, including martial arts. Though he does not know any particular fighting techniques at this time, he takes the initiative to learn the basic principles.

Johnny deliberates that maintaining a healthy body – internal and external – is key to living a happy life. He reasons that by refraining from unnecessary foods and repugnant actions shows that you care about yourself, your body, and your soul.

Nature and animals are one of his cherished aspects. He often goes to several parks during his spare time, taking treats with him to feed the squirrels and birds.

He holds many ecological places around the world in high esteem. He considers these locations "Sacred" because they are "Natural." The mystic quality of the elemental environments is what draws him toward it. He says that nature is unbiased. It accepts all as they are.

Ancient architecture is another one of his interest. He asserts that these ruins are fascinating because they possess excessive untold history.

Johnny has received many awards from the elementary, middle, and high school that he attended. His awards are as follows: Perfect Attendance, Honor Roll, Spelling Bee, and Most Improved Student.

He takes great pride in his achievements. He regards that pushing beyond your limits will always prove fruitful.

May 11, 1990 is Johnny's birthday. He has always been fascinated with astrology and science of numerous fields. Taurus the Bull, his astrological symbol, holds significant meaning to him.

To Johnny, Taurus represents valor, perceptiveness, passion, uniqueness, and tenacity – basically an icon that can withstand many of life's onslaughts – if the individual is willing to give themselves time to develop spiritually.

Being a diverse individual, Johnny sometimes cannot help but to piece random ideas together and create something innovative.

Video game instrumental music has enthralled Johnny for years. His arrays of electronic game influential compositions are Super Mario and various other melodies. Super Mario is the only character he has admired since childhood.

Super Mario and Tetsu'reidza Courage are his heroes. To him, they are the epitome of bravery.

Today, Johnny continues to live his life the way he chooses. He recommends that everyone do the same, for as long as you remain on the right path and outshine the wretched ways of this world, you should not have any regrets.

*"I am neither man, beast,
or god. I am me."*

 Chapter 1

The Transcendent One Cometh

There are two kinds of star beings throughout the universe: the *Melhounas*, who are the benevolent star beings.

Then, there are the *Azagnorpors*, who are the malevolent star beings.

Only those of very exceptional skill could defeat a star being.

Anyone of a lesser caliber could never hope to defeat them.

There was a legend of a green Sacred Star.

It was stated that it would one day appear and outshine all other star beings.

1

Countless people and species are doubtful of such an occurrence, as it was stated that such a phenomenon was impossible.

Star beings are created by the universe.

This process is extremely mystical, as there is no definite way of knowing how star beings emerge, let alone obtain their formidable powers.

Staraidus is the power each star being possesses.

Star beings do not possess a skeletal system or internal organs, nor anything that would hinder them.

However, they do possess *Livalaquia*, which is the sparkling silver life liquid that resides inside of them.

Star beings are very powerful spiritual entities.

They are energy personified.

Each star being has their respective constellation, which represents them.
Every star being has their own uniqueness and abilities.

The constellation that most reveres, the one that illuminates the night sky, is *Tauran'creima*.

This constellation is also known as the Celestial Bull.

An otherworldly aspect such as this has enthralled many for incalculable generations.

Its wonderful green brilliance often has a lasting impression on those who witness it.

As mentioned, green stars are rare, if not possible.

Yet, Tauran'creima defies such logic.

Though other constellations possess their respective color, green is the only one considered very exceptional among stars.

Flowerensia, Goddess of Life, is the creator of planet *Venusia* and *Velmelkia* Kingdom.

Her primary dominion is the *Floreopia* Continent.

The *Ovele'mulus*, which is Flowerensia's favorite flower, is the kingdom's symbol.

It is a flower that has iridescent petals.

It represents eternal virtue and prosperity.

Flowerensia knew of this special star.

She would observe it from afar, beholding its magnificence.

It was matchless.

"Great things come to those who exude patience," Flowerensia always said.

Flowerensia has long black hair with bangs, short tresses, flawless fair skin, a gorgeous visage, dark eyebrows, conspicuous dark eyelashes, iridescent green eyes, and a curvaceous figure.

Flowerensia often wore extravagant robes adorned with flower designs.

She also wore knee-high black sandals with an Ovele'mulus attached to the respective strap of each sandal.

She loved how the petals felt on her beautiful toes, as well as the overall appearance.

One day, during the afternoon, a shooting star pierced the exosphere of planet Venusia.

It was headed toward *Hydena* Mountain, which was of *Fereforei* Snowland, a frigid yet beautiful region north of Velmelkia Kingdom.

The shooting star's speed was incomprehensible.

Upon landing on Hydena Mountain, it shook the foundation violently, which caused an avalanche.

Multiple green shockwaves – the *Sacroncai* Shockwaves – which held green sparkles, flew from the wondrous star.

The Sacroncai Shockwaves extended beyond the horizon.

The otherworldly green light shrouding the beautiful star faded in and out of existence at intermediate intervals.

Flowerensia witnessed the spectacular occurrence from her temple.

She immediately went to investigate.

Upon arriving, Flowerensia observed the star.

She felt unimaginable power from it.

Interesting. Could this be the fabled star of legend?

The star gradually morphed into a humanoid.

Once concluded, it was that of a man.

However, the luminous green light was ever present, thus making his identity a mystery.

The entity was in a knelt position.

His left forearm rested on his thigh, and his head was bowed.

When the star being became aware, he slowly rose.

When the man noted Flowerensia, he merely stood there.

"Greetings," Flowerensia spoke. "I take it you're the *Transcendent One?*"

"My name is Courage. Tetsu'reidza Tauran'creima Courage Astrial'len."

His husky, otherworldly voice echoed throughout Hydena Mountain.

"Tauran'creima is my constellation. Pleased to make your acquaintance."

"Likewise. I've been observing your star for some time. It's the most notable of the lot."

"Truly? Surely you jest?"

"Nope. Not in the least. It's the brightest, most serene of the bunch. I'm not one to lie, dear Courage. What I say will always be true."

Though she could not see his face, she sensed his skepticism.

"I understand if you're doubtful of my statement. However, as the ruler of this planet and this kingdom, it is not in my best interest to misinform. Especially to you… Chosen…"

"You rule this kingdom? And… did you just refer to me as… Chosen…?"

"Indeed. It was preordained that we should meet. You've a bright future."

"What? Wait… Who are you? And what exactly are you talking about, lady?"

"If you would allow me to explain, I'll tell you all you need to know. Yet, care to join me at my temple? Though the cold doesn't bother either of us, I *hardly* consider this setting ideal for such a message."

She extended her delicate hand toward him, welcoming him to take it.

5

It was difficult for him to decipher whether she was flirting with him or being overly friendly.

"Really, lady? You want me to take your hand?"

"I know we're in a *cold* region, Courage. But surely you aren't going to be this *frigid* toward me?"

These puns of hers... Gracious...

"...I don't know who you are. In fact, I don't even know your name."

"The name's Flowerensia. *Goddess* Flowerensia. And... would it kill ya to lighten up? Surely you sense no harmful aura about me?"

"Well... Flowerensia. I would like to become accustomed to you before being excessively extrovert."

"Damn... I tried. Maybe next time..."

To compensate for his unwillingness to hold her hand, she merely stood next to him.

Fortunately, he did not protest.

Flowerensia teleported with Courage from Hydena Mountain.

Flowerensia and Courage emerged within the library of her temple.

Flowerensia sauntered toward the window.

She gazed upon her superlative garden.

A record player sat upon a desk near the library's entrance.

Very soothing music emanated from its horn.

Courage approached the record player.

He placed his hands upon the desk.

He closed his eyes.

He listened to the pleasing melody intently.

The echo of the piano soothed him.

Subconsciously, he tapped his fingers to the rhythm.

Even before the next note played.

Flowerensia looked over her shoulder.

She noted Courage's interest.

"It seems you have an ear for music…"

"Yes. Truly. It's very… uplifting. Inspiring…"

"The name of this tune is called 'Destiny'. Perhaps after I tell you what needs to be said, you'll listen to more of my melodies?"

"That would be wonderful."

"Lovely!"

Flowerensia looked toward her garden once more.

"Courage… you have a great destiny ahead…"

"A great destiny? Wait… this isn't more of your puns, now is it?"

"I'm afraid not."

"Then what gives? I landed on this planet by happenstance. And now you're telling me I have a great mission? What the hell is going on?"

"Calm down, love. I don't mean to be so sudden. However, I'd rather tell you certain things now than at the moment of truth."

"Fine then."

"Courage… I've already told you your star is the most splendid of the lot. You hold many admirable aspects that not even the gods can match. You're beyond comprehension.

"Throughout the ages, there has been bloodshed among the star beings and the deities of *Rhol'heima*, the heavenly kingdom. Personally, the star beings are innocent; certain deities other than myself believe that star beings are a threat.

"Yet, I believe it is mere jealousy that the deities aren't the only powerful beings in the universe. It's pathetic, honestly.

"To make matters worse, the malevolent beings of *Relmi'shira*, the hellish kingdom, have become very savage over the years. Though they've always been a bunch of ne'er-do-wells, they've never been this resilient.

"They have made numerous attempts to conquer *Zeinhailurein*, the spirit world, to force those that dwell there to join their chaotic cause. Not to mention cause mayhem on different planets to attempt world conquest.

"I think… I think this is an omen. An omen of something inconceivable. It's only logical."

The more Flowerensia spoke of this experience, the more uneasy she became.

Flowerensia was a very friendly goddess.

However, her intuition was usually very accurate.

The tales she accounted are not very common, as once villains were dealt with accordingly, that was the last they ever heard of them.

Unless certain individuals were very potent, or had strong ties to an influential organization, continuous assaults on planets were unheard of.

"Flowerensia… were these events really that dire?"

Flowerensia turned toward Courage.

Her once bright expression was now solemn.

Yet, her eyes, very subtly, held apprehension.

She wanted to conceal her fear.

The likes of a cosmic disaster was something Flowerensia shunned.

She catered to all forms of life, and to witness the conclusion of it all by an unfavorable circumstance scared her.

Yet, who or what, which would be responsible for such an unprecedented disorder, is the true reason for Flowerensia's distress.

She refused to imagine what the being behind such chaos would look like.

If that was even plausible.

Flowerensia rejected such notions.

"Yes. These circumstances grow dreadful as time proceeds. Now... I need you to look at me. I mean, *really* look at me. Remove your bright green cloak and show me who you are."

As instructed, Courage gradually unveiled himself to Flowerensia.

Once the resplendent green light ebbed, she gazed upon the legendary man all know as the constellation Tauran'creima.

Courage possesses short dark hair, fair skin, dark eyebrows, glistening yet fierce green eyes, and a muscular build.

He wore a red headband that has extended tails.

The headband has a silver image of Tauran'creima in the center.

The headband also has silver pyramid studs along either side of the tails.

He wore black sacred armor – the Sacroncai Uniform.

The Sacroncai Uniform has intricate silver designs – the *Vesorai* – on the entirety of the uniform.

These markings are known as Constellation Ascension Glyphs.

The attire has shoulder armor, as well as a short black cape that has the Glyph of Tauran'creima.

Courage wore a black bodysuit underneath the Sacroncai Uniform.

He also wore black forearm guards, a silver square plate on each knuckle, and stylish black boots that have five silver rectangular plates on either side.

The sole of the boots are silver as well.

Flowerensia smiled.

Her cheeks were flushed.

"My… the legends surely do you no justice…"

"Really now?"

"Nope. And all of what I said is true. If you're still skeptical, you'll see in due time."

"So what do I do now? Surely there's something of interest in your kingdom?"

"Yes. Let's take this one step at a time. Perhaps a tour is in order. Sightseeing, if you will."

"No one knows who I am other than you?"

"Don't tell me you're nervous, love?"

"What? No. Not by any means. It's merely… I think it may be a great idea for me to keep a low profile. You know, being this alleged 'Transcendent One'."

"There's nothing "alleged" about you. You're the real deal. And come on, you think it's common for a goddess to be among her people?"

"Uh, no. Not really."

"Precisely. So you have nothing to worry about. Other star beings may sense your exceptional nature and immediately know who you are."

"Great..."

"You make it sound like it's a bad thing, dear. Others would kill to be in your shoes. I think you'll come around eventually, dear. Things are still quite new to you."

Courage placed his fist on his hip.

He looked away.

"No it ain't..."

"Well damn. Edgy much?"

Flowerensia laughed.

"Courage. If you need me, I'll be in my garden. And by the way, your entire name again is... Tetsu'rei*ga* Tauran'creima Astri*hall*in. Right...?"

Courage frowned.

"You're butchering my name, lady. It's Tetsu'reid*za*-Tauran'creima-Courage-Astria*l*len. Understand?"

Flowerensia blushed.

"I do now. Such an astounding name."

"Yeah... thanks..."

"Come see me soon, love."

Flowerensia chuckled.

She teleported from the library.

After Courage enjoyed various melodies and read numerous stories, he decided to go see Flowerensia.

Once Courage arrived at Flowerensia's garden, he noted her standing in the center among her congregate of flowers.

Her back was to him.

She was looking toward the heavens.

The gentle breeze blew through her hair.

A group of small birds, each with its own color, landed at the feet of Courage.

One bird laid on his right shoulder.

And another one rested on his left shoulder.

All of them chirped cheerfully.

"Hey, Mister," a green bird spoke. "How ya doing?"

Star beings had the ability to understand animals.

"Great. Just trying to get down to the bottom of things. Nevertheless... Flowerensia?"

"A pleasure to finally have you out here with me..."

"Uh, yeah... you asked me to come out here..."

Flowerensia giggled.

"Yes. Of course I did…"

Why the hell is she so strange…?

"Regardless, nice garden. But can we get to the point?"

"Hmm… blunt much?"

"Very."

"I like you…"

"What? Why? What's with you?"

"You say what's on your mind. You say how you feel. Without beating around the bush. As far as I'm concerned, you're the pinnacle of manhood."

"Oh come now. You give me excessive praise. For no reason. We just met, for heaven's sake. Do I truly stand out *that* much?"

"Very."

"…Clever."

"As I mentioned before, if you don't believe me now, you will when the pieces start falling into place, meaning you'll see for yourself eventually."

"Uh huh. Yet, what other *destinies* do I have? Or are you just speaking nonsense because you find me intriguing?"

Flowerensia turned to Courage.

"You're familiar with Melhounas and Azagnorpors, yes?"

"Indeed. I happen to be a Melhouna. Fortunately."

"The divine community reflects the same aspects. There are good deities as well as bad ones. Yet, the one that's the most notorious of the lot is… Deathelena, Goddess of Darkness."

"Judging by the name, she seems like a real bitch."

Flowerensia laughed.

"My word! Such language for a *sacred* being!"

"I speak my mind. I'm not one to sugarcoat anything. And let me guess, she's the one that's causing so much strife. Right?"

"Yes. You're correct."

"Figures. Let me take a crack at it again. This Deathelena character led countless onslaughts on the most valued locations for resources. Most likely acting out of greed.

"You, and perhaps many others, sealed this woman. Yet, she persistently breaks free, and attempts the same, monotonous plans. Am I right again?"

Flowerensia gasped.

"Well damn… you pretty much beat me to it. It's like you witnessed the whole thing."

"No. It's just common sense. Some people like this individual you mentioned can't be too bright if they haven't succeeded in the number of times they tried. Pathetic."

"I wouldn't underestimate her. She may not have achieved her goals, but she's still a force. Trust me…"

"Will I encounter this Dark Goddess?"

"Indeed. As potent and exceptional as you are, you're bound to attract attention. In fact, I wouldn't be surprised if you already have, you know, due to the sheer intensity of your landing, as well as the incredible power emanating from you…"

"If I stay, I'll only cause this kingdom trouble. Do you think I should leave?"

Flowerensia scowled.

"No. Stay. Trouble has a habit of arising at the most inopportune moments. Don't blame yourself for what has already been happening since time began."

"I'm just saying. You seem… really nice. I'd hate to bring this place to ruin because of this Dark Goddess, or any other being who has nothing better to do with their time."

"Hmm… you're sweet. And edgy. A bittersweet combination, love…"

"Oh shut up…"

Flowerensia blushed.

"I really like teasing you…"

"Uh, yeah. I can tell…"

"How so?"

"It matters not. It's not smart taunting a bull. A celestial one at that."

"Oh right!"

Flowerensia softly struck her palm with her fist.

"I wouldn't want those horns up my ass, as I'm sure they'll hurt!"

Flowerensia laughed.

"On the other hand, I wouldn't mind you hurting me… in *that* way!"

"Gracious…"

Courage placed his hand over his face.

Flowerensia sauntered toward Courage.

Upon nearing him, she stood inches from him.

Her blush deepened.

"Sorry, dear. You set me up for those puns. You always do."

Look at me, acting like a horny school girl. This guy's the real deal. Yet, he's skeptical of his worth. Talk about modest. He seems rough around the edges, yet he has that noble quality. So remarkable.

"So, when ya wanna go sightseeing, dear?"

"I have no idea. Maybe I'm better off keeping a low profile for right now."

"Hmm… seems to me like you're nervous, love. That doesn't seem like you at all."

"Uh, hello? I'm not nervous. You're not being held to a high standard like I am. "Transcendent One" is what you called me."

"Perhaps in another time and place, things could've been different. Yet, this is what it is, dear. I'm so sorry, Courage."

"Forget about it. If what you're stating is true, then it is what it is. I just wasn't expecting this."

Suddenly, a malevolent laughter echoed throughout Flowerensia's garden.

Flowerensia and Courage attempted to locate the source, but to no avail.

"My, my!" the unknown individual stated. "A lovers' quarrel. How amusing."

"Place not your faith in mankind, but within your own power."

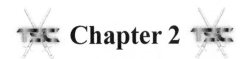 **Chapter 2**

Deathelena, Goddess of Darkness

"Say that to my face and we'll see if it's so funny," Courage retorted.

Flowerensia laughed.

"You're such a savage, Courage..."

"It can't be helped. I don't like idiots like this poor excuse for a comedian."

"Well... aren't you feisty?" the character stated. "Though you are *somewhat* intriguing, I'm not here for you. Flowerensia and I have unfinished business."

"And as you can see, she has a guest," Courage countered. "So you'll have to reschedule your appointment."

"You've a sharp tongue..." the entity said. "Let's see what all the fuss is about with you..."

Suddenly, purple and black smoke emerged.

The *Groimeida* Smog is smoke that conceals an entity's presence.

It also poisons those who enter its vicinity.

When the Groimeida Smog dissipated, a female figure stood upon dead flowers.

She grinned.

At the female's presence, the birds flew away.

They sensed danger from her.

"Who the hell are you?" Courage questioned.

"The nightmare of everyone. I'm the thing that haunts the subconscious of those that conceal fear. I am fear, the personification of darkness."

"That's Deathelena, Courage," Flowerensia informed. "Why the hell she would appear now of all times is beyond me."

"Fool... I just happen to be passing through when I felt a grand power in the distance. And to think it came from this wretch is inconceivable. I was about to investigate, but you beat me to the punch."

Dark Goddess Deathelena has long black hair with bangs, short tresses, flawless fair skin, an excessively appealing countenance, dark eyebrows, red eyeshadow, prominent dark eyelashes, penetrating purple eyes, purple lipstick, and a curvaceous stature.

She wore her black uniform – the *Hychineirian* Uniform.

The Hychineirian Uniform has incandescent lavender symbols – the Hychineirian Runes – on the entirety of the uniform.

The uniform has shoulder armor, dark gloves, and a long black cape.

The cape also has the Glyph of *Scorpreikia*, the Dark Scorpion.

She wore knee-high black boots.

She also wore dangling ruby *Estrohas* Earrings, which are magical earrings that would detonate whenever Deathelena threw them.

However, they would instantly regenerate on her ears once more.

Killoseigas, which are celestial flames, and *Killoswi'is*, which are celestial sparks, would permeate the vicinity for some time and burn whomever nears it.

Killoswi'is are red, blue, and purple.

She can also charge her *Divionagai*, which is the power all deities possess, with the Estrohas Earrings.

She can increase her Dark Divionagai to insane levels.

Overall, Deathelena is the strongest among the deities.

Deathelena rules the dreadful *Hychineira* Kingdom of planet *Gwempteya*, the celestial body she governs.

She also rules Relmi'shira.

Planet Gwempteya is surrounded diagonally by a single gaseous ring – the *Parlonias*.

Deathelena believes she is beyond everyone, especially those of Rhol'heima.

She desires all beings to know of her boundless malignant power.

She wants those who are strong to join her formidable Hychineirian and *Relmi'shirian* Army.

If there is an opportunity to gain power, Deathelena will cease at nothing until she claims what she seeks.

She is not beyond sacrificing those who assist her to meet her ambitions.

However, those close to her will be spared.

Deathelena does foul deeds to expand her influence.

She wants to give her nation, the *E'valgeileihon* Continent, as well as the entirety of planet Gwempteya, what others forbid.

Yet, her subordinates must pledge eternal servitude, lest their very being be eradicated from existence.

Regardless, Deathelena felt as if she knew Courage.

Yet, it was farfetched.

Because she never met him.

She delved into her mind.

She attempted to decipher where, and when, she could have met him.

Courage was ready to fight her.

"I can be a wretch. I can be whatever the hell you want. But, at least I'm not a bitch. Put that in your pipe and smoke it, you fucking failure."

Flowerensia covered her mouth.

She was shocked.

But she also tried not to laugh.

"…Hmph… damn you," Deathelena said. "I'm going to enjoy cutting out your tongue, you sacred bastard…"

"Good luck with that," Courage stated. "I'll cut you too short to reach the heavens you o' so desire to take over, yet fail every time.

"You don't know me, and I don't know you. Yet you being here is trouble, obviously. So here's my warning: leave here. Your company isn't wanted."

"Bastard! The nerve to address me as such! And why do I feel as if I know you?"

"Don't kid yourself. I've never met anyone as repugnant as you. Ever."

Deathelena studied the Vesorai upon Courage's Sacroncai Uniform.

Then, she noted Tauran'creima, the celebrated constellation of them all.

All became clear.

"The hell are you looking at?" Courage queried. "I'm not someone to gawk at. Keep your eyes to yourself."

"Ah… so *you're* the Legendary Tauran'creima…" Deathelena realized. "I remember having a bout with you eons ago. Not that you would remember being in that perturbing beast form. Pity I couldn't kill you…"

"…What? That was you? You were the disgusting presence I felt? No wonder I attacked you. You should've stayed clear of my region."

Deathelena closed her eyes.

She reminisced of their fight.

"That sacred manifestation. That bright, otherworldly green light. That colossal Celestial Bull. And that bothersome divine power…"

Deathelena opened her eyes.

She stared through Courage.

"Tauran'creima… why do you exist…?"

"I should be asking you that. Halfwit bitch."

"Where there's life, death soon follows…"

"I disagree…" Flowerensia said.

"Denial is always the first stage…" Deathelena countered. "So you'd rather the idiotic bad humans to exist alongside the good ones for eternity? Overpopulation isn't a fictitious matter.

"You also condone the butchering of animals so these peasants can feast. Care to explain your position on this, Ren?"

"There's nothing to defend, Lena…" Flowerensia stated. "Leave my domain. At once…"

"You've gotten a little bravado about you since your new boyfriend arrived," Deathelena taunted. "You think he's protecting you. You look at him with *utter* admiration.

"So many… indescribable images churn through your mind. Of you and him. Very explicit and sexual images unbecoming of a Flower Goddess. How shameful…"

"The pot calling the kettle black. You've always been a hypocrite and the true meaning of evil. Go die…"

"I have. Plenty of times. Yet, as always, I return, *much* stronger than I was. It's only a matter of time until I rule all existence. The divine community is only biding their time."

"Flowerensia is far from a damsel," Courage interjected. "And though the deities of the Great Beyond may not have put you in your place yet, you will know what it truly means to be on the receiving end of all your depravity."

"Yet it hasn't happened," Deathelena said. "And why're you no longer the Celestial Bull? Did you grow tired of being an astral bovine?"

"Perhaps. I've been needing to expand my horizon. *And*, I've been dying for a good fight. And your mouth is the perfect thing I'd like to seal.

"And by the way, just because your defeat hasn't happened yet doesn't mean it isn't forthcoming. Karma works when you least expect it."

"I recall Ren calling you Courage. Is that your new name?"

"The entirety of my name is Tetsu'reidza Tauran'creima Courage Astrial'len. Remember it, for I believe we'll meet again."

"I intend to. Because after I'm through beating you within an inch of your life, your name will change from *Courage* to *Coward*."

"That was so funny I forgot to laugh. Surely you can come with a more savage remark than that?"

Courage did not want to show it, but he was immensely hostile.

He greatly despised being called something that was the opposite of his very name.

Flowerensia sensed Courage's subtle yet unparalleled temper – Tauran'creima's Wrath.

She was skeptical he would lose control.

"Courage... don't engage her..."

"Are you kidding me? She was warned by both of us. And she hasn't left yet. And you say don't fight her? There comes a time when people need to be put in their place the hard way. I don't have the patience for ignorance and idiots. And she's one of them."

"You're an interesting one..." Deathelena said. "I have time to spare. I could use you as a stress reliever. Let's see if you still hold up to what you were eons ago.

"I would've had my rematch sooner at that cold mountain if it wasn't for Ren. Honestly, I don't see what's so special about you star beings. How you're able to match deities like me is blasphemous.

"We're creators while you're... a tiny spark in the sky that we put there. And then there's you, the pinnacle of star beings. Abysmal..."

"False," Courage asserted. "You didn't put a damn thing in the sky, the solar system, or whatever have you. Star beings were *always* there. You fail to realize that star beings are on a different level entirely.

"It doesn't matter if you're a deity, a demi-god, or a microscopic organism. Quite frankly, I don't give a shit. The point is star beings aren't limited.

"We are who we are, and nothing can kill us. Only those who are of our caliber, or those of a very exceptional nature, could match us.

"Even then, the odds are still not in their favor. We possess something most organisms don't. You included. There aren't many that can keep up with us, which should tell you something about us entirely."

"Hmph. You're a proud star being. Your theory will be put to the test. We'll see if it's true. Or if it's a lie like everyone's lives."

Courage marched toward Deathelena.

However, he stopped in the center of the pathway.

He did not want to step on Flowerensia's flowers.

"*Aw!* How adorable!" Deathelena teased. "You care for your girlfriend's flowers. Here, maybe this will motivate you."

Deathelena lifted her foot.

Before she could crush another set of flowers, she was sent flying across the garden by an aerial kick by Courage.

Then, he floated above the flowers.

Flowerensia looked at Courage in disbelief.

She was unable to fathom what just happened.

What in the actual…! I didn't even see him move! What in heavens…!

Flowerensia outstretched her hands toward Deathelena.

She used telekinesis to keep Deathelena aloft.

This was to keep Deathelena from landing on her flowers, in addition to restricting her mobility.

When Deathelena regained focus, she realized she was being held in the air against her will.

Sensing that it was Flowerensia restraining her, she became upset.

Deathelena effortlessly broke Flowerensia's attempt to contain her.

Flowerensia recoiled.

Deathelena floated inches above the flowers.

She prepared to fight Flowerensia and Courage.

Deathelena looked back and forth between Courage and Flowerensia.

She was deciding who she would attack.

Realizing she would be able to overwhelm Flowerensia, she flew toward her at an incredible speed.

Flowerensia summoned a transparent yet iridescent flower barrier – the *Swa'reikei* – before her.

Deathelena raised her fist.

She shrouded her fist in purple energy – the *Telti'leigrus*.

Deathelena was preparing to punch through the Swa'reikei and end Flowerensia's life.

"Payback's a bitch!" Deathelena said. "You're not the only one I intend to unleash my wrath upon! Those who assisted you in defeating me time and time again will be brought to a sudden end!"

Abruptly, Deathelena was knocked off course toward Flowerensia.

Deathelena glided toward a cherry blossom tree.

She struck the tree trunk.

She grunted.

Then, she fell on the ground.

She was unconscious.

The Telti'leigrus dissipated.

Flowerensia noted Courage before her.

His fist was extended where he struck Deathelena.

Flowerensia looked into his eyes.

They were calculating.

Flowerensia dispelled the Swa'reikei.

"Hey, don't let your guard down yet," Courage warned. "She's down, but not out."

"Of course," Flowerensia replied.

Deathelena groaned.

She gradually opened her eyes.

Then, she slowly rose to her feet.

She snarled.

She hissed in pain.

She held her head.

Damn. I felt an incredible shock when he struck me. It... wasn't just the punch itself. I think he added part of his sacred power to it... and released it upon impact. I can't believe this... yet I'm not leaving until I truly figure this damned star out. Damn you...

"Protecting your precious girlfriend, eh? Pathetic. The lot of you."

"Instead of saying that down there, you should come up here and say that," Courage said.

"Gladly!"

Deathelena flew toward Courage.

When she neared, she raised her fist.

He easily telegraphed her.

He grasped her fist when she attempted to strike him.

She tried to punch him with her other fist.

However, he grasped that one as well.

Deathelena headbutted Courage.

He mildly flinched.

She pressed her forehead against his.

She clenched her teeth.

"Never had a woman this close to you in all your cursed life?"

"If I did, it sure as hell wouldn't be someone like you."

"Aw. And just when I thought that opposites attract."

"Keep dreaming, crazy bitch."

"Correction. I *don't* dream. I *make* realities."

A dark sword – the *Ni'egoraga* – emerged behind Courage.

The Ni'egoraga possessed illuminate purple Hychineirian Runes that gradually faded in and out of existence.

Flowerensia saw the Ni'egoraga behind Courage.

She conjured three spinning flower razors – the *Reizonias*.

She launched them toward the stationary Ni'egoraga.

The Reizonias ricocheted off the dark sword.

Flowerensia became frustrated.

Ha! Trying to save your boyfriend, you worthless dumbass?

To hell with you!

That's where everyone will end up eventually. Because I have the means to make it happen!

Leave Flowerensia alone.

Why you…!

Deathelena telekinetically launched the Ni'egoraga toward Courage.

Courage swiftly changed their positions.

He threw Deathelena toward her incoming sword.

The Ni'egoraga pierced Deathelena's back.

The blade emerged from her abdomen.

However, Deathelena did not wince.

Due to the dark nature of the Ni'egoraga, it did not injure Deathelena.

Deathelena telekinetically withdrew the Ni'egoraga from herself.

She grasped her sword in her right hand.

She took a fighting stance.

Black blood dripped from the blade onto the flowers below.

The flowers wilted.

Flowerensia grimaced.

This bitch just keep finding ways to piss me off! Stop killing my flowers!

Deathelena chuckled.

Flowerensia scoffed.

…Yet, I shouldn't complain. Courage is putting himself on the line for me. And everyone else. People he doesn't even know…

"Tauran'creima! If you've got a sword, draw it!"

Courage ignored Deathelena.

"Hey! Are you denying my challenge? That's cowardice!"

"No. It's not. I don't consider you worthy of such a bout."

"What? How dare you!"

Deathelena charged at Courage.

She swung the Ni'egoraga horizontally.

She attempted to decapitate him.

Courage ceased her attack with his index finger.

Deathelena gasped.

Courage felt the negative nature of the Ni'egoraga.

It rejected him.

He instantly shoved the sword away with his index finger.

Deathelena spun about.

Yet, she recovered.

She lunged toward Courage.

She raised her left fist.

The Telti'leigrus emerged about her extremity.

Courage struck the Telti'leigrus-covered hand away.

Deathelena recovered once more.

She thrust the Ni'egoraga toward Courage.

He evaded the attack.

He kicked the sword from her hand.

The Ni'egoraga fell toward the garden.

Then, he followed up with a kick to her abdomen.

She grunted.

She glided backward across the garden.

When the Ni'egoraga neared the garden, Courage telekinetically stopped it.

Flowerensia summoned five Reizonias.

She launched them toward Deathelena.

Unfortunately, they disintegrated.

A purple and black force, a ripple-like barrier that faded as quickly as it appeared, was the cause.

This barrier was called the *Pronzeimius*.

Once Deathelena recovered, she returned to confront Courage.

She dispelled the Ni'egoraga.

"Hmph, well aren't you full of pizazz..." Deathelena said.

"Hmph, well aren't you full of shit," Courage mocked.

"Bastard... you and Flowerensia will rue this day..."

"I highly doubt it," Courage stated. "You're all talk. Yes, you're powerful. But you're only powerful to those who aren't stronger than you. Meditate on that."

Deathelena raised her hands toward the Estrohas Earrings.

She closed her eyes.

She wriggled her fingers.

The Estrohas Earrings commenced sparkling.

Her Dark Divionagai slowly rose.

She conjured a purple shield around herself – the Scorpreikia Barrier.

Dark clouds appeared in the sky.

They eclipsed the sun.

It started raining.

Flowerensia became dejected.

This bitch has to ruin everything. Why can't she just leave people alone?

Flowerensia, I can handle this. Raise your happiness once more.

O-oh... O-of course, dear...

He outstretched his right arm sideward.

He turned his palm upward.

A small amount of life force emerged from the flowers and trees of Flowerensia's garden.

The small orbs varied in color.

Courage looked toward Flowerensia for approval.

May I?

Yes. Take as much as you need.

Courage closed his eyes.

He telekinetically brought the small orbs to him.

The life force shrouded his arm.

It shined an iridescent brilliance.

The life force faded in and out of existence at intermediate intervals.

Egramanagri is the ability to absorb life from plants.

Lifortei Tresaidas was a basic level purification attack.

Deathelena steady rose her Dark Divionagai with the Estrohas Earrings.

Courage scoffed.

I've had enough of this boring bout. Time to end this.

Courage flew toward Deathelena.

When he neared, he stopped.

"You can't hope to get by my Scorpreikia Barrier, love," Deathelena said. "It's over for you and your girlfriend. As well as this entire planet."

"Wrong. Now please shut up."

Courage placed a small amount of his Sacred Staraidus in his left fist.

The Sacroncai Punch was a very lethal attack.

He struck the Scorpreikia Barrier with the Sacroncai Punch.

The Scorpreikia Barrier shattered.

Deathelena was shocked.

Her concentration was interrupted.

As a result, her Dark Divionagai stopped increasing.

And the Estrohas Earrings stopped sparkling.

Then, he struck her abdomen with his right palm.

She choked.

The Lifortei Tresaidas shrouded her.

It faded in and out of reality at low intervals.

She screamed in agony.

She fell toward the garden.

Courage grabbed her wrist.

He slowly descended toward the pathway.

Then, he landed on the pathway.

He laid Deathelena on her back.

Flowerensia approached.

She stood near Courage.

The rain stopped.

And the dark clouds dissipated.

The sun shined once more.

Deathelena groaned.

She looked toward Courage through partly opened eyes.

"Damn you. How could I lose to you…? Again…"

"Truth be told, I wasn't attacking you with *all* my strength. If I did, you'd either be dead or crippled. You should've left when we warned you."

"I hate this. I hate everything. And I hate this sacred power nullifying me…"

"Come off it. You were sealed countless times. Surely that was painful as well?"

"No. Nothing like I feel now…"

"You and I were holding back more than tenfold. Yet, this is the right conclusion for one such as you."

"I'll… get you, Courage. Trust me…"

The Lifortei Tresaidas not only debilitated an adversary's strength, but it prevented them from accessing their powers temporarily.

Deathelena moaned.

She attempted to stand.

Unfortunately, she could only kneel on one knee.

She breathed heavily.

Her head was bowed.

"Lena… leave here and never return," Flowerensia stated. "I'm tired of your attempts to kill me and those who helped me subdue you. You never learn!"

"Damn both of you…" Deathelena said.

"What was your *true* reason for coming here?" Courage asked.

"The hell you think? Revenge!" Deathelena confessed.

"Why do you want revenge?" Courage queried. "Surely power isn't your main goal?"

"No… I want the best for my people…" Deathelena replied. "Those who are worthy in my eyes deserve the blessings I bestow upon them."

"But you're a goddess," Courage stated. "You can give them whatever you want, *without* causing harm to others. What's your deal?"

"The hoity-toity divine community thinks that power should be balanced. Yet, said balanced power isn't displayed throughout the universe. The weak die while the strong thrive. So I want to strip those uppity fuckers of their powers and supply it to my people. In doses, of course."

"In essence, you're selfish," Flowerensia said. "As always."

"That doesn't make any sense," Courage stated. "You might as well keep the powers for yourself, as you'd be skeptical of mutiny from the very ones you claim you care for.

"Common sense, Deathelena. You're not fooling me. Even if you care about your people, you wouldn't give them such a privilege of having the divine community's powers."

Deathelena scoffed.

"Yet, should something happen to me, my kingdoms need a proper leader in my stead."

"But you're death," Courage said. "You'll come back, regardless. Unless otherwise completely obliterated."

"That doesn't mean my kingdoms can manage themselves in my absence, fool. Nevertheless, I've said enough. I won't forget this.

"Ren… I could've easily taken you if it wasn't for your boyfriend. I would've made an example of you before your feeble people. Like I did eons ago. You know this.

"You're not as strong as you claim without any assistance. You don't have the right to rule a kingdom, let alone a planet, if you can't properly defend yourself. You're too soft. Yet… that's to be expected from a *Flower* Goddess.

"If it wasn't for your boyfriend, who you covet so dearly, history would've repeated itself. This very day."

"Rot in the abyss, you psychotic bitch…" Flowerensia scolded.

"You know what I say is true. You lust for, perhaps even love, Courage, a man you just met. You want to do all kinds of sexual things to him.

"Yet, since you're the submissive type, he'd be the one dominating you. Between your legs or otherwise. And you'd love it. All of it."

Flowerensia blushed.

She looked away out of shame.

"You're disgusting…"

"Ha. I hit the nail on the head, bitch. In addition, you're not fit to rule a nation if someone like me can come along and easily take it from you.

"Grow a bigger cunt and do something to stop beings like me on your own. Don't expect your hero to always be here for you. Pathetic."

Then, Deathelena glared at Courage.

She grinned.

"I anticipate our next bout. And you're right, we held back. Yet, you did so more than you know. You're a very dangerous being. Yes, incredibly lethal. Which makes this all the more exciting. Until next time…"

Deathelena teleported from planet Venusia.

Courage dispelled the Lifortei Tresaidas.

The life force returned to the flowers.

Courage approached the flowers that wilted from Deathelena's blood.

He stooped.

He placed his hands above them.

Green particles – the *Harminas* – emerged about his hands.

The Harminas merged with the flowers.

Gradually, the flowers recovered.

Flowerensia observed Courage's kind deed.

Her blush deepened.

She folded her arms.

She arched her fingers near her lips.

"C-Courage… thank you. You don't have to…"

"Nonsense. I took life from these flowers. It's only right I give it back, especially since two sets of flowers died because of Deathelena: one from her blood and the other when she first appeared."

"I'll take care of the other ones when I get the time..."

After Courage healed the flowers, he dispelled the Harminas.

Then, he stood.

The group of small birds from earlier returned.

They landed in front of Courage while one bird rested on his right shoulder and another one relaxed on his left shoulder.

They chirped happily.

"They like you, dear..." Flowerensia noted.

"I see..."

"You're special to them..."

And you're special to me. You're so amazing, Courage. Thank you so much for saving me...

Deathelena emerged in the laboratory within the depths of her castle.

She limped toward a large capsule filled with purple liquid – the *Iodinicron* – which assist in rapid recuperation.

However, the Iodinicron Capsule was not for Deathelena.

The capsule housed an unconscious individual she held dear.

The capsule possessed a young adult female, whom Deathelena took into custody.

Her name was Asai Rionai.

She was a Melhouna.

Asai was often misunderstood, thus becoming an outcast.

Since then, Deathelena became like a mother figure to her, as well as a mentor.

Asai has long purple hair with bangs, extensive tresses, fair skin, a pretty visage, and purple eyebrows.

She possessed no clothing while she occupied the capsule.

Asai was gravely injured during a confrontation with another star being.

She was on the verge of death.

Lamentably, Deathelena's healing capabilities could not subdue Asai's critical wounds.

However, Deathelena took the liberty of placing her in the Iodinicron Capsule to heal.

Asai had been in a coma for as long as Deathelena could remember.

No matter what she did, Asai would not awake.

All of her injuries were mended.

Yet, she remained asleep.

Deathelena was worried.

She despised being fatalistic, but she feared for the worst, even though Asai's vitals were positive.

The Lifortei Tresaidas ceased fading in and out of existence around Deathelena.

Deathelena placed her hand upon the glass of the Iodinicron Capsule.

Black tears cascaded down her cheeks.

The tears struck the floor.

She felt as if she failed the only one she grew fond of over the years.

Deathelena did not mind that Asai was a Melhouna.

Asai had potential unlike most in her army.

As a result, Deathelena trained and cared for her as if she were her daughter.

"Asai... I'm sorry. I'll find a way to bring you out of this damned coma. I promise..."

Deathelena placed her forehead against the glass.

She wept for some time before her battered body needed rest.

Deathelena collapsed on the floor.

She was unconscious.

Her black tears steady streamed down her face.

"I am my own sanctuary."

 Chapter 3

Rhol'heima,
The Great Beyond

"You're very strong, Fesforia!" Asai declared. "But I'm stronger!"

Asai wore the Hychineirian Uniform, as tribute to Deathelena.

She was sparring with Fesforia Meilorei, a female General of Deathelena's army.

Fesforia was one of Deathelena's top ranking fighters.

Asai, Fesforia, and Deathelena were in the training yard of her castle.

The Hychineirian Army observed the bout between Asai and Fesforia.

Fesforia had long red hair, short tresses, impeccable fair skin, a beautiful countenance, dark eyebrows, bluish green eyes, and a shapely body.

Fesforia wore a black choker with a Killoseiga pendant attached to it.

It was a symbol of her passionate lifestyle and personality.

She was garbed in a very revealing red outfit that displayed part of her ample breasts and half of her firm buttocks.

She also wore red thigh-high boots.

She was considered one of the sexiest girls of Deathelena's army.

Asai admired Fesforia as if she were her older sister.

However, Fesforia had a difficult time reciprocating her affection.

She felt as if Asai was a threat to her position.

Not to mention Asai being a Melhouna was something Fesforia could not accept, as Fesforia was an Azagnorpor.

The prejudice between the Melhounas and Azagnorpors was immense.

In essence, Fesforia harbored resentment toward Asai.

However, there were those that accepted beings as they are, as the individual's character was what mattered most.

Fesforia chose to serve Deathelena because she saw it as a means to gain power and notoriety.

However, Fesforia would occasionally depart and pursue other aspects independently.

These were aspects she kept private.

Fesforia was very powerful.

However, she was not strong enough, should she decide to overthrow Deathelena, who has outmaneuvered Fesforia on numerous occasions.

A star being Fesforia may be, but she was extremely far from Courage's caliber to actually pose a threat to him or Deathelena.

Fesforia, as well as countless beings throughout the universe, wanted to see the legend that defeated Deathelena eons ago.

When it was stated that Tauran'creima effortlessly defeated Deathelena, there was massive controversy in numerous parts of the cosmos, including Rhol'heima, Relmi'shira, and Zeinhailurein.

Even before the bout between Tauran'creima and Deathelena, most knew or dared not to approach Tauran'creima without a good reason, lest they had a death wish.

Tauran'creima was the Guardian of the Universe.

As such, he was not one to take lightly at all.

Regardless, Deathelena noted the disgust in Fesforia's eyes as the latter stared at Asai.

Deathelena became indignant.

"Fesforia! What the hell is wrong with you? She's your team member! Why look at her with such animosity?"

"Because she's a Melhouna! She's a goody-two-shoe star being! As death itself, you shouldn't affiliate yourself with people opposite of us!"

"Watch your tongue, girl! Lest you want me to cut it out! Know your place! And even if what you say is true, if there is use in someone, regardless of their background, I'm going to make use out of them!"

"If you try to maim me, it won't matter! Star beings' body parts regenerate, anyway! Stars never die!"

"I have my ways, girl! Don't test me! Now act like a senior and teach Asai what you know! We're all a team here! I don't expect any division among our own!"

"But that's just it! She's not one of us! She's the same as the legend! Hell, she doesn't even have an evil vibe about her..."

43

Astral Tears welled in Asai's eyes.

They sparkled as they fell down her cheeks.

"Do you hate me, big sister? I... I just want to please you. I love you... like Mama Deathelena..."

"See?" Deathelena said. "Look at what you did. Because of your irrationality, you made her cry. Such an asshole."

"Damn it..." Fesforia stated. "Can we finish this some other time?"

"No!" Deathelena replied. "You stay and teach Asai, you ingrate bitch! Get your shit together!"

While Fesforia was distracted, Asai outstretched her arms frontward.

She set her hands several inches from each other.

She closed her eyes.

She focused.

Purple light emerged between her hands.

Its rays rotated rapidly.

Once she had adequate power, she quickly propelled the attack – the Estaidaras – toward Fesforia.

The Estaidaras was a potent attack that could severely hamper most life forms, especially star beings.

Not only does it inflict major damage; it also restricted that individual's power.

In fact, this was a basic level attack, yet it had advanced effects.

The Estaidaras rapidly approached Fesforia.

When it neared her, it exploded.

Fesforia, who was caught by surprise, was blown across the training yard.

She screamed in agony.

She glided backward until she struck the black brick wall.

She was embedded within the wall.

Dust covered her.

Deathelena and the Hychineirian Army was appalled at Asai's unexpected yet powerful attack.

They also noted a difference in her demeanor.

Though her Astral Tears remained, her determination was apparent.

She took a fighting stance.

She awaited Fesforia to return to the center of the training yard.

When Fesforia regained her composure, she levitated from the wall.

She groaned.

She had several wounds about her body.

Livalaquia leaked from the injuries.

She planted her feet on the ground.

She snarled.

"Lucky shot! Now I'll get you! Let's see if you can handle this!"

Fesforia placed her right foot forward.

She outstretched her arms to either side of her body.

Suddenly, a red aura – the Ramonicos Aura – framed her body.

Several apparitions of her constellation – Ramonicos, the Celestial Ram – flew skyward as her Staraidus increased incredibly.

Ramondei was the first stage of Fesforia's transformation.

"Fesforia, stop!" Deathelena shouted. "She's still developing her powers! She can't quite control it yet! No need for overkill here! This is training, you imbecile!"

"Damn it, your highness!" Ramondei Fesforia protested. "You take her side more than anyone! What's with the favoritism? That shit packed a punch!"

"Stop your bitching!" Deathelena retaliated. "It's not about taking sides! I already informed you of her lack of being able to control her powers, which is why we're here! To assist her!"

"Hey wait!" Asai stated. "Your Staraidus is supposed to be suppressed! What gives?"

"I'm far stronger than you!" Ramondei Fesforia said. "If I'd have been weaker, maybe it would've affected me, but it didn't. It only hurt me. I must say, it hurt like a motherfucker. Now, it's your turn to feel pain. My pain!"

Ramondei Fesforia flew toward Asai.

When she neared, she threw a punch at Asai.

Asai grasped Ramondei Fesforia's wrist.

Then, she struck Ramondei Fesforia's lips with her elbow.

Ramondei Fesforia yelled.

She glided backward.

She landed on her back.

Yet, she immediately recovered.

She leaped to her feet.

When Ramondei Fesforia was ready to counterattack, she was unable to, as Asai already closed the distance between them.

She hovered before her.

Asai threw a punch at her.

The assault connected with Ramondei Fesforia's nose.

She yelled in pain.

She glided backward across the training yard once more.

She fell through the wall.

She lied on the floor.

Asai's morale greatly improved.

"You're stronger than me, huh?" Asai mocked. "What a joke. I might not have suppressed all of your Staraidus, but the Estaidaras affected you. Whether you want to admit it or not."

Then, a purple aura faded in and out of existence about Asai's body at a low frequency.

Auderesa, the Celestial Rabbit, was Asai's constellation.

The Auderesa Aura was taking some time.

As such, the Auderesa Aura kept fading in and out of reality.

Ramondei Fesforia groaned.

Disgruntled, Ramondei Fesforia placed herself on all fours.

She snarled.

A fiery red circle with strange glyphs emerged beneath her – the Syphomethus.

The Syphomethus appeared below Asai as well.

It paralyzed her.

Then, Killoseiga erupted from the Syphomethus.

Asai's screams of anguish echoed throughout the training yard.

Aspects of celestial or extraordinary existence could harm star beings.

However, the summoner of the celestial aspect would be unharmed.

The Auderesa Aura disappeared.

Grinning, Ramondei Fesforia flew toward the Killoseiga.

She entered it.

She punched Asai.

Asai yelled.

Asai glided out of the Killoseiga.

She struck the wall.

She was embedded within it.

She was injured.

However, she managed to dispel the flames shrouding her.

Ramondei Fesforia immediately pursued her.

When she neared Asai, she held her by her neck.

Asai struggled.

"Let me go, big sis! I'm not done beating your ass yet!"

"Shut up and be still, little cunt! It's over for you! No escape!"

Ramondei Fesforia opened her mouth.

She gradually withdrew Asai's life from her.

The Egramana was the process of extracting the life from any living being and becoming much stronger.

This was common among star beings.

The Auderesa Essence – Asai's life force – slowly entered Ramondei Fesforia's mouth.

Asai gradually became weaker.

As a result, her struggling slowed to a stop.

Deathelena, along with the Hychineirian Army, were alarmed.

Highly upset, Deathelena intervened.

With a wave of her hand, she extinguished the Killoseiga and the Syphomethus.

Deathelena summoned her Ni'egoraga.

The Telti'leigrus shrouded the sword.

Then, she teleported.

She emerged behind Ramondei Fesforia.

She pierced her back.

Ramondei Fesforia yelled.

Her Ramonicos Essence rapidly depleted until there was a very small amount remaining.

The Telti'leigrus was capable of withdrawing life from any being.

As a result, she released Asai.

Asai collapsed on the floor.

She was unconscious.

She had burn marks on her face.

And her Hychineirian Uniform was scorched in several places, exposing parts of her body.

Ramondei Fesforia collapsed unconscious as well.

Her Ramonicos Aura vanished.

They laid parallel to each other.

The healing ability for star beings – the Meheiloreilia – commenced gradually mending their wounds.

Deathelena gently lifted Asai bridal fashion.

"Hey... someone take this worthless bitch Fesforia to a cell. Now..." *Deathelena ordered. "I'll take care of Asai..."*

One of the red and black armored Hychineirian Soldiers lifted Fesforia bridal style.

The Hychineirian Soldier walked toward the dungeons, which was below the castle, while Deathelena headed toward the laboratory, which was in the very depths of the castle, a place she was very secretive about.

When Deathelena arrived at the laboratory, she gently placed Asai on a bed.

Then, she activated the Iodinicron Capsule.

While the capsule was preparing, Deathelena stripped Asai of her clothing.

She tossed the tattered Hychineirian Uniform aside.

Then, a red and black energy shrouded Deathelena's hands.

Deathelena attempted utilizing her healing power – the Edomonas – to assist Asai.

She placed her hands upon Asai's chest.

Unfortunately, it was inadequate.

Perhaps since Asai was a Melhouna and Deathelena was of a dark origin, her healing power was not compatible.

Consequently, she had to rely on the Iodinicron Capsule to support Asai's recovery.

Deathelena placed Asai into the Iodinicron Capsule.

She secured her into it.

Then, she closed the door.

She pressed a button, which allowed the Iodinicron to pour onto Asai.

Once the capsule was full, Deathelena sat on a chair.

She attempted to refrain her black tears.

But it was futile.

"She called me… Mama Deathelena. How adorable…"

It was nighttime.

Courage laid on a bed within a room of Flowerensia's temple.

However, he was restless.

Flowerensia and Courage agreed that they would go to Velmelkia Sanctuary tomorrow for his formal introduction to the kingdom.

She spent the remainder of the day informing the town of the special event being held tomorrow at Velmelkia Sanctuary.

Damn, I'm bored. There's nothing to do. Ugh… though I'm grateful Flowerensia's letting me stay here, I really need my own building. Someplace far away. My own privacy.

Yet, I can always return to my constellation. However, since I'm on this planet, I might as well make the best of it.

His bout with Deathelena did not sedate his excitement.

Not to mention, he pondered of his purpose.

Though Tauran'creima is the Guardian of the Universe, Courage did not know what to do.

Though both are one, he still felt lost.

His only interests were fighting and anything pertaining to creativity.

Transcendence was all he knew.

Dissatisfied with the lack of action, Courage leaped off the bed.

He walked toward the window.

Then, he gazed toward the sky.

He saw a Melhouna couple dancing in a very slow, fascinating way.

Then, Courage played the song 'Destiny' from his conscious.

He memorized every note perfectly.

He listened to the beautiful tune as he observed the spectacle of the Melhounas.

He allowed the tune to be external.

Staraidus *Museala Extere'al* allows others to hear Courage's melodies.

Staraidus Museala *Intere'al* allows only Courage to hear the tunes.

Instrumental music affected Courage in great ways.

It increased his Sacred Staraidus to extraordinary heights.

In addition to his phenomenal adrenaline – the *Selsengra* – it would be disastrous if he were in a fight.

Tauran'creima is considered the most powerful being throughout the cosmos, so being an enemy of Courage would be very dangerous.

In fact, being an adversary of any star being would be devastating, no matter who the opposition was.

They were on a scale that superseded any entity.

The Melhouna pair heard the wonderful melody.

They stopped dancing.

They looked toward the source.

Then, they waved toward Courage, who reciprocated their acknowledgment.

The Melhounas started dancing once more.

The female Melhouna released iridescent sparkles from her body in intermediate intervals – the *Ethroheidas* – as a result of the melody.

She was elated.

Courage continued observing the Melhouna duo.

Then, he noted Tauran'creima galloping across the sky.

Like all constellations, Tauran'creima is enormous.

He has piercing green eyes.

He has a long tail.

Green sparkles faded in and out of existence around him.

He was shrouded in an otherworldly green brilliance.

And his Sacred Staraidus was beyond astronomical.

Tauran'creima looked toward Courage.

Tauran'creima released a powerful bellow of salute.

This was known as Tauran'creima's Bellow.

Courage felt an unbelievable surge of power throughout his body.

That was the Selsengra.

However, he contained it.

Courage flew into the air.

Then, he released Tauran'creima's Bellow, which shook the foundation of Velmelkia Kingdom.

Tauran'creima chuckled with immense approval.

Courage flew onto Tauran'creima's head.

He placed his hand on one of his colossal horns.

Tauran'creima paced across the sky as the Melhounas and humans below observed in awe.

"How goes it?" Courage asked. "Taking a nightly stroll?"

"Far from it," Tauran'creima replied.

His authoritative voice echoed throughout the region.

"I came to see how you were, Courage."

"You're me, so you should know."

"Agreed. Yet, I could not help it."

"What's my purpose? Why am I here?"

"That you should know. We have been around long enough for you to grasp your nature."

"However, this is my first time being on a planet. We may have traversed the universe, yet we've never done anything like this. So come on, there has to be something."

"It is obvious. I am the Guardian of the Universe. You likewise with me. You are a Divine Guardian. A Sacred Melhouna. The Sacred Star of the Cosmos. The Epitome of Transcendence. You are the beacon of light to those who are lost in darkness and gloom."

"Hey... I firmly believe that people are in charge of their own destiny. They are responsible for picking themselves up whenever they fall. The universe is a cruel place, and anyone who isn't prepared for its trials will surely fail. Miserably."

"True. Yet, there are those who need a helping hand. Not everyone is like you. Sometimes, it takes someone who has experienced life and its many hardships to assist another in need. Not everyone has the courage to press on when they feel as if they have been beaten entirely.

"However, I do agree that once help has been given, those individuals must grow stronger from then on."

"That I very much agree with."

"You can always return to me. Yet, I think it is good for you to travel about. Not just here, but the cosmos as well. Like always."

"Why? What's the point when we've been doing this for eons?"

"Be your own being. Ever transcend."

"That's second nature."

"You should rest. You have much ahead of you."

Courage released Tauran'creima's Bellow in reverence.

"You make me proud," Tauran'creima said. "I am always with you. Now please. Rest."

Courage laid between Tauran'creima's horns.

He stared into outer space.

Eventually, Courage fell asleep.

He dreamed of being the greatest among the star beings.

The next day, Flowerensia stood before her people at Velmelkia Sanctuary.

"Greeting, everyone!" Flowerensia said. "I'm glad you all are here today! I have one question to ask all of you. Did you feel that violent earthquake yesterday? Crazy, right?"

"Yeah, what the hell was that?" a male member asked. "It happened once during the afternoon and three times at night!"

"That was my stomach growling," Flowerensia stated.

The congregation laughed.

"Nah, I'm just joking," Flowerensia said. "We all know deities don't have to eat."

"My goddess!" a female member called. "A massive green bull was seen in the sky last night!"

"Does anyone recall the legend that's been around since time began?" Flowerensia queried.

"Yeah!" the congregation replied.

"Well, believe it or not, it's come to pass," Flowerensia stated. "I'd like to introduce the one the legend spoke of."

Flowerensia blushed.

Everyone noticed this, as well as her sudden change in body language.

They whispered among themselves.

Flowerensia placed her hand on her chest.

"I feel... like I've known him all my life, even though we just met. He... saved me recently. Please... I'd like for him to come forth. His name... is Courage, Tetsu'reidza Tauran'creima Courage Astrial'len. Please... come forward..."

"Wait a minute..." the male member said. "That giant bull was the famous Tauran'creima? Are you kidding me?"

"No, this isn't a joke," Flowerensia assured. "Regardless, this man, this legend, is the personification of Tauran'creima. Now, please... Tauran'creima... Courage. Come forth..."

Courage entered the room.

He marched boldly down the aisle.

His expression was indifferent.

Everyone gawked at Courage.

Some denizens gasped out of shock.

Other residence gasped out of fear.

They felt the incredible authority he possessed.

When they noted the image of Tauran'creima on the back of his cape, they knew the legend was true.

Flowerensia watched as Courage ambled down the aisle.

Her blush never receded.

And her hand remained on her chest.

She tried not to allow her mind to drift into immorality.

Courage stood before the altar.

He looked at Flowerensia.

She tried not to divert her eyes.

It was as if he could see through her.

You look upset, dear. What bothers you?

Nothing. Just want to get this over with.

Courage... I'm doing this because I don't want you to be a stranger here.

I'm already a stranger here.

Of course. That's how it always starts when someone is at someplace new. Everyone goes through this.

...Alright.

And before I forget, the deities of Rhol'heima wish to see you.

The hell they want?

They saw the bout between you and Deathelena and wish to speak with you personally.

This better not be a waste of my time.

Don't worry. I'm coming with you.

Courage grinned.

Why? You don't want me to get savage on their asses? Is that it?

Flowerensia's blush deepened.

She turned her head.

Courage!

Courage chuckled.

"Mommy…" a prepubescent female called. "Are Lady Flowerensia and the Hero kissing? Do they love each other? Are they getting married?"

"Uh…" the mother said. "They're… probably whispering, dear…"

Alright, Courage. Let's finish the ceremony. We can continue this afterward.

Of course.

Flowerensia flew into the air.

She conjured a scrolled.

She unfolded it.

Then, she read the following passage she recorded long ago:

"Over the course of my time stargazing, I witnessed a sight unlike any other. A green star. A star very uncommon. Upon closer inspection, the star was that of a bull. The star beings are a fine lot, but something about this green, beautiful star…

"There's more to it than what others have deemed over the years. Perhaps one day, this phenomenal star will make its motive apparent to all in the cosmos. I know it'll be something unforgettable."

Flowerensia dispelled the scroll.

She extended her hand in Courage's direction.

"This man, the one you see before you, is the legend! The Transcendent One! Courage… Do you have anything you wish to say?"

Flowerensia… really?

Come on, Courage. Please. Speak from the heart.

Damn it. Fine.

Courage turned toward the congregation.

"Strength lies dormant in all. Don't let anyone tell you otherwise. I'm not here to be a savior, but a messenger. A guide. You all have the ability to lead. If Flowerensia can lead, so can you.

"You all are the reflection of how she manages her kingdom, and surely she's not going to tolerate ne'er-do-wells. So, in the end, strength lies in you. However, it's up to you to use it in a favorable way.

"That is all."

Flowerensia blushed once more.

Thank you, Courage. That was sweet.

Most of the congregation gave Courage an accolade.

Others remained quiet, as they feared him.

The ones that appreciated him and his words of encouragement tossed flowers at him.

Courage was very grateful.

However, there was one skeptic.

"Hey," a male member called. "How do we know you aren't just some dude playing dress up?"

Silence immediately fell upon the vicinity.

Everyone looked at the male who made his absurd assertion.

Courage looked toward the male.

His eyes reflected great ire from his claim.

The male felt indescribable dread as he gazed into Courage's penetrating eyes.

Flowerensia disapproved of the male's perspective.

"How rude…"

Courage raised his hand.

He interrupted Flowerensia's statement.

He wanted to speak for himself.

"So basically, you're calling not just the legend that's been around long before you were thought of a liar, but Flowerensia as well. The nerve of you.

"Do you really think, for one goddamn second, that I would waste my time being someone I'm not, you wretch? Think before you speak!

"Whether you're jealous or just being the odd one out makes me no difference. The point is I am who I am, and I don't give a damn who believes me or who doesn't! Know your damn place!"

Terrorized of Courage, the male ran out of the chamber.

Flowerensia, as well as the congregation, was speechless.

Courage's anger was something to be feared.

"Well, everyone..." Flowerensia said. "That concludes this ceremony. Regardless of what just transpired, Courage means well. He's just not to be provoked. Under any circumstances. Nevertheless, if you all wish to speak with Courage, you may. Otherwise, you may leave."

After Courage's celebration, he and Flowerensia teleported to Rhol'heima.

Flowerensia and Courage stood upon the clouds.

Mist shrouded the vicinity.

Yet, they were still able to observe the beautiful, otherworldly kingdom.

A divine tune echoed throughout the heavens.

The harmony only played a piano, a xylophone, and a violin.

Upon hearing the melody, Courage began memorizing the composition.

Flowerensia looked toward Courage.

His eyes were closed.

She felt him learning the notes of the melody.

Thus, she left him alone.

You never cease to amaze me, Courage. You seem to treasure things pertaining to music and the arts. Fascinating.

After several minutes, Flowerensia spoke.

"C-Courage… my apologies for interrupting you. But those of this kingdom await us."

He opened his eyes.

"Damn… just when it was getting good, too."

Flowerensia and Courage proceeded until they reached *Hyrenal* Summit.

Gods and goddesses stood about.

They gazed at Courage and Flowerensia.

Yet, they mostly observed Courage.

The deity who ruled Rhol'heima was sitting on the elaborate throne.

Three male star beings stood nearby.

They observed Courage.

The very effeminate star being blushed.

Then, he giggled.

He stroked a tress of his hair behind his ear.

He fantasized about Courage.

Flowerensia stood near Courage.

Courage placed his fist on his hip.

"The hell is this, a rally?"

Flowerensia laughed.

"Courage, please. Don't start. You're going to get us in trouble."

"Congratulations, Transcendent One!" the ruler of Rhol'heima said.

"Uh, who are you?" Courage asked.

"My apologies. My name is Feloreigro. I am the ruler of Rhol'heima. I am the God of Time."

Feloreigro was an elderly yet powerful man.

He has long white hair, fair skin, bushy white eyebrows, a lengthy white beard, and hazel eyes.

He has an invaluable oval gold jewel – the *Zeidandai* – implanted in his forehead.

Feloreigro wore a long white robe and brown sandals.

He wore a gold necklace with a gold clock on it – the *Omni'saion*.

His arms have eight gold bands – the *Gromonolors* – secured around them.

He held a gold staff – the *Utelezar* – in his right hand.

An illuminate lightning bolt – the *Igranz* – was on the head of the Utelezar Staff.

The Omni'saion was the trademark of Rhol'heima.

"We all saw how you effortlessly eliminated Deathelena," Feloreigro stated. "She's been more trouble than we could ever imagine."

"Yeah well, she was being a nuisance, and a sociopath…" Courage said. "And I didn't kill her. Just beat her into submission.

"Regardless, Flowerensia was kind enough to fill me in on the details. It's been stated that she, as well as those who assisted her, had sealed Deathelena every time she escaped. Sounds like a pest control problem."

Flowerensia, Feloreigro, the male star beings, and the deities laughed at Courage's jest.

"What? I'm just saying," Courage continued. "How can someone so powerful keep begging to be sealed repeatedly? It's the prime definition of insanity. She's a glutton for punishment. A masochist."

"You are right, Transcendent One," Feloreigro said. "We sealed Deathelena in *Lymbolesia*, a place of perpetual nothingness. Yet, after some time, she always manages to escape and cause havoc once more.

"Regardless, we of Rhol'heima are ever grateful you put a stop to her. Even if it is temporary peace, we are glad you stopped her before she did any serious harm."

"Another thing that's an issue…" Courage stated. "Why have the deities and star beings been at odds? Surely there's a reason behind such madness?"

"Besides Deathelena, other deities think that star beings are insignificant to them," Feloreigro replied. "They believe that gods and goddesses are the only true powerful beings throughout the universe."

"Flowerensia mentioned that as well," Courage said. "And that's just too damn bad, because star beings are in a league of their own. And with me around… well… let's just say it's not going to go in anyone's favor but for star beings.

"The audacity to assume that deities are the only powerful beings in the universe is just asinine.

"Star beings have been around longer than any entity. Not to mention our phenomenal power, our Staraidus, exceeds the imagination. These are facts. *We* are the Original People.

"It doesn't matter if someone can detonate a solar system, or perform mind-boggling feats. It doesn't matter who, or what, someone is. In the end, star beings have *always* been very exceptional. The *very* best. After all, we are the Chosen People of the Universe."

"But you are not invincible..." a goddess said.

"And neither are you," Courage rebutted. "And we don't have to be unbeatable, but we're close enough.

"Unlike most organisms, stars *never* die. Even if we're defeated, we'll always return. I mean, did you hear what I said? We're the *Chosen* People of the *Universe*. In essence, we aren't like anything ever created. We are on a completely different aspect of existence.

"We could be beaten until we're incapacitated, as well as being stripped of our senses. However, star beings *always* have an ace up their sleeve. Just when our opponent thinks they have an advantage, we unleash one of many counterattacks.

"*That* is what makes us special! *That* is what makes us the greatest! We're a species that's unlike *any* other! And it's been proven! Time and time again across the ages!"

"Be the star that never ceases scintillating."

 **Chapter 4**

Tension

"How does the star reproduction process work again?" Kimiko asked.

"You're really asking that?" Ulanahar countered.

"Perhaps she forgot," Velcrimia said. "Or maybe she just hasn't had sex in years that it's no longer second nature to her."

Velcrimia Celestia, Kimiko Lybena, and Ulanahar Gekonia were at Lofty Plains of Velmelkia Kingdom.

After Courage's introduction ceremony, they decided to relax.

Velcrimia and Kimiko are Melhouna while Ulanahar was an Azagnorpor.

Like Asai, Ulanahar was greatly misunderstood.

She was often ostracized for being an Azagnorpor.

Even when Ulanahar emerged eons ago, she never committed violent acts.

She only defended herself when it was necessary.

Velcrimia has short blue hair with bangs, perfect blue skin, a beautiful visage, dark eyebrows, glimmering blue eyes, and a slender yet curvy body.

She has a triangular sapphire jewel – the *Pele'vuoleen* – embedded in her forehead.

She wore a cloak that was light blue on the left and black on the right.

The Pele'vuoleen Sapphire, which was surrounded by a silver frame, acted as a fastener for the cloak.

She wore a purple blouse, a light blue mini skirt, and black stockings that had her Constellation Ascension Glyphs on it – the *Belsi'reiga*.

She also wore black low-heel shoes.

Velcrimia's constellation is *Teretri'aga*, the Celestial Maiden.

"What's that supposed to mean, Velcrimia?" Kimiko asked. "You say it as if I'm dry down there! The hell is wrong with you?"

Kimiko has short dark hair with bangs, which covered her left eye.

She also has blue highlights throughout her hair.

She has smooth brown skin, a pretty face, dark eyebrows, hazel eyes, and an athletic body.

Kimiko wore a short sleeve jean jacket, black forearm guards with metal studs, a black sports bra, a black sash, jeans, and black tennis shoes.

Kimiko's constellation is *Rinaigora*, the Celestial Hawk.

"Maybe Kimiko means that as the years go by, people become more experimental in their sexual ways," Ulanahar replied. "Some are fixed in their sexual preferences than others."

Ulanahar has short white hair with bangs, immaculate brown skin, a very appealing face, white eyebrows, amethyst eyes with red pupils, and a sexy body.

She has a powerful gem in her hair – the *Lemynhas* Ruby.

She wore an elaborate silver breastplate with her Constellation Ascension Glyphs on it – the *Itali'malus*.

She also wore gold wrists and armbands, a black miniskirt, and black boots with gold embellishing.

Ulanahar's constellation is *Eidomularus*, the Celestial Snake.

"You're close, Ulanahar, but not quite," Kimiko said. "I mean, I never really understood how we maintain ourselves. We're very different than any other species."

"Do you want the science or the sensual version?" Ulanahar asked.

"Give me the juicy details," Kimiko stated.

"Honestly, you should know the science before anything," Ulanahar countered.

"Then why the hell you ask me, then?" Kimiko said.

"Like humans, star beings mate the same way," Ulanahar stated. "However, once the star man ejaculates his *Leikaitas*, or star essence, into the star woman, the process known as *Iloreiyus*, or the crystallization of the *Keileimia*, the starlight inside of us, commences.

"The crystallization happens to protect the Keileimia while it's developing.

"The development process takes a month before the star woman ejects the Crystallized Keileimia from her womb. Then, the star couple can either safeguard the Crystallized Keileimia themselves or send it to one of their constellations to further its maturity."

"Wait, hang on…" Kimiko interjected. "Does it develop into an embryo or what? What if the star woman is an Azagnorpor? This is kind of complex."

"We don't have embryos," Velcrimia said. "We have Keileimia. And it matters not if the star woman is an Azagnorpor. We are the Light of the Universe, regardless. We don't have cycles like female humans, nor any other complications they have.

"Also, when the Crystallized Keileimia matures, the crystal shatters. Then, the star takes its form. Depending on certain circumstances, they'll either look that of a teenager or an adult. However, the teenage ones can still grow into adults.

"They're usually referred to as Millennial Stars. In rare cases, toddler star beings can be a factor. And like the teenage star beings, they'll gradually grow into an adult."

"When the star woman pushes the Crystallized Keileimia out of her, does it hurt?" Kimiko queried.

"We barely feel anything," Ulanahar replied.

"What about any other problems humans and other species have?" Kimiko questioned. "Do we have them?"

"No," Velcrimia answered. "We don't have the same issues as humans or any other species. We don't age. We don't have to eat. We don't have to go to the restroom. We don't experience agonizing childbirth.

"We don't die from diseases and any other inconveniences most species have. We aren't regarded as the most powerful for no reason.

There are more benefits to being a star being than anything. After all, we are the First People."

"Whoa, fucking cool!" Kimiko stated. "Alright, trick question for ya! Ulanahar, does the same logic apply when a star man mates with a female human or a goddess?"

"Yes. Star men have very dominant genes. Iloreiyus still applies, as well as sending the crystallized egg to his constellation should he choose to do so. Since the female human or goddess is not a star being, they do not possess Keileimia.

"However, if the star man mates with a female human, their child may require nourishment, since it'll be half human, half star.

"And as for the star man mating with a goddess, the same logic applies, except their child will be half deity, half star."

"Which is stronger, though?" Kimiko inquired.

"Full-fledged star beings, of course," Ulanahar replied.

"...You know, we sound like some bigot motherfuckers..." Kimiko said.

"No, these are facts, Kimiko," Ulanahar stated.

"Okay, another trick question," Kimiko said. "Does the same logic apply to star women who mate with a human man or god?"

"The Keileimia in us acts as the star man's Leikaitas," Ulanahar said. "Meaning when the god's or human man's sperm come into contact with our Keileimia, the Keileimia will crystallize itself, a process known as *Iloreimiac.*

"Afterward, the process is essentially the same as if we made love with a star man. Overall, no matter the gender, we star beings are very dominant and complex entities."

"What's the difference between sperm and Leikaitas?" Kimiko asked.

"Leikaitas houses spiritual and unique properties that benefit not just the Keileimia, but us as well," Ulanahar replied. "It also sparkles. Sperm is only subjected to the worldly plane of existence and doesn't possess the assets Leikaitas has.

"Not to mention making love with another star being... being skin to skin with them... it's like being transported to another aspect of reality entirely. It can't be rivaled. It's *that* good.

"And if we aren't ready for children, either the star man can place a temporary star barrier, or *Ethomeist*, around our Keileimia or we could do it ourselves.

"Overall, most star beings prefer to mate with their own species. We're very selective about who we choose to have sex with. Whether if it's casual sex or spiritual lovemaking, we're careful about who we lie down with.

"In addition, sexual chemistry is paramount. The more akin the star beings are in various aspects, the better the sexual experience. Their smell. Their taste. How attractive they are. The sound of their voice. How they make us feel when we touch.

"And most importantly, how our clairvoyance interprets them.

"If the sexual chemistry is present, the sex will be incredibly intense to the point the star couple doesn't want the lovemaking to end. It's *that* serious for us. We can endure for days, maybe even weeks. In fact, the star couple could possibly have sex for as long as they're willing.

"No other species can handle us sexually or otherwise. Our potent sex drive and powers would severely overwhelm them.

"We also want the best for our star offspring should a star couple decide to have any. Our genes are very powerful, after all."

"You're really smart, Ulanahar," Kimiko said. "But I know you're a freak in the bed."

"Of course. I love the spirituality behind making love. It's beautiful. We're the Masters of Existence, the Masters of the Arts for a reason. Sex is one of our strong aspects."

"You're like the older sister I never had," Kimiko said. "You're smart. And shit rarely gets under your skin. I mess with you because I like you, but damn, you just brush off my pestering comments."

"Because I know you mean well, Kimiko," Ulanahar stated. "Had I thought otherwise... well... I'd rather not get into scenarios."

"Hey wait..." Kimiko said. "Is it possible for star beings to have siblings, or have twins?"

"Of course," Ulanahar stated. "Star beings can have brothers and sisters. But twins are a rarity. Yet, as of right now, we and Courage are the Originals, the First Star Beings."

"Here's my question, Ulanahar," Velcrimia said. "We're the strongest. The best, correct? Well, what if a human or god tries to subdue us?"

"It's impossible for a human to defeat us in any way. For example, a man can punch us in the face. We won't feel anything, but he will. He'll most likely break his hand.

"Even if he tries to stab us in the eye, it won't work. And as for a god, he better be all he says he is. Otherwise, his defeat is imminent."

"Is it possible that if our constellation is eliminated, then we'll cease to exist?" Kimiko asked.

"Anyone dense enough to fight our respective constellation has a death wish," Ulanahar said. "Those Supreme Beings are ridiculously powerful.

"Each of them has their own powers and range of attacks that can annihilate countless celestial bodies, as well as universes. And under the right circumstances, we can *become* them. We *are* them.

"We have various transformations that can give us a substantial advantage. We'll also have access to a wider range of incredible powers. We're already insanely powerful, so imagine what it's like being under the influence of our variations.

"Star beings don't possess any weaknesses our opposition can exploit, so almost any attempt to subdue us will likely fail.

"We also have a very exceptional healing factor.

"However, if the worse occurred, the elimination of our constellation doesn't, in turn, kill us or severely hamper our powers. It may not even lessen the chances of our return should we ever face defeat.

"In fact, I think our constellation may take a while to return. Like us. The Chosen People of the Universe isn't just something we say, after all. It's what we are."

"What can we survive?" Kimiko asked.

"Many things," Ulanahar said. "The list is too extensive to name everything. From magma, incredible ocean depths, radiation, outer space, black holes, to cosmic explosions, there's not much that can kill us. Our opponent has to be of *our* caliber. There's no in between.

"We're the Chosen People of the Universe. All other life forms pale in comparison to us. We were gifted since the beginning. And we use our talents wisely.

"However, things of a celestial nature can harm us. Nothing more."

"You have my respect, Ulanahar," Kimiko said.

"Likewise," Velcrimia stated.

"It's my pleasure to enlighten," Ulanahar said.

"So what now?" Kimiko asked.

"We could wait for Courage to return," Ulanahar suggested. "After the ceremony, he and Flowerensia disappeared."

"He's probably fucking her relentlessly," Kimiko said. "You know, making her have *multiple* orgasms."

"Sounds sweet," Ulanahar stated. "Though I highly doubt Flowerensia could handle Courage. He's too much for her."

"You like Courage, Ulanahar and Velcrimia?" Kimiko queried.

"Yes, I like him," Ulanahar replied. "I want to make sweet love to him. He's so dominant. And very attractive."

"So you like the pretty boy type?" Kimiko joked.

"It doesn't matter," Ulanahar said. "As long as a man is dominant and sincere, he could be a pretty boy or rugged."

"He's definitely one of a kind," Velcrimia stated. "But... I have my thoughts on another wonderful star man..."

"Courage's alright," Kimiko said. "But I've had my eyes on Janeiholm for a while. He said he was going to Rhol'heima to finally meet the legend."

"That's right," Velcrimia stated. "Helipak and Gravulkim said they were going with him."

"That's probably where they are right now," Kimiko said.

"What about Transidyus?" Velcrimia blushed. "Anyone hear from him?"

Kimiko snickered.

"Well, look who likes who. You getting wet down there, Velcrimia? Not so much of a "Celestial Maiden" with *those* thoughts, now are you?"

"Kimiko... shut up..." Velcrimia retorted.

"Transidyus only comes about when it's urgent or when he has something important to relay," Ulanahar said. "Not to mention, besides Courage, he's one of the most powerful star beings ever.

"He has an absurd amount of Staraidus. Even if he tries to mask it, it still manages to make its phenomenal presence known. It's... really scary. Regardless... he's very attractive..."

"What about Leiku?" Velcrimia queried. "I haven't seen him in a while, either."

"Like Transidyus, the same applies to Leiku," Ulanahar said. "Those two are… my gracious. They're beyond remarkable. Courage may have his work cut out if he attempts to fight two Grandmasters of the Universe."

"Being a Grandmaster of the Universe is incredibly profound," Velcrimia stated. "You're absolutely right, Ulanahar. Courage is one of the greatest, yet a Grandmaster Star Being is one of the many exceptions."

"Well instead of standing here yapping, we should see if they're at Rhol'heima," Kimiko said.

"Agreed," Ulanahar stated.

Velcrimia, Ulanahar, and Kimiko teleported to Rhol'heima.

"The audacity…" Feloreigro said. "You speak with such passion, yet you disregard the powers of the deities. Such rashness…"

"I beg your pardon?" Courage asserted. "I don't see you speaking highly of us, either. You damn right I'm going to place star beings before anything because that's who I represent.

"No one in the cosmos can compete with us since we're on an entirely different playing field. Again, these are facts.

"And I can see the hate in your eyes, old man. Don't try to hide it. I wouldn't be surprised if you're one of the many deities that despise us.

"You're the God of Time, yet have the audacity to feign ignorance about star beings being the *First* People. The *first* brilliant, spiritual people ever."

Courage pointed toward the three male star beings.

"Those three over there. I don't know them, yet I know damn well they have abilities unlike any other. *That* is what makes us a force in our own right."

"You..." Feloreigro said. "Transcendent One, what you say is all fact. However, I *highly* disapprove of your hostile tone. No one has done anything to you. I brought you here to congratulate you. Not scold you, or any other star being."

Courage scoffed.

"If you have such resentment toward us, why did you allow them passage here?" Courage questioned.

"I never stated I hated star beings," Feloreigro defended. "And they came here to meet with you, since they missed an opportunity to meet you at your ceremony. They were busy with other matters and received word that you would be here eventually."

"Is that so?" Courage queried. "Hold on. I want to finish this discussion, but I want to see what these three are about."

Courage approached the three male star beings.

The very effeminate one gasped.

Then, he blushed.

He placed his hand on his chest.

"Oh sweet stars, he's coming!" Helipak said. "What should we do?"

"Calm down, man," Janeiholm stated. "Learn how to take a breather."

"Right," Gravulkim agreed. "You get worked up over your own shadow sometimes."

Helipak, Janeiholm, and Gravulkim are Melhouna, as well as Original Stars.

All three waited with great anticipation to finally meet Courage, especially Helipak.

Courage stood before them.

"Gralokmara. (Greetings). My name is Courage. Pleasure to make your acquaintance."

Astrailese is the official language of the star beings.

Meilinese is the universal dialect.

"Hey, man. How ya doing? The name's Janeiholm Secremel. I appreciate you sticking up for us."

"Of course," Courage said. "I'm passionate about who we are and what we represent."

Courage and Janeiholm shook hands.

Janeiholm has a high top fade hairstyle with a braided ponytail.

He has brown skin, dark eyebrows, brown eyes, and a muscular physique.

He wore a tropical shirt that has a depiction of an ocean with numerous palm trees on an island.

He wore yellow fingerless mix martial arts gloves, yellow sweatpants, and brown sandals.

Janeiholm's constellation is *Epi'phinahas*, the Celestial Jaguar.

"H-hi, handsome! Pleasure to meet you as well! The name's Helipak Zetesteen, but you can call me *Heli* or Helinara!"

Helipak has short blond hair with bangs, pristine fair skin, blond eyebrows, prominent dark eyelashes, a highly feminine face, green eyes, and a slim, graceful figure.

He also has a very womanly voice.

Helipak wore a black scarf, a blue vest, black arm length fishnet gloves, blue shorts, and blue shoes.

He also wore blue glittering polish on his fingernails.

Helipak's constellation is *Wyen'deishia*, the Celestial Deer.

Helipak approached Courage.

He stopped inches from him.

Helipak looked into Courage's eyes.

It was love at first sight.

"My... you're better than I expected..." Helipak said. "It's *definitely* a *pleasure* to meet you, love..."

"Thank you, ma'am..." Courage replied.

Helipak gazed at him seductively.

He raised his hand near his lips.

He arched his fingers.

Then, he giggled.

"Aren't you something special, dear? So sweet of you, honey..."

"Hey uh... Courage?" Janeiholm intervened. "Helipak's not a... girl. He's a dude..."

"Janeiholm's right, Courage," Gravulkim said. "Helipak has a very... feminine appearance."

"What?" Courage questioned. "But... how...? This has to be a female..."

Helipak laughed.

"I love you already, sweetie. I look forward to taking *good* care of you, Precious Star of my Heart. Narosasei aront..." (Delectable honey...)

"Helipak, stop..." Janeiholm said. "You're embarrassing yourself. And us as well."

Gravulkim sighed in disbelief.

"Regardless, my name is Gravulkim Sydemyic. It's an honor to meet you, Courage."

Gravulkim has long red hair, green skin, bushy red eyebrows, a short red beard, yellow eyes, and a large muscular build.

Gravulkim wore a long beige overcoat.

Under the overcoat, he wore a black vest that has several black belts secured around it.

He wore massive silver gauntlets, and blue pants that were tucked into his silver boots.

Gravulkim's constellation is *Doncil'doras*, the Celestial Bear.

Helipak chuckled.

"Oh don't worry about these two, dear Courage. They're just jealous that my admiration of you exceeds theirs…"

"What?" Janeiholm said. "We respect him for being an outstanding dude! It's you who's taking it too far!"

"He's right, Helipak," Gravulkim stated. "Showing respect and being obsessive are two different things."

Helipak conjured an Ovele'mulus.

He gently placed the stem between his forefinger and middle finger.

He handed it to Courage, who was very skeptical.

"From me, to you, love…"

"My goodness, man…" Janeiholm said. "Please stop. This is so unnerving. I can tell he finds you weird. He doesn't want to bend you over and fuck you in your ass, Helipak. He doesn't want to lay between your legs and rub dicks with you, either.

"Stop flirting with him. Shit, if anything, he could kill you without even trying."

"I can be either a female or a male if I so desire," Helipak said. "I have an affinity for the feminine. Nevertheless, I'd rather die by his hands than anyone else's. Anything otherwise is unacceptable…"

"Fucking hell…" Janeiholm relented.

"I agree with everything Janeiholm said," Gravulkim stated. "Anyway, can we move along before Helipak takes his obsession to another level? I don't want to imagine what's going through his conscious right now. It's so… ugh. Forget it…"

"Helipak…" Courage said. "This isn't a good time. I have important matters to attend to with the deity of this kingdom."

"Will you still accept my offer, love…?"

"I'm neutral when it comes to this particular matter."

"I see…"

Helipak was disappointed.

He loved Courage more than anything or anyone.

Courage was his inspiration.

He dispelled the Ovele'mulus.

"Well, love. If you ever change your mind, I'm always waiting for you. 'K?"

"It's best not to get your hopes up," Courage stated. "Don't set yourself up for failure. Move on and find the one who'll reciprocate your love. Or become independent and grow stronger than you are now."

Helipak hung his head in shame.

He closed his eyes.

He shook his head.

"I can't… you're all I've thought about…"

Courage sighed.

"Helipak… look at me…"

Helipak slowly lifted his head.

Then, he slowly opened his eyes.

He was on the verge of tears.

"You're not weak," Courage said. "I refuse to believe that. Push yourself and I *promise* you'll see progress. You just have to believe. You just have to put forth the effort. May the universe provide for you, Helipak."

Astral Tears fell from Helipak's eyes.

"T-thank you… honey…"

"Great day to you, Helipak. To all of you."

Courage marched away.

Helipak watched as Courage walked away.

He placed his hand on his chest.

He closed his eyes.

Thank you, beloved. I won't forget you, Courage. Ever.

Courage approached Feloreigro.

"Now, where were we? Oh right. You claim you don't hate star beings, yet it seems you're denying our history for the sake of your own. Am I wrong?"

"Of course you are. All I stated was that you have a lack of regard for the might of the deities. All of the deities here surely do not take kindly to your crudeness."

"I couldn't give less than a fuck what they think of me, or star beings. You expect me to apologize for feeling passionate about who I am? No. Not going to happen. Ever.

"I don't want, nor expect, someone else to speak highly of us. Yet, our history is ingrained throughout the universe, so I'd expect the God of Time to acknowledge that. Not mince words.

"The deities, as well as any other species, that chose to confront countless star beings over the years had a point to prove, which I find beyond pathetic.

"Star beings never had to prove a damn thing to anyone. Star beings' duty is to safeguard the cosmos, create, and grow as a people. In perfect harmony. That's more than I can say about any other species."

Flowerensia grasped her arm.

She looked away.

"Courage... you're right, dear..."

Feloreigro was highly upset by Courage's condescending demeanor.

He abruptly rose from his throne.

"Arrogance!"

Courage immediately took a fighting stance.

Feloreigro was surprised.

This star being... the Transcendent One. Indeed... he is a very dangerous kind...

Everyone throughout Rhol'heima was shocked.

"Is he really going to fight Feloreigro?" a god queried. "He can't be. There's no way he'd win. That pompous bastard's gonna regret speaking out of term. Feloreigro might be old, but he still got skills."

"You're a fucking idiot," a goddess countered. "If he dealt with Deathelena, mind you while holding back the majority of the time, what makes you think he can't hold his own against Feloreigro?

"I'm not biased. These are just simple facts many of you are choosing to ignore for the sake of your bruised ego."

"If you're sticking up for your sociopathic boyfriend, then why don't you go join him?" another god said. "Fucking traitor. And you have the nerve to be a goddess. You're no better than the peasants."

"Again, you're proving my point," the goddess stated. "Such an emotional response. Why would the Transcendent One even be here if he feared us? I respect him for speaking his mind, as well as knowing his history. He loves himself and those like him.

"He's not saying he has a lack of regard for any other species. Yet, he'll always place star beings first, since that's what he is. You dumbasses fail to realize his point of view. You emotional fucktards."

"Melharina… thank you…" Flowerensia said.

Melharina leaped toward Flowerensia.

She landed next to her.

"Long time, no see, old friend!" Melharina said.

Melharina is the Goddess of Light.

Melharina has long brown hair with bangs, beautiful fair skin, dark eyebrows, blue eyes, and a lovely shape.

She wore a lavish pink robe, a yellow sash, purple pants, and violet shoes.

Melharina rules *Leidonia* Kingdom, which resides on planet *Ki'ordyna*.

Ki'ordyna is surrounded diagonally by two vibrant rings – the *Ki'ordyntrias*.

The emblem of Melharina's nation is the *Paralinquia*, which is an illuminate blue circle with eleven spiritual gates on its parameter and holy glyphs on the interior.

It represented enlightenment.

Rhol'heima is utilized as a meeting vicinity whenever Feloreigro has something of importance to convey.

"You're so lucky, dear," Melharina stated. "The Transcendent One landed in your kingdom. Get it? He *landed* in your *kingdom?*"

"You're still perverted as always..." Flowerensia blushed.

"Damn right," Melharina said. "And so are you."

"Ah... you know me so well..."

"Of course. So, is there any way to calm the hunk and the old fart down?"

"C-Courage... please. Let's not do this. Let's resolve this peacefully."

"I sense the fangirl in you, Flower..." Melharina teased. "You'd do anything to fuck him. Or, you'd love for him to completely dominate you and have his way with you for hours, maybe even days.

"I wouldn't be surprised if you're wet in the panties thinking about him now, *if* you even have anything on under that robe..."

Flowerensia's blush deepened.

She released a very low moan.

She looked away.

"Now's not a good time, Melharina..."

"Silence, you two!" Feloreigro ordered. "Surely you do not wish to fight me, Transcendent One? I mean you, or any star being, no harm. However, it is you who has the hostile attitude."

"Don't try to get by me with that nonsense," Courage said. "If you don't want to acknowledge the facts I've stated, that's fine. But living in denial doesn't do anyone any good."

"Your history is clear as the sky," Feloreigro stated. "I do not know why certain deities would belittle themselves into attempting to rival the star beings. Mayhap their ego got the better of them and sought to make their point."

"Well, for so-called "almighty beings", they sure made a fool of themselves," Courage said. "I'm sure the star beings laid waste to their asses."

"Transcendent One… enough…" Feloreigro stated. "If you wish to fight, I will not be the one who will engage you. If you want, pick one of the gods to face you. It will be to the death. Should either of you choose to do so."

Courage looked toward the crowd of deities.

Some of the gods and goddesses glared at him.

The other deities remained silent.

Courage chuckled.

"Hmph. One's not enough. Give me three of them."

Everyone gasped.

"What?" Flowerensia shouted. "Have you lost your mind, Courage? We can resolve this peacefully!"

"So you doubt me?" Courage queried.

"Never! But there's a time to fight and a time to be diplomatic!"

"True. But when there are beings that believe they're better than star beings, and try to prove they are by attacking them, that's where I draw the fucking line. Had I known about this sooner, I would've intervened.

"I didn't want to be gruff, yet when it comes to the wellbeing of my people, I don't need anyone thinking they can walk over us and believe there won't be any consequences. *Everyone* is cast under judgment. Deities included. No exceptions.

"It's not in my interest to start a war. However, when you fight with *one* star being, you fight with *all* of us. With the exception of Azagnorpors who haven't conquered their evil tendencies."

"Are three gods truly what you want, Transcendent One?" Feloreigro asked.

Madness! What "is" this being? He wants to take on three gods all by himself! I bet he really wants to fight the entirety of Rhol'heima! I would not put it past him if he wants to fight me as well. This man breathes fighting!

"Let's get this show on the road," Courage replied.

Courage pointed to the three gods he wanted to engage.

They were of considerable size.

"You, you, and you. Come on. Let's go."

The three gods stepped forward.

They snarled.

The God of Wind.

The God of Earth.

And the God of Fire stood before Courage.

They wanted to end him.

"You three can either attack all at once or one at a time," Courage said. "Makes me no difference."

"Hey, shut your mouth!" the God of Wind said. "Such impudence!"

"It's impudent that I care about my people being belittled by idiots like you?" Courage countered. "Wow. That's some *great* logic you possess."

"You're a psychopath," the God of Earth stated. "You're blaming us for other deities' problems. Not cool."

"I'm not blaming anyone, since I don't know who specifically attacked my people," Courage said. "It makes me no difference. The point is you three idiots took the challenge, when all you had to do was decline.

"If what I stated doesn't apply to *any* of you, then why is everyone so upset? Is it because there's truth to what I said? Those who are silent during a wrongdoing are just as guilty as those who actually committed the crime! No excuses!"

"Maybe some heat will help you cool out," the God of Fire said.

The God of Fire raised his hand.

A fire sphere emerged above his palm.

The God of Fire threw the fire sphere at Courage.

Everyone thought Courage would be burned to cinders.

Yet, that was far from the truth.

Courage summoned the *Gwi'denahala*.

The Gwi'denahala is a purple, sacred geometric circle that has very eccentric symbols and glyphs around the parameter.

The Gwi'denahala is a multi-dimensional rift that can send anything Courage wants to where he deemed suitable.

The Gwi'denahala emerged before Courage as the fire sphere neared him.

The fire sphere passed the threshold of the Gwi'denahala.

Then, another Gwi'denahala appeared beneath the God of Fire.

Frousanei – which is celestial freezing wind – erupted from the Gwi'denahala.

The Gwi'denahala can also convert whatever element that enters it into something else entirely.

The God of Fire screamed in agony before his yell was abruptly halted.

The Frousanei froze him completely.

Then, Courage's eyes briefly illuminated solid purple – the *Fellordimia* – which, if the adversary was incapacitated, could instantly kill them.

The God of Fire shattered into pieces.

The *Frouzai* – which is celestial ice – fell into the Gwi'denahala.

The hint of red within the Frouzai were the remains of the God of Fire.

Courage dispelled the Gwi'denahalas.

"Y-you killed the God of Fire...?" the God of Wind queried. "H-how...?"

"Instead of asking questions, attack me," Courage replied. "The same goes for you, God of Earth. Both of you attack me at once."

Indignant, the God of Wind swung his colossal sword horizontally at Courage.

When the assault neared, it struck Courage.

Everyone gasped.

The God of Wind defeated Courage.

Or so the God of Wind thought.

What he perceived as Courage was nothing more than an astral clone – a *Fedmori'ia* – which disintegrated into green particles when the God of Wind struck it.

The God of Wind looked about before noticing the genuine Courage stooped on the head of his sword.

"Bastard! What in the…! How is this even possible?"

The God of Wind summoned a spiral of wind around his sword.

Swiftly, Courage punched the God of Wind between his eyes.

The God of Wind felt indescribable agony.

His eyes popped out of his head as he glided across Hyrenal Summit.

The God of Wind fell off the edge.

He plummeted below the clouds into nothingness.

The God of Wind's eyes fell near Courage.

Courage utilized Fellordimia to eliminate them.

Only the God of Earth remained.

The God of Earth punched the cloud.

Courage summoned the Gwi'denahala below himself as a countermeasure.

A stalagmite emerged below Courage.

The Gwi'denahala reversed the stalagmite.

Another Gwi'denahala appeared on the cloud a few feet away from the God of Earth.

The stalagmite emerged from the Gwi'denahala.

Then, it arched rapidly toward the God of Earth.

The stalagmite pierced his abdomen.

It emerged on the other side of his body.

The God of Earth screamed in pain.

Courage summoned three metallic cubes – the *Tru'ethra* Cubes – which rotated in any direction from its stationary position.

Next, the Tru'ethra Cubes slowed to a stop.

Then, a piercing green eye with a reflection of the universe – the Eye of Tauran'creima – emerged on the Tru'ethra Cubes.

The Eyes of Tauran'creima glared through the God of Earth.

The *Meidoreha'agreda* is a powerful sacred attack capable of shattering any living being's will.

It forces them to relive the anguish of their past, the pain of the present, and the agony of their future simultaneously.

It also revealed their fears, secrets, and weaknesses, which causes them substantial agony.

The God of Earth's anguish was inconceivable.

Courage displayed no remorse.

Each Eye of Tauran'creima on the Tru'ethra Cubes warped into a green vortex – the *Zie'onra*.

Then, the God of Earth disintegrated into each Zie'onra.

His screams of anguish became distorted as his fragmented body passed through the Zie'onras.

Once the God of Earth was completely eliminated, Courage dispelled the Meidoreha'agreda, the Gwi'denahalas, and the Tru'ethra Cubes.

Next, Courage released Tauran'creima's Bellow, as a celebration for his victory.

The entirety of Rhol'heima shook.

When the quake ebbed, Courage stood in silence.

He watched the clouds drift by.

"Tauran'creima's Pride… lives on…" Courage stated.

Then, Courage looked toward the deities, who immediately backed away from him.

Next, Courage looked at Feloreigro, who was paralyzed with fear.

I… I cannot believe it. He actually killed three gods on his own. T-there is no way someone like him should exist. Yet… here he is. He is beyond logic. He is… too dangerous…

Moreover, Courage looked toward Flowerensia and Melharina, who were also scared.

Lastly, Courage looked at Helipak, Janeiholm, and Gravulkim.

All three were completely shocked.

Yet, Helipak giggled.

And his blush was prominent.

So sexy… so powerful…

He sighed.

So dreamy…

However, as a result of having very lustful thoughts of Courage he could not control, he fainted.

He landed softly on his back on the cloud.

"You dumbass…" Janeiholm scolded.

Gravulkim placed his hand over his face.

He shook his head.

"Good grief."

Then, Courage noticed three star females standing near Helipak and co.

They witnessed the entire bout as well, and were utterly surprised.

Courage approached the three star females.

"Gralokmara. (Greetings.) I take it you three are frightened as well?"

"Uh… k-kinda…" Kimiko admitted.

"All I can say is that you're very powerful beyond any doubt," Velcrimia said.

"Courage," Ulanahar said. "You proved the legend to be true. The power you possess is unprecedented. And, you have our respect for having the star beings' best interest at heart."

"You're an Azagnorpor," Courage noted. "Yet, I'm glad you aren't like the rest of them."

"My respects, Courage," Ulanahar stated. "Thank you very much."

"If I may ask, what are your names?" Courage queried.

"Ulanahar Gekonia."

"Velcrimia Celestia."

"Kimiko Lybena."

"Pleased to meet the three of you," Courage said.

Suddenly, a mysterious star being, a Melhouna, emerged.

"Transidyus…" Velcrimia said.

The entirety of Rhol'heima felt Transidyus' presence.

His inconceivable Staraidus presented substantial fear.

Transidyus has short dark hair, brown skin, dark eyebrows, intense yellow eyes with narrow pupils, and an athletic build.

Transidyus wore a black headband that has lengthy tails, a black elaborate overcoat that has small chains connected to metal rings, a corresponding black vest, black pants with small chains, and black boots.

He also wore black leather fingerless gloves.

Transidyus' constellation is *Fireiya*, the Celestial Horse.

He is an Original Star.

The Glyph of Fireiya was in the center of his headband and on the back of his overcoat.

"That power… who are you?" Courage asked.

"Transidyus Misohareila is my name."

"This may be sudden, but I'd like to have a match with you," Courage said. "I've been looking for an exceptional challenge for a long time."

"I'm afraid I can't do that. There are crucial matters that I must attend to."

"Pardon? As customary of star beings, when one of us challenges another to a duel, it must be taken, lest that individual be ever seen as a coward. You have astonishing power. I feel as if I can learn much from you by having a proper duel."

"Courage. I promise that you'll get the match you deserve. But right now, it can't be helped. Not to mention, you still have much to experience."

"…I'll accept your words. I look forward to the day we face each other."

"Likewise. In the meantime, you should go to Zeinhailurein. Someone wishes to see you."

"Really? Who?"

"I can't say. You'll find out once you get there. That person will relay the details to you."

"Fine. Thank you."

"Great day, Courage. And I intend to keep my promise."

"It's great to see you again, Transidyus…" Velcrimia said.

"Likewise, Velcrimia," Transidyus replied. "Take care, Celestial Maiden, Teretri'aga."

Transidyus marched away.

He teleported from Rhol'heima.

"See beyond your horizon."

 **Chapter 5**

Zeinhailurein, The Spirit World

Deathelena stood on the balcony of her castle.

She pondered.

Asai... I promised that I'd find a way to awaken you. And that's a promise I intend to keep. Little dearest... just hang in there. For me.

After Deathelena awoke, she proceeded thinking of a way to awaken Asai.

Since dark beings' therapeutic capabilities have no influence upon Melhounas or beings of divine origin, Deathelena was truly worried Asai would remain in a coma for eternity.

95

She assumed Asai would awaken once her wounds healed.

Yet, lamentably, that was not the case.

Deathelena gazed toward the horizon of the sea of *Killosogma* of Hychineira Kingdom – the *Marligrat'chia* Sea.

Killosogma is celestial magma.

Killosogma is the most sweltering aspect throughout the universe.

Deathelena continued thinking of Asai.

She desperately wanted to find a solution to her plight.

Her only means of awakening Asai would be to abduct a Melhouna and force them to use their power to awaken her.

The only Melhouna she could think of was the one who defeated her twice.

That Melhouna was Courage.

She figured it would be suicide trying to fight him on her own again.

Yet, she had to think of a plan that he could not outmaneuver.

I warned him I'd get him. Yet... he's so damn powerful. I hate it. Perhaps I'll send someone in my stead... and get him when he least expects it. Hopefully, after countless years, I'll finally do away with him.

She thought of using one of her Hychineirian female minions as a decoy.

She thought of sending one of them as a messenger.

They would tell Courage of a misfortune.

Yet, unbeknownst to him, they would lead him to Deathelena's Castle, where he would awaken Asai.

Afterward, Deathelena would abruptly emerge and eliminate Courage.

She did not have an additional plan if Courage managed to outmaneuver her.

Regardless, Deathelena was known for effectively improvising.

"Elaimia!" Deathelena called. "Get your ass out here!"

The mysterious individual Deathelena called appeared beside her.

Elaimia Besolei has short brown hair, flawless fair skin, brown eyebrows, a pretty face, red eyes, and a slim frame.

She wore a fitted mesh bodysuit that covered her from her neck down to her thighs.

Over this, she wore a long black overcoat with a red inseam, a dark blue mini-skirt, a black belt that has several weaponry pouches attached to it, black knee-high sandals, and violet shin guards that have the Glyph of Scorpreikia in the center.

The Glyph of Scorpreikia was also on the back of her overcoat, as well as in the middle of her light blue headband, which has extended tails.

Her fingernails and toenails were painted red and black respectively.

A Hychineirian Kunai Knife holster was secured about her thighs.

Elaimia is one of Deathelena's most faithful female fighters.

She is a Lieutenant General.

She is not as powerful as Fesforia.

However, she is most certainly talented.

"Yes, Goddess Deathelena. How may I be of service?"

"Go find that nuisance Courage. Make up a story and lead him here. I want him to awaken Asai. I've tried everything I can think of, yet she hasn't awakened. Now, I'm forced to swallow my pride and seek outside assistance with this matter."

"Hmph. So the lousy legend has come to pass. And he's more than we bargained for. You're right. What a nuisance. Regardless, leave it to me, Goddess Deathelena. I'll lead him straight to death herself."

"He's crafty, Elaimia. Don't get overconfident. There's no way you'll beat him directly. Hell, I nearly died fighting him…"

"Say what? You lost? Again? How powerful *is* this dude?"

"Stronger than you care to know, dear. When he was Tauran'creima eons ago, it was a tremendous pain. I couldn't do anything to him. He was impervious to everything I threw at him. As such, I was forced to retreat before he killed me.

"These star beings, especially him, far surpass deities and many other species. It's unnerving. How can anything outshine gods and goddesses is beyond me…"

T-this is crazy! Deathelena lost to the legend's constellation first. Then, she lost to him again? I think it's unwise to lead a ticking time bomb like this legend to our base of operation.

Though Deathelena has a plan, if it goes wrong, he could kill everyone here. My goodness… I hate the thought of it…

Elaimia refused to display fear.

Yet, Deathelena's experience had her apprehensive.

Deathelena sensed her subtle anxiety.

She chuckled.

"Fear not. You'll be fine. Just be careful. He's far from the idiot I assumed, yet you have to use your mind and intuition more than usual. If he senses any kind of deception, you may undergo intense interrogation, or he might just kill you. He's a ruthless prick."

"O-of course, Goddess Deathelena…"

"If he does see through your lie, who knows, he might just fuck you mercilessly as punishment."

Deathelena laughed.

Elaimia blushed.

"S-say what? He'd *never* do that to anyone, my goddess! That's... unheard of!"

"You're very pretty. So it stands to reason he may substitute killing you for pleasure. Something you'd surely like, especially coming from him. He'd enjoy breaking your scrawny ass."

"Hell no! He's the enemy! Why would the enemy fuck me?"

"To get information out of you. You know this. It's a form of torture. Not to mention the more sexually appealing the captive, the better reason they have for fucking them senseless. War isn't just about bloodshed; it's about who's smarter and the most ruthless."

"Well what about you? Even though you hate his fucking guts, surely you've thought of fucking him, or vice versa? Hate and love are two sides of the same coin.

"We've had our pick of the litter over the years, but that was just meaningless sex just to weaken our victims. I know you, Deathelena. You're merciless. And immoral."

"I'm sure he'd fuck me good. I can tell. Yet, I know for certain he'd *never* meet a woman that's freaky like me. Ever."

"Like you just told me, Goddess Deathelena, don't get overconfident. Forgive me. Yet, everyone of this army needs to keep that in mind."

"Fesforia could learn many things from you, dear. Though she's one of the strongest I have, she can be a complete idiot sometimes, which works against her significantly. Regardless, be careful around Courage, lest you want kinky things done to your three holes."

Deathelena cackled.

"Even though I don't want to entertain such a thing, you're right. Though I don't see how you can find humor in such horrific things."

"It's part of life, dear. Anyone who's ignorant enough to ignore such gruesome aspects is bound to fall prey to them. Heroes or not, no one is above ruthlessness. Furthermore, I created most of you, so surely you find humor in the darker aspects of life?"

"Yes. To a degree."

"I see. Nevertheless, be careful. One false move, and it's over for you."

Deathelena turned to Elaimia.

She walked toward her.

When she neared, she gently placed her hands on her cheeks.

Elaimia gasped.

Her blush deepened.

Deathelena closed her eyes.

Then, she embraced Elaimia.

She kissed her lips.

She moaned into her mouth.

Elaimia was shocked.

Yet, she submitted to Deathelena.

She returned her embrace.

She closed her eyes.

She receded into bliss.

Deathelena and Elaimia have a history of being intimate.

They are bisexual, as with many women in the Hychineirian and Relmi'shirian Army.

Fesforia is receptive to bisexuality as well.

The Hychineirian males are mostly heterosexual.

However, there are a few who are bisexual, or strictly homosexual.

Deathelena slowly withdrew from Elaimia's lips.

A string of saliva stretched between their lips.

Deathelena licked the saliva string into her mouth.

Elaimia kept her eyes closed.

She never wanted the intimacy to end.

Deathelena chuckled.

"Should you succeed, love, I'll treat you to a love session you'll never forget. You'll be treated tenderly, from your pretty face to your beautiful toes…"

"A-and… s-should I fail…?"

"You won't. But if you do, and manage to survive, then it's in the dungeon you go. And I'll have Fesforia join you. I'm sure she'd love to have endless hours of fun with you.

"You told me how exceptionally good she is, so I know you don't want her to extend that astronomical pleasure…"

Deathelena kissed her lips once more.

Elaimia shivered with glee.

"Now go. Courage should be in Flowerensia's kingdom. She's always following him like a lost bitch or a desperate whore. An utter fangirl she is. However, if you truly don't know where to look for him, ask those peasants of her kingdom. They should know.

"Evale." (Farewell.)

Deathelena and co. often spoke *Hychineirese* when it was convenient.

Then, Elaimia magically changed her clothes in a flash of light.

She was garbed in a black robe with a hood, which covered her eyes.

She vanished from the balcony.

Courage and co. walked through the mystical, misty spirit world of Zeinhailurein.

"Damn it," Courage said. "Does anyone know who the hell Transidyus was referring to?"

"He could be talking about the gorgeous Celestial Spirit, Serenity Addlebeen," Flowerensia replied. "She watches over this surreal world. Remember what I told you, Courage. Zeinhailurein was one of the many places foul beings attacked in the past."

"Indeed, you did tell me that. Yet, my question is how the hell does she know I exist? I can't go anywhere without someone knowing who I am. Very strange."

"You're famous, man," Janeiholm said. "You're the legend people spoke of. As such, being well known comes with the territory. I know it seems like a pain now, but just roll with it."

"You're right, Janeiholm," Courage stated. "I know it sounds like I'm complaining, but it's one of many reasons why I told Flowerensia I wanted to keep a low profile. I never knew I was so vital."

"One thing I love about you Courage is that even though you're rough around the edges, you have a modest spirit," Flowerensia said. "Yet, those rough edges are also what makes you special."

"Flowerensia... please stop..." Courage said.

"What?" Flowerensia stated. "I mean every word, dear."

"Ah-ha!" Kimiko stated. "I knew you loved him! Boyfriend and girlfriend! Sacred Star and Flower Goddess sitting in a tree! K-i-s-s-i-n-g! Yeah!"

"S-shut up, Kimiko!" Flowerensia blushed.

"You got her, Kimiko!" Melharina instigated. "Keep at it!"

"Oh yeah!" Kimiko said. "I'll get her some more!"

"Yeah..." Helipak stated. "Though they may look like a great couple, he's better off with me. My tenderness can't be rivaled."

"My goodness..." Janeiholm groused. "Dude, really? I bet you'd swallow everything he has, wouldn't you?"

"Of course," Helipak affirmed. "I bet it'd taste really sweet. He can have his way with me whenever, and however, he wants. I'd treat him like the Sacred Star he is."

"Helipak... give it a rest..." Gravulkim stated.

"Never," Helipak asserted. "Courage is mine. Always."

Melharina laughed.

"You've got your work cut out for you, o' Sacred Hero. Not only do you attract countless women, but you're a magnet for beautiful guys like Helipak."

Helipak blushed.

He twirled a lock of his hair around his index finger.

"Thank you, Goddess of Light."

"No problem, Celestial Deer."

"Melharina," Courage called. "Don't you start with me, either."

Melharina chuckled.

"You think Serenity's alright?" Velcrimia asked. "It's been awhile since I've been here. I'd hate to think something terrible happened when we weren't aware. She's incredible."

"She's fine, Velcrimia," Ulanahar replied. "She's not a pushover. Far from it."

Suddenly, two figures emerged near a tree.

Transidyus and an elderly man stood before Courage and co.

And like Transidyus, the elderly man is a Melhouna, an Original Star, and possesses unbelievable Staraidus.

"Transidyus," Courage said. "Nice to see you again. Who's the sage?"

"My name is Leiku Gania."

Leiku has white hair, fair skin, white eyebrows, a white pointy beard, solid white eyes, and a lean build.

He wore a black martial art robe, a red sash, black martial art pants, and black shoes.

Leiku's constellation is *Ole'donmori*, the Celestial Owl.

"What the hell are you two?" Courage asked. "Both of your power greatly exceeds mine. If you wanted, you could crush practically anything with your power alone."

"They're the Grandmasters of the Universe," Ulanahar informed. "You're very powerful, but these two are on another level. Like you, they're heavily revered.

"It takes exceptional discipline to reach their caliber. Make no mistake, we star beings exceed all else, but being a Grandmaster of the Universe is a league of its own."

"...I see," Courage said.

"I see the look of a fierce warrior in your eyes, Lofty Courage," Leiku said. "You only want to face those of your magnitude or greater. For that, you have my respect. Yet, like Transidyus stated, you have much to experience before you can become a Grandmaster like us."

Courage scoffed.

"Whoever said I wanted to become one?"

"With your potential, you will only become greater," Leiku said. "You are a Master Star. You are not the kind to be complacent. You are not admired as the Transcendent One for absolutely no reason."

"You read me like a book," Courage stated. "Yet, I'm wondering. Have you and Transidyus ever had a duel?"

"Yes," Leiku replied. "It ended in a stalemate. Neither of us could land a single strike. Whatever magic or martial art we utilized, we canceled each other out.

"We could have proceeded for decades. Centuries, even. Yet, there was always the possibility that the universe would have collapsed had we decided to get serious."

"What?" Courage said. "How the hell is that even possible?"

"You should know this, Lofty Courage," Leiku stated. "You are not a Grandmaster. Yet, you have extraordinary power. You are an anomaly among the star beings."

"So I've been told," Courage said. "But what about you two? Your power is beyond ridiculous."

"We are powerful, yes," Leiku stated. "Yet, you are the exceptional star. A Sacred Melhouna. Tauran'creima. All believed to be a myth. Yet, here you stand before us.

"And, even though you are the Transcendent One, you lack experience. There is much for you to learn."

"So I'm immature…" Courage said. "Is that it?"

"You are who you are," Leiku stated. "Yet, gaining experience will help you gain insight. In various ways."

"You're right," Courage said. "However, I have a question. If star beings don't age, why are you elderly?"

"Though I look old, I am not weak, as you can very well tell. I have my reasons for being this way."

"Perfect," Courage stated. "Because I look forward to fighting you as well, Leiku. You and Transidyus are what I've been looking for: a true challenge. I know it'll be enthralling. A genuine learning experience, to be sure."

"What are we, weaklings?" Kimiko said. "Come on, Courage. Don't do us like that."

"In comparison to these two, I'm afraid I won't settle," Courage stated. "Kimiko. Don't misunderstand. I know you and everyone here are powerful. In your own ways.

"However, in order for me to become much stronger, I must fight those at or above my skill level. That's the only way."

"O-of course…" Kimiko conceded. "But, don't be surprised if one of us challenges you, the Great Sacred Legend, to a duel as well. You're stronger than all of us, yet we could learn some things from you as well. Just like you may learn from Leiku and Transidyus. It's a cycle."

"Very clever, Kimiko," Courage said. "Indeed. I look forward to a bout with you. Or any of you who decide to challenge me. Come prepared."

Leiku chuckled.

"Likewise, Lofty Courage. Come prepared. Yet, once again, as Transidyus stated, you will get your match. In due time. However, in the meantime, Madam Serenity awaits you."

"Grandmaster Leiku…" Kimiko called. "If Courage is a Master Star, then what are me, Helipak, Gravulkim, Velcrimia, Janeiholm, and Ulanahar? Common Stars?"

"No. Like Lofty Courage said, every one of us surpasses the rest. That is a known fact. However, within every species, there is a hierarchy. Grandmaster Stars are at the apex. Master Stars are below Grandmaster Stars. All other stars are Acolyte Stars.

"Grandmaster Stars are extremely rare. Transidyus and I are the only Grandmasters throughout the universe. It takes phenomenal power, skill, and knowledge to become one. However, in Transidyus' and I's case, we were Grandmasters since the beginning."

"Well, Courage is the only star who isn't like us," Kimiko said. "He's extremely rare. He proved the legend true. So, by right, Courage should be a Grandmaster as well."

"Indeed," Leiku agreed. "However, he does not possess the experience, or wisdom, to be known as a Grandmaster yet."

"Without hardship, there is no learning experience," Gravulkim said. "What you say is true. Yet, how can you and Transidyus just become Grandmasters without any trials?"

"It is an enigma, Sir Gravulkim," Leiku admitted. "Some stars are just exponential from the beginning. That is merely how we are. Yet, there is always an opportunity to learn something from others. Learning is perpetual for everyone.

"Regardless, allow me to continue. Master Stars are somewhat rare. Grandmaster Stars are very rare. Acolyte Stars are those that have much to experience.

"In summary, think of these as ranks. It is a judgment of one's power. However, to all other species, we are a massive threat, regardless of the power that star may possess at that time."

"Thank you, Grandmaster Leiku," Kimiko stated. "There's so much I can learn from you. Heh. Courage was right, you are a sage. Good call, Courage!"

"Much appreciated, Kimiko," Courage said.

"Lofty Courage, Madam Serenity wishes to see you," Leiku stated. "We will surely meet again. Until then, take care."

Transidyus and Leiku teleported from Zeinhailurein.

Courage and co. stood before a pond.

A very beautiful woman was sitting in the glittering water.

This is celestial water known as *Aqualyra*.

It is the purest liquid in the cosmos.

It possesses healing properties beneficial to star beings.

The woman's eyes were closed.

And her legs were crossed.

"So... you've finally arrived, Courage..." the woman said. "A pleasure."

"Yeah..." Courage stated. "Are you Serenity? The one who rules this domain?"

"Yes. I'm the one who wants to speak with you."

Serenity rose to her feet.

Then, she slowly opened her eyes.

Serenity has short black hair with bangs, pale skin, dark eyebrows, light auburn eyes, and a thin figure.

A lavender robe was all Serenity wore.

The *Dironcreia* Orb is Zeinhailurein's emblem.

The Dironcreia Orb is a blue spiritual sphere that possesses nine powerful spiritual jewels – the *Zedithia* Gems.

Each Zedithia Gem varied in color.

The Dironcreia Orb symbolized spiritual growth and the Zedithia Gems represented the auras.

"Flowerensia and Melharina," Serenity acknowledged. "Glad to see you."

"Likewise," Flowerensia and Melharina said.

"You as well, Velcrimia and Ulanahar," Serenity stated.

"Thank you," Ulanahar said.

"I'm glad you're safe as well, Serenity," Velcrimia stated.

"To the rest of you, I welcome you to my world," Serenity said. "A world of eternal peace."

"It's not really peaceful if your world's been attacked…" Courage interrupted.

Janeiholm, Melharina, Flowerensia, and Kimiko were surprised at Courage's bold remark.

They covered their mouth in shock.

Yet, they also wanted to refrain from laughing.

Flowerensia blushed.

Really, dear? What a great way to make an impression. So savage.

Velcrimia, Helipak, Gravulkim, and Ulanahar placed their hand over their face in disbelief.

However, they could not deny that Courage had a good point.

Regardless, Helipak giggled.

Sweet Courage doesn't hold back at all. So beautifully handsome yet extremely rugged. So very sexy...

"Amusing," Serenity said. "So, not only is the Sacred Star very dangerous, but he's also witty. A sharp of the tongue, indeed."

"Basically, she called you a smartass, dude," Janeiholm stated.

"Not necessarily, dear," Serenity corrected. "He's very different. And that's very refreshing."

"Uh-huh, right..." Courage said. "It's the truth, regardless. If someone's territory is attacked once, there's a chance it could happen again, thus my reason behind my statement. Peace is compromised when losses are experienced."

"He's right, Serenity," Flowerensia stated. "I nearly lost my kingdom and my planet to Deathelena eons ago. Though we can learn from each assault, it still leaves us open to harm because other malevolent forces may find a way to breach our defenses and cause chaos."

"I see..." Serenity said. "Courage... may I speak with you alone?"

"Pardon? Why?"

"It's very vital."

"Fine. Let's go."

Janeiholm whistled his approval.

Then, he bobbed his eyebrows suggestively.

"Bullshit, Janeiholm," Courage rebutted. "And you know it."

"Yet, you *don't* know it," Janeiholm countered. "You're not in private with her yet."

"Clever," Courage conceded. "Yet, I stand firm on my statement."

Serenity extended her hand toward Courage.

"Transcendent One. Please. Come."

"It's alright for me to step in the Aqualyra?"

"Yes. Come forward."

Courage stepped into the pond.

Then, he marched toward Serenity.

He stopped a few feet before her.

"Why so skeptical, Courage?" Serenity asked. "Come closer and take my hand."

"Nah, I'm good. I'll tell you the same thing I told Flowerensia. And I quote: *"I would like to become accustomed to you before being excessively extrovert"*. End quote."

"I see... you do say what's on your conscious. Alright, I respect your choice. Let us go."

Serenity and Courage teleported from the vicinity.

"So what the hell are we supposed to do, Serenity?" Kimiko and Melharina protested. "Stay here like sitting ducks? Come on!"

"The pond's right here," Janeiholm joked. "So you don't have to worry about being a "sitting" duck when you can just "swim" like one."

"V-very funny, Janeiholm," Kimiko blushed. "Not to mention the water's too shallow."

"Man, Courage sure has a mean streak, eh Flower?" Melharina said.

"Indeed," Flowerensia agreed. "But that's part of what I love about him."

Serenity and Courage arrived in the middle of *Sarenadia* Sea.

Sarenadia Sea is an ocean of Aqualyra.

They both stood upon the shining water.

The sun was at its zenith in the clear blue sky.

"So, we're in the middle of an ocean, I see," Courage said. "Is this your ideal place for conveying messages?"

"You truly are amusing, Transcendent One…" Serenity stated. "And… I guess you could say it is…"

"And you say I'm the amusing one. You take that title tenfold. Yet, I'm receptive to this atmosphere."

"Thank you…"

"So what must you tell me?"

"I'm sure Flowerensia already informed you of what we've experienced over the years…"

"She did. She believes a bad omen is why numerous places were attacked by Azagnorpors and other assholes."

"Indeed. Even though attacks are common throughout the cosmos, they've never been on this scale."

"Why wasn't the rest of the team able to hear this?"

"I don't want to worry them…"

"Nonsense. We've all been through some kind of hell. In one way or another. Are you placing your faith solely in me for some reason?"

"Y-yes. You're the Sacred Star of the Cosmos, after all."

"So you're using me?"

"No, dear. Never. I'm sure all others you meet will regard you highly as well. Not just me. Regardless, your power exceeds most, so you're able to do things others cannot."

"In case you aren't aware, Transidyus and Leiku got me beat by light years when it comes to power. Why didn't you ask them for assistance?"

"Because they have their own trials to deal with. Being a Grandmaster Star is not a luxury."

"Say what…? Wait… Transidyus did say he was rather busy, which is the primary reason he wasn't able to face me in a proper duel…"

"Not to mention your Sacred Staraidus surpasses the lot. Evil stands no chance against you."

"Right… so what else is there? Surely that wasn't it?"

"No… I believe that there's someone rare. Like you. But evil and utterly ruthless…"

"Sounds like Deathelena."

"She's dust compared to this being."

"That speaks volumes. How do you know this?"

"I do periodic strolls throughout outer space. And I've gotten the same disgusting feeling every time. I don't get the same peaceful vibe anymore.

"Something's out there… and it's plotting. It doesn't just want to end the strongest like yourself, but all of existence. And perhaps it'll build an empire from the remains of the universe, if there's anything left should this being succeed, that is…"

"Your hypothesis may hold some validity. I mean, I believe you and Flowerensia, but until I see proof of this enigmatic galactic being, this is all conjecture."

"Call it a woman's intuition."

113

"That's a hell of an intuition, lady."

Serenity laughed.

"You really are refreshing, Courage. Really. Thank you for listening to what I had to say. You're welcome here anytime."

"Much appreciated, Serenity."

Suddenly, red and black clouds appeared.

They eclipsed the sun.

The foreboding clouds shifted rapidly across the sky.

"What the hell?" Courage questioned. "Is this dreadful aspect part of your world?"

"A-absolutely not... what's going on?"

Then, Sarenadia Sea gradually changed into an ocean of Killosogma.

Courage and Serenity quickly flew upward to avoid being burned.

"What the hell is going on, Serenity?"

"I don't know! I... I... I think that... *thing*! That *devil*! Is here! It's completely taken over the atmosphere of my world!"

Serenity placed her hands on her head.

Then, she grasped her hair.

She was terrified.

"Serenity, please remain calm. Alright? As a ruler, you have to think rational in times of stress. Even when taken by surprise. Your people depend on you."

"O-of course. I... I'll try..."

Suddenly, a metallic, demonic laughter echoed throughout Zeinhailurein.

"Tauran'creima… you have finally come…"

"I've been around for eons. The hell are you on about?"

"Trust me. I know. Like the simple-minded Celestial Spirit said, I have only been biding my time…"

"For what purpose, goddamn it? If your beef is with me, then what was stopping you from taking me on eons ago? Like Deathelena. She didn't know what she was up against and lost."

"I have my ways. I have studied all of you. You, and only a few others, are worth noting. However, you are the legend. Therefore, you possess power like no other. Sacred Star… we shall see if you are worthy of being called a legend…"

"Wait… I'm not the strongest. Transidyus and Leiku are astronomical."

"Matters not. All will perish before me. And, given time, you may rival them. Maybe even surpass them. Which is why I deem you the strongest. Consider it an honor."

"But you don't give a damn about us. Why not just kill us now?"

"Courage, stop!" Serenity intervened. "Don't egg him on! He has the power to back up anything he says!"

"He hasn't shown himself yet."

"He doesn't have to! He's that powerful!"

"Of course… hey, asshole. Why don't you show yourself? Let's talk face to face."

The mysterious being emerged.

He was floating several feet from Serenity and Courage.

His arms were folded.

He was very tall and muscular.

The evil entity wore the *Helligaiyon* Armor, which is red and black, and it covered his entire body.

The Helligaiyon Helmet is red on the left and black on the right.

It also possesses two pairs of horns.

His symbol, the *Kreseirumana* Crystal, which is shaped like a wolf, illuminated mildly on the forehead of the Helligaiyon Helmet.

The Kreseirumana Crystal is the strongest, most powerful gemstone in the universe.

His eye sockets are orange and his eyes are yellow.

The Helligaiyon Armor possesses three spikes on the shoulders, outer forearms, knees, and shins.

It also has a spike on the elbows.

Lastly, it has a spike on each knuckle.

The Glyph of Kreseirumana, the Turbulent Wolf, is on the back of the Helligaiyon Armor.

It illuminated in correspondence with the Kreseirumana Crystal.

Serenity recoiled.

She felt his astonishing power.

"Hey, Serenity," Courage called. "You alright? You don't seem well."

"It's this… devil. I hate the foulness he emanates. It's sickening…"

"How pathetic," the being stated. "Like two peas in a pod."

"You're hiding your true self!" Serenity said. "Don't be a coward, you devil!"

"I have no need to answer to the likes of you, *weakling*. Know your place."

"Who are you?" Courage asked. "What are you? You aren't a star being. You're not a god. What the hell are you?"

"My name is Oblivionu'crei. I create and destroy universes. I have existed for as long as you, Tauran'creima. Yet, star beings claim to be the First People, but are as worthless as all else."

Courage scoffed.

Tauran'creima. Do you know who this asshole is?

No. I am afraid not.

He's talking some pretty mean shit. Not to mention his power is ridiculous.

Is it like Transidyus' and Leiku's respectable might?

...I believe so. Yet... I'm excited. Regardless of the stakes.

You have what it takes. We have what it takes. Ever transcend.

Always.

"Talking to yourself, Tauran'creima?" Oblivionu'crei taunted.

"Mind your business, you bastard," Courage retorted. "Regardless, the nerve to insult star beings is beyond laughable. You stated your damn name, but *what* are you? Out with it!"

"I am an amalgamation of countless, powerful aspects. I am an *Altreigromian*. I am the first and only of my type."

"So, you're like the First Star Beings of their respective constellation. Like myself. Interesting..."

"I can say the same thing about you, Tauran'creima."

"What's your purpose? Surely it isn't just to rule over the universe? You have to be more ambitious than that."

"To bring balance to the cosmos. There are innumerable flaws that have yet to be addressed since time began. Star beings, gods, demigods, humans. Everything. Flawed. Utterly disgusting. The lot of you."

"And your vicious actions are supposed to bring order? Oblivionu'crei… you can't be this delusional…"

"Silence! I am far from delusional! Within every society, there is a hierarchy. A food chain. However, those who are in power misuse their might to oppress those less fortunate. They do not know how it feels to be underneath someone's government."

"Your theory is sound, yet your actions speak otherwise. As such, take Serenity for example. She isn't abusing her power. Yet, here you are tormenting her world. Your logic is flawed."

"Far from it. Star beings have difficulty accepting one another. Both Melhounas and Azagnorpors. Deities seek worship. And humans are just as, if not more pitiful than the rest of you.

"If those peasants are not fighting over money, or other meaningless nonsense, then they are waging wars for the most asinine reasons."

"If a responsible deity or star being rules a planet that has humans and other species, said wars would be prevented. It's that simple."

"Tauran'creima, the universe is *heavily* flawed. You know this, yet you choose the subtle route. And your sweetheart here is no different.

"Given the opportunity, I am certain she would drastically change Zeinhailurein into a living hell. Like how you see now. The irony of eternal peace."

"That's false!" Serenity protested. "I'd never mistreat those who passed on! Let alone anyone who visits my realm! Have you lost your mind, you devil? I've always been a kind spirit!

"I believe this is your attempt to persuade us, as well as yourself, that what you're undertaking is right! Yet, in reality, it's all a lie so you can control everything with impunity!"

"I do not need impunity. I can just make what I see suitable for the universe come to fruition. My vision. My empire… will be realized: a universe of genuine balance and true peace."

"You and Deathelena are the only ones I've met that seem to have a great motive," Courage said. "Yet, your actions say otherwise. If your philosophies are true, fine. I respect that. But I don't respect the harsh measures taken to fulfill your goals."

"Some things cannot be taken lightly, Tauran'creima. I do not respect the subtle route you choose to take in maintaining balance."

"So, you expect me to force my ideologies down people's throat? Like you? Sounds legit."

"It seems we have different perspectives. I am direct while you choose to be covert. Despicable."

"There's nothing "covert" about me. Yet, you're right in saying our point of views are different. However, I'm not the type to force people to believe or do what they don't want to. That simple. I have my way. And they have theirs. That's how the universe works.

"Nothing is perfect, which is what you seek. There is no such thing as perfection. You can't have light without darkness. Everyone can invest in their respective utopia. Yet, when it harms the masses, then we have a problem."

"Your philosophies hold weight, to be sure. Yet, it leaves you vulnerable. To be taken advantage of."

"Wrong. I'm not narrow-minded. Or a bigot. I respect different perspectives as long as it's feasible.

"Listen, I don't respect you as a being. However, I do respect your power. Know this. I most certainly anticipate a fight with you, as I only duel those stronger than me."

"Courage... be careful..." Serenity said. "You're the only one who can best him..."

"Don't count the others out," Courage stated.

"True, but he's on a different level," Serenity said.

"I respect your code, Tauran'creima. I rarely overestimate anyone. You have a high wager on you. Luckily, I do not seek bloodshed this day. This is but a forewarning of what is to come.

"However, when the time comes, I will return. And then, the entire universe will see whether or not the legend is truly all he is praised to be."

Courage grinned.

Then, he chuckled.

He was excited.

He was elated to finally meet beings who were worthy of a duel.

It mattered not whether his adversaries were good or evil.

All that mattered was their power.

That would determine if he would receive the thrill he valued.

Then, the Selsengra proceeded circulating throughout his body.

Serenity sensed Courage's change.

She disapproved.

She gently grasped his forearm.

Courage snapped his head toward her.

Serenity was startled.

Yet, she did not release him.

She slowly shook her head.

She wanted him to calm down.

Fortunately, Courage conceded.

The Selsengra gradually subsided.

Oblivionu'crei chuckled.

"I have noted that about you as well, Tauran'creima. You get ecstatic when facing stronger beings. You love fighting. You live for it.

"You may be taking the subtle route, but you will not decline a challenge should one present itself. If the circumstances were different, you would engage me now. Yet, your sweetheart protests, and I have already given my warning.

"...Those gods you fought, including the Dark Goddess. They did not appease your fighting drive. You laughed internally at how pathetic they were. Yet, the Grandmasters and I are what you truly seek. You know for certain you will get the fight you desire. You are indeed fascinating.

"...You are most certainly the odd one of the stars. There was a brief boost in your power. Yet, you did not power up manually. At all. Intriguing.

"Tauran'creima, the fight between us begins when I return. I am certain it will be one you will not regret. Do not fail, for the universe... nay, *multiple* universes, lie on your shoulders."

"May the best man win," Courage said.

"...Likewise," Oblivionu'crei agreed.

Oblivionu'crei vanished.

The red and black clouds slowly dispersed.

The Killosogma gradually reverted to Aqualyra.

The sun beamed and the Sarenadia Sea sparkled once again.

All was well.

For now.

"Serenity, we need to inform the others."

"Right!"

"Are you feeling well?"

"Now that he's gone, I feel much better."

"Alright. Let's go."

Serenity and Courage departed from Sarenadia Sea.

Serenity and Courage returned to the pond.

Everyone looked bewildered.

"Courage and Serenity, are you alright?" Ulanahar asked. "The atmosphere suddenly changed. There was also a strange laughter, as well as an unspeakable power. Now, everything's normal. What happened?"

"Long story short, Deathelena is not the only threat," Courage said. "A being named Oblivionu'crei arrived. He's an Altreigromian. And he's absurdly powerful. I'm fighting him sooner or later."

*"Forever face the light, and the
darkness will wither away."*

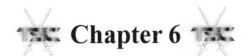 **Chapter 6**

Asai Awakens

Flowerensia and Courage were at Velmelkia Peninsula.

They observed the islands out at *Crozeni* Ocean.

A group of seagulls wandered around Courage.

He also had one seagull on his respective shoulder.

Courage attracted all types of animals and entities.

"So…" Flowerensia said. "You want your own place of residence.
…I see. W-which island would you like…?"

Flowerensia was depressed.

Yet, she understood his perspective.

Courage was very independent and very private.

"The one without the volcano," Courage replied.

"Most of them lack a volcano, Courage. And that's Celestial Magma Mountain."

"Why on Venusia would you have an active volcano?"

"It's a natural part of Venusia. It's not harming anyone. It has a purpose."

"Like what? Boiling whatever it touches until there's nothing left? Flowerensia... Killosogma is incredibly dangerous. It's nothing like normal magma of other universes.

"Anything of celestial nature will harm the likes of many. Including star beings. And we're the force of the universe."

"So... whaddaya want me to do? Put a large cork in it?"

Courage sighed in disbelief.

He conceded.

The seagulls laughed.

"Hey birdies, pipe it," Courage ordered.

"I'm joking, dear," Flowerensia stated. "Lighten up. For as long as I can remember, it hasn't erupted at all. And if it has, the celestial magma created the other islands you see before you. That's when I came along and gave it the floral beauty you witness now."

"Do these islands have a name?"

"Of course. To the east, that's *Ulenar* Island. To the northeast, that's *Asthromei* Island. And to the southwest, that's *Kreileimenar* Island.

"Deep in *Pareizyma* Jungle on Ulenar Island lies an ancient temple I call the Temple of Transcending. There's also a garden leading to an exceptional view of Crozeni Ocean."

Flowerensia placed her hand on her chest.

"...I... think you'll love Ulenar Island more than... anything..."

"Very interesting. I can't wait to see for myself. If I like what I see, I'll inform you."

Courage looked toward the seagulls on his shoulders.

"Alright, birdies. Time for me to go."

"*Aw...*" the seagulls drawled.

Reluctantly, the seagulls flew off of his shoulders.

Next, the group of seagulls flew away.

Then, Courage flew toward Ulenar Island.

The water parted as he flew several inches above it.

Flowerensia watched as Courage headed toward his new residence.

Her sadness unveiled.

She placed her hand on her chest once more.

It hurt to see the one she grew fond of withdraw from her.

Even though he would be nearby, it would not be the same without his physical presence near her.

She felt as if she lost her first love.

"Courage... I hope you like it here. In Velmelkia Kingdom. With you here, there's a light that I could never hope to match. A light no one could ever surpass..."

Tears fell from her eyes.

Then, she teleported to her temple.

One week later.

Courage was quite comfortable on Ulenar Island.

He often sat at the edge of the garden, which ended at the peak of a cliff.

He gazed toward the horizon of Crozeni Ocean.

He was meditating.

To assist with his contemplation, he would listen to melodies, most of which he created.

Then, there were times Courage would train most of the day above Crozeni Ocean.

He created and fought an astral clone of himself – a blue, glistening version of his astral clone – the Staraidus Fedmori'ia.

This proved very exceptional, as Courage received the thrill he longed for, in addition to testing his powers.

And in the process of this, he learned countless aspects.

He communicated with Tauran'creima as well.

Upon nightfall, Courage would either remain on the cliff or return to the Temple of Transcending.

Within this mystical black building, there was a large circle that had advanced sacred glyphs around the borders, as well as within it.

This was the *Vevolomurus*.

Whenever Courage entered the Temple of Transcending, the Vevolomurus illuminated different colors at a low frequency.

Then, he stood in the center of the Vevolomurus.

Next, he closed his eyes.

Finally, it felt as if he was being transported elsewhere.

The Vevolomurus chose Courage.

And whoever left such a powerful symbol intended for him to utilize it.

The Vevolomurus drastically enhanced Courage's meditation, as well as every aspect of his being.

One week on Ulenar Island felt as if it were eons.

Yet, Courage appreciated the seclusion.

It gave him the opportunity to reflect and expand himself in countless aspects.

When Courage and co. returned from Zeinhailurein, Elaimia spied on them.

Currently, she was on Ulenar Island.

As she continued observing Courage, she became incredibly fearful of him.

She was petrified.

It was daylight.

Courage was sitting on the edge of the cliff.

He was meditating.

Elaimia could feel his remarkable Sacred Staraidus from a great distance.

She felt nauseous.

Regardless, Elaimia very slowly approached Courage from behind.

"Excuse me, Sir Courage..."

"You have a disgusting aura about you, woman..."

He knows...

"Of course I've sinned. No one's perfect."

"Shut up."

Elaimia quivered.

"You've come here for a foul purpose. You defile my island with your *repugnant* presence. How dare you..."

Elaimia heard the anger in his voice.

And she felt the sting of his insult.

Then, Courage slowly rose to his feet.

She gasped.

"What brings you here?" Courage interrogated.

Elaimia was very afraid to say anything.

Courage turned toward her.

"I asked you a question, woman."

She gasped once more.

She froze.

She felt as if he could see through her.

Courage observed her.

"Hmm… you're indeed a foul sort. Only those in the occult or a dark clan would garb themselves in a black hooded robe. You're pitiful."

"I've come to ask a favor of you…"

"Hmph. What would someone like you need to ask of me? *Wretch*."

"It's… someone close to me. She's completely recovered, but she hasn't awakened. I think she's in a coma. She needs someone of great power to awaken her."

"Interesting… have you tried anything to offset this coma?"

"Yes. But nothing works. At all."

Then, Courage slowly approached Elaimia.

She wanted to retreat.

Yet, she knew that would reveal her true intentions, thus risk being killed.

When he neared her, he stopped.

He placed his index finger under her chin.

He forced her to look at him.

Then, he summoned a Tru'ethra Cube.

An Eye of Tauran'creima appeared on it.

It peered through Elaimia.

She knew she was exposed.

Suddenly, the Tru'ethra Cube illuminated solid red.

That meant the one the Eye of Tauran'creima glared through was wicked.

Courage scoffed.

"I knew it… all has been revealed."

Elaimia became very worried.

"P-please, Courage! Don't kill me! Only you can help the girl! I'll… I'll do anything you want! Anything!"

"Shut up…"

Elaimia obeyed.

Courage dispelled the Tru'ethra Cube.

"It's not going to end well for you and the one you serve. Yet, I'll assist the one that needs my help. *However*, if you even *think* about attacking me, I'll extinguish you from existence. Understand, woman?"

"Y-yes…"

"Now take me to where the one you care for needs my help."

Terrified, Elaimia teleported to Deathelena's Castle with Courage.

Elaimia and Courage arrived at the large steel double doors of Deathelena's Castle.

Courage observed the dismal environment.

"Damn, woman. You really are evil. Well… this should be fun…"

"W-what do you mean? Yes, I'm a dark being, but do you have to be so cruel to me…?"

"Yes. I do. Until you prove otherwise, you're just a wretch. Regardless, it's been awhile since I fought. But... the likes of you wouldn't even be an appetizer for my fighting force."

"Yes... I know that..."

Deathelena. I have him here. Make sure everyone is out of his sight, as well as making sure their power remains off his radar. If he finds out this is a ruse before he gets the opportunity to awaken Asai, he'll kill us all. So please, hurry and get this ticking time bomb away from me...

Alright, calm down. Take him to the laboratory. That's where Asai is.

I'm on it.

"Before we proceed any further, where the hell am I?" Courage questioned.

"Hychineira Kingdom of planet Gwempteya," Elaimia replied. "I cater to this type of atmosphere."

"Yeah. I see that. To each his own, but this place is depressing. There's an ocean of Killosogma. Countless volcanos. And a dark sky. The hell were you thinking inhabiting a place like this?"

"I don't know. I just... like it..."

"And is this your castle?"

"Yes. I inherited it when my mother and father passed."

"So you're a princess...? But you dress like you're in a clan..."

"It's a preference. Now... please come with me. The one that needs your care is in the laboratory."

"Wait. How the hell do you know about me?"

"Courage... you're famous. You're the legend foretold throughout the cosmos."

"How did you know where to find me?"

"I have psychic powers."

"I don't trust you worth a damn."

"I know. We're opposites. It's understandable. Now please. Come.

"No."

Elaimia was shocked.

"W-what? Why? Courage, she needs you!"

"You haven't told me who you are, let alone who this "she" is."

"My name's Elaimia Besolei, and the girl I need you to awaken is Asai."

"How did the girl get put into a comatose state?"

"She was sparring with a high ranking soldier, but things didn't go as expected."

"That was pretty stupid. That soldier should be demoted to a mere grunt worker. When one spars, they don't *actually* hurt their opponent. Seriously. Whoever this high ranking dumbass is needs a demotion. Just my perspective."

"…Courage… sometimes… there can be tension among our own. Not everyone gets along. Not everyone sees eye to eye."

"That's life in its entirety."

"…Indeed. Now, if you have no further questions, Asai needs you."

"Trust me. I can interrogate for days. You just happen to be lucky. For now."

"Yes…"

He's so scary. Deathelena was right. If he doesn't trust someone, he'll interrogate that person until he finds a loophole in their argument. Then, should he find that flaw, he'll exploit it and use any reason he can conjure to eliminate that individual. Utter ruthlessness.

Then, Elaimia teleported with Courage to Deathelena's Laboratory.

Elaimia and Courage were in Deathelena's Laboratory.

They stood near the bed the unconscious Asai laid upon.

There was a black towel secured around her.

After Deathelena awoke, she removed Asai from the Iodinicron Capsule.

Regardless, Courage sensed that Asai was a Melhouna.

He became more suspicious of Elaimia.

"Asai is not one of you. She's a star being. A Melhouna. Like me. You and no soldier of your army is capable of putting someone like her in this state.

"I can tell she has trouble controlling her powers, but she's still a force. So my only guess is that it must have been another star being, or someone fairly exceptional that did this to her."

Damn. His detective skills are incredible. It's like he knows everything. This legend... he's beyond scary...

"Yes. We do have a few very exceptional fighters of my army. And you're right. The one who put her in this condition was indeed not careful of how they handled the sparring session."

"How did she get here? She wouldn't willingly join a bunch of evil bastards like you."

"...She was alone. She wanted comfort. She wanted a place to call home. So I took her in. I didn't force her to do whatever she didn't want to. And… if we're so evil, how come we didn't kill her? She's one of you, yet she's here. Alive.

"I respect your power, Courage. But I don't respect your tone about us. You don't know me, yet you treat me less than dirt. Consider the circumstance before you and see if it doesn't add up."

"You're evil, you bitch. What else is there to prove? Your disgusting vibe is a dead giveaway. And you fucks couldn't kill Asai, let alone *any* star being if you tried."

"What about your friend Ulanahar? She's an Azagnorpor. An evil star being. Yet, you embraced her without a care."

"How do you know about her?"

"All those affiliated with you instantly become popular."

"Ulanahar's different, you despicable wretch. She doesn't intentionally cause harm like other Azagnorpors, or other assholes. Not to mention, her genuine vibe completely overshadows the fact that she's an Azagnorpor. Get your facts straight before you speak of someone you don't know."

"The same logic applies, Courage. Be fair. You don't know my nation, yet you speak ill of us."

"Like I said before, until you prove otherwise, you're a wretch. Nothing more."

"So I'm guilty until proven innocent?"

"Damn straight. My Tru'ethra Cube revealed all about you. Hell, I knew you were no good when you approached me."

"What if the shoe was on the other foot?"

"I wouldn't give a shit. I know where my foundation lies and what my standards are. I have nothing to concern myself with."

Suddenly, Asai groaned.

Elaimia gasped.

Then, Asai slowly reached for Courage.

However, he evaded her caress.

"Hey, what the hell are you doing, girl? Don't touch me."

She wriggled her fingers when she could not reach him.

"Sacred... presence... near..." Asai whispered. "Very... pure. So... nice..."

"What the hell is she on about?" Courage questioned.

"Don't be mean to her, Courage," Elaimia said. "She likes you. This is a miracle. She hasn't moved, let alone spoke in years."

"So due to my presence, she starts moving? The hell is this about?"

"Yes. You two are star beings, correct? So, it's only natural you'd complement one another."

"So now that she's alright, can I go now?"

"Courage, she's not awake yet."

"So I'm her caretaker now?"

"No. But you are a hero."

"Yeah right..."

Then, Courage cupped his hands.

Suddenly, a luminous green orb – the *Harminagias* – emerged.

The Harminagias is capable of revitalizing incapacitated individuals.

Courage telekinetically shifted the Harminagias toward Asai.

When it neared, it merged with her.

Then, Asai moaned.

She slowly awoke.

When her vision cleared, she gradually sat up.

Her purple eyes sparkled.

Next, she looked at Courage and Elaimia.

However, Asai took a keen interest in Courage.

"You… saved me. Master…"

"Master? I'm nobody's master, girl. Let's get that straight."

"Sies. Lu driat," (Yes. You are,) Asai said.

"Hitros. Seq goie," (No. I'm not,) Courage stated.

Asai giggled.

Then, she gazed at him seductively.

Courage ignored her blatant passion.

However, Elaimia noticed Asai's love for him immediately.

Asai… she's fallen in love with Courage. Interesting. Star beings are truly fascinating entities. However, I highly doubt Deathelena would approve of her affection, since she despises Courage.

Asai will likely be Deathelena's second-in-command. She's investing so much time and grooming her for the position.

Yet… with how Asai's taken a liking to Courage, things may not bode well for Deathelena should Asai choose to follow Courage and his friends. If that happens, Deathelena will likely groom Fesforia for the position since she's a General.

"Rinameiz... Courage..." (Master... Courage...)

"Tetritas!" (Hush!)

Asai blushed.

Then, her pupils changed to hearts.

"What the hell is wrong with this girl, princess?" Courage asked.

"Isn't it obvious, Courage? She loves you."

"For what? We don't even know each other. Ugh..."

"Love at first sight, perhaps?"

"I don't give a damn what it is. I came here to awaken her. Whatever she does from here is her call. However, should any of you persuade her to commit violent acts, I won't hesitate to deal with her harshly."

"Courage, I already told you we haven't made her do anything she's against."

"I don't think you people would have her here without a good reason. Some kind of contribution is mandatory. There's a price for you all coddling her, especially someone who isn't evil to begin with."

"There is no contribution she's forced to comply with. I chose to take her in because she was alone. There is no price she has to pay. She's family here. The Hychineirian Nation accepts her."

"You *seem* alright, princess. But don't get your hopes up. There's something greater here. Something darker than you. And once I find out what it is, your credibility will be shot to shit."

"I understand... Sacred Star..."

Then, Asai grasped Courage's forearm.

"Master Courage... come with me..."

Courage sneered.

"Shut up, girl. I'm not your goddamn master."

Suddenly, Asai vanished with Courage.

Elaimia looked around confused.

"W-what the hell? Where'd they go? Courage? Asai? Damn… this is bad…"

You better find them fast. Or else you're going to be punished instead of pleasured.

Y-yes, Goddess Deathelena.

Elaimia hurried out of the laboratory in search of Asai and Courage.

Courage appeared at a meadow.

Several types of trees were scattered about.

Mountains were in the distance.

Clouds slowly drifted across the sky.

And the sun beamed.

A breeze blew across the serene meadow.

Courage admired the fantastic landscape.

He felt at peace.

Then, he closed his eyes.

That weird girl… she transported me here. Why? And where the hell is she? Ugh… I couldn't just be left alone on my island. If it isn't one thing, it's another.

…I feel very light. It's like I'm in a dream. Very strange…

Regardless... this environment feels like... home. My constellation...

Then, a pair of arms softly secured themselves around his waist from behind.

"Hey, what the..."

"*Shh*. No need to be alarmed..."

The voice was feminine and seductive.

The mysterious female held Courage close to her.

Then, she placed gentle kisses upon his neck.

Courage stifled a moan.

The female giggled.

Courage recognized that giggle.

Yet, it was different.

"Who the hell are you? If you're that girl, what's your problem? And get the hell away from me."

"I'm the one you rescued. My name is Asai Rionai. My constellation is Auderesa, the Celestial Rabbit."

"Where the hell are we?"

"In my universe. Within my constellation."

"...Really now?"

"Yes. This is *Essensai* Meadow."

"Why am I here?"

"To show you my appreciation. Master... I welcome you to my universe..."

"Damn it. My name is…"

"Courage. I know exactly who you are. Have you forgotten what we are?"

"Goddamn it. No, I haven't."

"I call you my master because you're the strongest of the lot. You can kill almost anything without much effort. You're the ruler of the universe."

"Oh cut the nonsense. Yes, I'm powerful. But so is every other star being."

"You're different than us. You're a special type of star."

"Ugh… do you *not* know that there are two star beings that put my power to shame? They are Transidyus and Leiku. They're Grandmaster Stars."

"And you're a Master Star. An uncommon one… a Sacred Master Star. You're interesting, indeed. And given time, you'll be a Sacred Grandmaster Star. Master… you're beyond blessed. You're beyond wonderful."

Asai was fascinated with Courage.

She saw limitless potential in him.

A Grandmaster Star is very exceptional.

Yet, since Courage is the legend, should he ever become a Grandmaster Star, he would be beyond any entity throughout the universe – a Sacred Grandmaster Star.

"Acolyte Star… what is the meaning of this?"

"Acolyte Star? I think you're misjudging my power, dear."

Courage interpreted her Staraidus again.

And she was right.

She is a Master Star.

Courage scoffed.

"So sweet you are, Master..."

"Shut up."

Asai chuckled.

She released him.

Courage turned toward her.

She looked completely different.

She is an adult.

She has a slim, shapely figure.

She wore a violet towel around her and a gold tiara on her forehead.

The gold tiara has an amethyst in the center.

She also wore dangling amethyst star earrings, as well as a purple choker.

Courage noted she was mildly glowing purple, as well as having purple sparkles about her.

Then, Asai giggled.

"You have the same thing as well. Are you now noticing?"

He looked about himself.

He noticed he was moderately glowing green, in addition to having green sparkles around him.

"Wait... what the hell? Where's my body?"

"Worry not. Our bodies are safe. Wherever we go, all else about us follows. I chose to have us in our *Kizaloras*, or star spirit form, for a specific reason."

"And that is?"

"To test you. Intimately."

"…First and foremost, I don't know you. Second, this is complete irony. We're in our star *spirit* form, yet you want to engage in a *carnal*, or *physical*, act. Right… very telling…"

"You're my master. I'm giving myself to you willingly. Do with me what you will…"

"How many times I gotta tell you? I'm not your, or anyone's, master. And… why would you choose to serve me? I don't need it. I don't want it. I don't need someone catering to my every whim. Whatever I need, I'll get it myself."

"Love. Have you ever thought about it?"

"No. It doesn't concern me."

"Even if you don't ever love me, or anyone intimately, you can make love to me whenever you need to. This is my way of showing you my appreciation."

"Bullshit. I don't *need* anything. You're going to love someone else someday. So stop wasting your time with me."

"No, Master. I won't. I respect your logic. Your cold truth. But we aren't like anyone else in the universe. We may have just met, yet as star beings, we can tell a lot about an individual just by looking at them. I feel as if I've always known you."

"That's a load of bullsh-"

"And before you denounce my statement, I'm not wasting your time. You'd be able to tell if I was feigning all of this. You're highly skilled and very wise."

Courage scoffed.

He remained skeptical.

"Before we proceed any further, why the hell did you choose to stay with Elaimia and her evil army? She has a disgusting vibe."

"Mother Deathelena took care of me while Lady Elaimia assisted."

"Say what? Deathelena? So Elaimia's a follower of Deathelena?"

"Yes, Master."

"I knew it. I knew she was lying. She told me her mother and father owned that castle. She even said she is a princess. I wanted her to admit that she is a lapdog, but she remained true to her nature. Pathetic.

"I knew she was vile when she approached me, yet my Tru'ethra Cube revealed *all* about her. I merely played along the entire time. People are still playing checkers while the masters play chess. Idiots."

"Master. Not everything she said was false. She's a Lieutenant General. She's very skilled and authoritative. But, she's also very kind."

"I don't care. Deathelena is the lowest of the low. I have no respect for her. We fought. Twice. The first time we fought, it was eons ago when I was in Tauran'creima form. Then, I fought her again when she tried to kill Flowerensia for sealing her away.

"…I understand if you respect her for taking care of you. But she's bad news. She doesn't care about anyone but herself. And maybe a select few of her minions who are worthy in her eyes."

"…I see. Mother Deathelena was always kind to me. Yet… this revelation is surprising. I was never on the field of battle. Since the beginning, I had a very difficult time controlling my Staraidus. Mother Deathelena noted this, so she always kept me within the castle.

"She had tutors attempt to teach me how to utilize my Staraidus. I got the comprehension of it, but when applying it, it was difficult. I would either use too much or too little. It was frustrating. Now, I don't think I have that dilemma anymore. If I'm safe in saying, it's all thanks to you."

"I doubt that. You did it on your own. I don't deserve credit where it isn't warranted. I only awoke you from a coma. That's it."

"Agreed. And the one who put me in that depressing state will get her just desserts in due time. I might just pay her a visit when the time is right."

"Asai, think about this carefully. You respect Deathelena, yet you know of her nefarious ways. And you're a Melhouna. You can't be good and serve evil. At the end of the day, the choice is yours.

"If you choose the Transcendent Path, I congratulate you. However, if you choose to go back to Deathelena, then I don't know what other advice I can give you. And, if you obey her orders and commit disdainful acts, I think you know I'm going to have to step in. Right?"

"Yes, Master. Should I disobey you, let alone offend you, you have a right to end me. It's because of you that I'm alive.

"Mother Deathelena might have briefly taken away my loneliness, but you gave me something more when you reinvigorated me. It's indescribable. It's just… beyond inspirational…"

Asai kissed his lips.

Courage was shocked.

She secured her arms around his neck.

She moaned into his mouth.

Then, she slowly withdrew from his lips.

"Take me. Master."

"I can't believe I'm entertaining this. This better not be a waste of my time, woman."

"It won't. I promise. Star beings are Masters of the Arts, after all. Lovemaking is one of them. Whatever we experience, we'll always learn and incorporate it into our lives somehow. We're brilliant in countless aspects."

"If you really want to do this, take us someplace private."

"We are in private. This is my universe."

"So you want to fuck outside?"

"…I see. You're into creature comforts. Indoor lovemaking is what you desire?"

"I guess. I've never done this, let alone thought of it. Let's just get this over with."

"It will all become natural once we begin, Master. I'll take you to a comfortable location at once."

Asai teleported with Courage from Essensai Meadow.

Asai and Courage appeared in a lavish bedroom.

The beautiful nature scenery was noted through the window.

"This feels like a dream," Courage said. "Or an illusion. This is all so damn strange…"

Asai slowly kissed down his neck.

She and Courage moaned.

Then, she whispered.

"Yes. It seems that way. Yet, I have you here with me for the reason I mentioned: to show you my gratitude. Everything of me belongs to you."

"No it isn't. Servants don't impress me."

"I can show you better than I can tell you, Master. It is *respect* I have for you. Nothing otherwise."

Asai dispelled her tiara, earrings, choker, and towel.

Then, she dismissed Courage's Sacroncai Armor.

They stood before each other naked.

She gasped.

She studied the Vesorai on his entire body.

The Vesorai are black symbols that are relative to Tauran'creima.

Each star being possesses their unique type of Constellation Ascension Glyphs.

However, their motifs would not emerge unless they were undergoing certain transformations.

Courage is the only star being whose emblems always mark his body.

"Beautiful…" Asai admired.

She touched his chest.

She traced the intricate patterns gently with her delicate fingers.

Courage closed his eyes.

He moaned.

Then, she fastened her arms around his neck once more.

She kissed his lips.

She moaned into his mouth.

Courage gradually reciprocated her kiss.

Then, he slowly embraced her.

They admired each other's natural scent.

They admired each other's unparalleled touch.

It was beyond stimulating.

Courage moaned once more.

Dream or illusion, this feels weird. Yet... it feels good. Very, very strange...

Master... this is only the beginning. I assure you, it will only get better.

...Of course...

Asai slowly licked his lips.

She wanted entry into his mouth.

Courage slowly opened his mouth.

Her tongue touched his.

She began licking around it.

She tasted him.

She moaned approvingly.

Courage mimicked her actions.

She tasted very sweet.

He caressed her back.

Asai placed her hand on his abdomen.

She gradually shifted her hand downward.

She gently grasped his manhood.

Then, she proceeded, very slowly, masturbating him.

Courage released a prolonged groan of bliss.

He deepened their kiss.

He slowly moved his hand down her back.

He fondled her firm buttocks.

Then, he gently squeezed them.

Asai giggled against his lips.

Such a bad boy...

You started it. I'm finishing it.

I expect nothing less from you.

Without breaking their kiss, Asai ambled backward toward the bed.

She released his member.

He released her buttocks.

They fell onto the bed.

She secured her legs around him.

Courage slowly withdrew from her lips.

Then, he kissed her neck in several places.

Next, he nibbled her neck.

Asai moaned.

She arched her back.

As the act proceeded, the passion between them escalated.

Courage gently parted her legs from around him.

He rolled onto his back.

He placed his hand on her head.

You first.

Asai understood his implication.

She slowly kissed down his body until she reached his manhood.

She opened her mouth.

She took part of his member into her mouth.

Then, she bobbed slowly.

Courage groaned.

Her warm, salivated mouth felt incredible.

When she became accustomed to him, her bobs increased.

She would occasionally moan, so the vibrations would give him excessive bliss.

He moaned.

He held her head firmly.

She slid the tip of her tongue underneath his member to further stimulate him.

Then, she began deep-throating him.

Her rhythm was painstaking.

With how well she was performing, he felt his climax approaching.

Asai sensed this.

She slowed her bobs.

Yet, she remained accurate in her diligence.

Courage relented.

"Alright, alright, enough."

Asai slowly withdrew his member from her mouth.

She grasped his manhood.

Then, she slowly masturbated him.

She purred.

"Were you about to climax?"

Courage moaned.

"…What do you think?"

"I take that as a yes."

"Cut the nonsense. You knew I would climax if you persisted."

"Of course. I couldn't help myself. Your sacred bull *horn* tasted really good."

Courage raised an eyebrow in question.

"S-sacred… bull horn…?"

Asai chuckled.

"A joke it is, Courage. A foul taste in humor, love."

"…Uh-huh…"

"What's the matter, dear? Rabbit got your tongue?"

"…Shut up…"

"Maybe I'll stick this sacred bull horn back in my mouth, so I can "shut up"."

"No. It's my turn. I'm sure you want some attention."

"You don't have to."

"Hush. I insist. Now lie down."

"Yes, Master."

She laid on her back.

She set her head on a pillow at the head of the bed.

She gazed at him seductively.

She was eager for him to take her body.

Courage crawled between her legs.

He laid on top of her.

He kissed her lips.

They moaned.

Asai caressed his back.

He kissed and nibbled her neck.

She moaned.

Then, he lightly sucked on her neck.

She screamed.

Next, he proceeded downward.

He fondled her erect pink nipple on her left breast while sucking the nipple of her right breast.

She panted.

She groaned.

She whimpered.

A euphoric sensation spread throughout her body as he continued relishing her breasts.

Then, he continued southbound.

He kissed her abdomen and caressed her waist.

She moaned.

Courage reached her shaved womanhood.

Her sweet secretion leaked from her.

First, he kissed her womanhood.

She moaned.

Then, he licked her femininity very slowly.

She screamed.

Courage loved her natural sweetness.

Asai clenched the blanket in her hands.

She groaned loudly.

Moreover, she gasped in ecstasy.

Next, Courage used his tongue to spell his name in her womanhood.

He also utilized different tongue techniques to maximize her bliss.

Asai was rapidly approaching her climax.

M-Master... I...

I know. Release it.

But…

Release it.

He nibbled, sucked, and licked her clitoris.

As a result, she was mentally pushed over the edge.

She screamed as she climaxed.

Courage pressed his lips against her womanhood.

He swallowed her secretion.

Oh… Master Courage…

Hush. Relax.

During her afterglow, Asai panted heavily.

Her eyes were half open.

She gazed at the ceiling.

As she recuperated, Courage massaged her dainty feet.

Next, he kissed each of her pretty toes.

Then, he slowly sucked each of her toes.

Occasionally, he moaned as he sucked on them.

She tasted delicious.

She moaned.

And she periodically giggled.

Then, Courage licked between her toes.

Asai sighed.

Afterward, Courage laid between her legs once more.

He kissed her lips.

Asai eagerly reciprocated his affection.

She fastened her arms around his neck.

Courage withdrew from her lips.

He looked into her eyes.

You ready for me to enter you?

Of course. As soon as I saw you, I wanted you inside of me.

Damn, really? You're a strange one.

So are you, Sacred Master Star. Now, take what belongs to you. And remember, this is Star Spiritual Lovemaking, or Thelomon'seila. This is the highest form of love. There is no comparison.

...I have to agree with you. This feels so strange... yet so right. It's indescribable.

So take me, then.

Wait... are star children a factor? I refuse to bring any into existence.

No. In Kizaloras form, the star female will not bring forth Millennial Stars. It's strictly an unrivaled bonding between the star man and the star woman.

Courage placed his index finger on her abdomen.

So there's no need for an Ethomeist?

No. There's no Keileimia within me in this form. And even if we were in our bodies, you'd have a right to put a star barrier around it if you weren't ready to bring forth the future generation. The choice is yours who you decide to make your lover.

That's a big "if". I don't normally think about these things. I decided to take your offer because you're interesting. And I didn't want to be disrespectful and decline your hospitality. However, I could've left at any time if I didn't feel inclined. Even if this is your universe.

That I knew for certain. Now please... I don't know how much longer I can wait, Master. Take me.

Reciprocating Asai's sentiment, Courage slowly pushed inside of her.

She drawled a moan.

Her vaginal walls gradually yielded as he entered her.

Asai and Courage are virgins.

However, certain factors did not apply in Kizaloras form.

Nevertheless, Courage completely sheathed his member within her.

Asai moaned loudly.

And Courage groaned.

Then, he slowly thrust into her.

They kissed each other.

When her vaginal walls adjusted to him, he changed his pace methodically, which drove her insane.

He grunted whenever he completely sheathed himself within her.

She whimpered.

She groaned.

She screamed.

Asai and Courage completely forgot where they were.

They felt as if they were on a transcendent plane of existence.

Then, he started thrusting aggressively when her vaginal walls embraced him.

Asai yelled.

She perfectly timed her bobs with his thrusts.

And each time they collided, she screamed.

And he grunted.

She yelled exceptionally loud whenever he struck her sensitive spot.

They kissed passionately.

Asai appreciated his dominance.

She loved his complete power over her.

Then, he rotated his hips.

This stimulated her vaginal walls.

She panted.

She prolonged a moan.

Her eyes rolled toward the back of her head.

She massaged her fingers through his hair.

And she caressed the back of his neck.

Courage slowly licked her neck.

Then, he nibbled it.

He also inhaled her luxurious natural fragrance.

Her scent intoxicated him.

As a result, he thrust into her vehemently.

Asai screamed.

She grasped his shoulders.

She never wanted to release him.

She never wanted the bliss he was giving her to end.

Then, he placed her feet on his shoulders.

He deepened his penetration and power.

She moaned loudly.

Moreover, she yelled whenever he struck her erogenous zone.

Then, Courage licked the side of her feet very slowly.

He moaned.

He loved her taste.

He gave her a seductive gaze from his peripheral.

Asai giggled.

I hope my feet are to your liking, love. And I hope I taste good as well.

Your feet are beautiful. And you taste delightful.

Next, he placed one of her legs on the bed.

He held her other leg up as he thrust into her.

She panted.

She moaned.

She whimpered.

She screamed.

She hissed.

She released these erotic sounds uninhibitedly.

As he dominated her, the sensuality shrouded her conscious.

He gently pinched her nipples.

She screamed.

Then, he leaned down.

He licked the nipple of her right breast.

Next, he suckled it.

Asai quivered.

With his brilliant performance, she felt another climax approaching.

M-Master... I... it's happening again...

Hold it a little longer.

B-but Courage... I don't know if I can...

Courage slowed his thrust.

He lifted her bangs.

He kissed her forehead.

Then, he looked into her eyes.

Don't climax just yet. Trust me. You'll enjoy it all the more when you do.

Y-yes, honey...

Courage steady thrust into her at a slow pace.

Asai touched his chest and abs.

She admired his tautness, as well as the Vesorai.

Next, Courage placed her other leg on the bed.

He held her waist.

He rolled onto his back.

Now, display your prowess.

O-of course…

Asai placed her hands on his chest.

Then, she slowly bobbed.

They moaned.

Courage caressed her waist.

He slowly moved his hands downward.

He set his hands on her hips.

Then, he rested his hands on her buttocks.

He squeezed them.

She groaned loudly.

When she became accustomed to this position, she increased her speed.

She kept a steady rhythm.

Then, she leaned down.

She placed her hands on either side of him.

She closed her eyes.

Then, she kissed his lips.

As they continued bonding, their moans grew frequent.

Next, Courage leaned up.

Asai did the same.

He slowly withdrew from her lips.

He buried his face in her neck.

She embraced him.

He kept his hands on her buttocks.

He steady thrust upward as she moved downward.

This position made it much easier to stimulate her erogenous zone.

They were close to climaxing.

It was becoming extremely difficult to suppress it.

Courage kissed her lips.

Asai reciprocated.

Then, Courage laid between her legs once more.

They did not break their kiss.

He thrust into her intensely.

She wrapped her legs around him.

They moaned into each other's mouth as their impending orgasm neared.

With several powerful thrusts, Courage ejaculated his green Sacred Leikaitas within Asai.

He grunted.

He clenched the blanket in his hands.

Then, the Vesorai illuminated green.

Suddenly, it covered Asai's body.

Every part of her being was completely overwhelmed with ecstasy.

Then, the Vesorai gradually faded.

Asai climaxed.

She groaned against his lips.

Her secretion soaked his member.

As her bliss continued, he steady thrust potently into her.

During her afterglow, Asai closed her eyes.

Courage slowed his thrusts.

The sound of their fluids as he entered her continued.

They moaned.

Some of his Sacred Leikaitas poured out of her.

It pooled beneath them.

Then, Courage buried his face in her neck.

Asai steady held onto him.

She loved him very much.

Courage... don't stop. Please. I need more of you.

My pleasure.

Thank you so much, Master.

Hours later, Asai bent over.

She placed her hands upon the bed.

Then, Courage held Asai's hips from behind.

Next, he thrust into her womanhood.

She screamed.

Occasionally, Courage sheathed his member inside of her.

Her eyes rolled toward the back of her head.

Yes... dominate me, Master...

Then, Courage laid on top of her from behind.

He held her wrists.

He thrust into her aggressively.

The sound of his collision with her buttocks echoed throughout the room.

Her endless screams of ecstasy chimed with the clashing of their bodies.

It was early evening.

Courage laid atop Asai.

She held him close.

They looked into each other's eyes.

They kissed each other.

Then, he lifted her by her buttocks.

He walked toward a wall.

He placed her against it.

He kept her at eye level.

Then, their respective aura shrouded them.

Next, they vacated the bedroom.

Asai and Courage emerged in outer space.

From different aspects of the universe, countless beings noted a green and purple star.

On numerous planets, many beings saw the same, even during the day.

Courage and Asai drifted throughout the cosmos.

Courage remained certain this entire occurrence with Asai was a dream.

Yet, it was an experience he appreciated.

Even if this was the last time he saw Asai, he would never forget such a profound encounter.

However, if by chance they ever saw each other again, Courage would be neutral.

He respected Asai for being honest with him.

She was indeed interesting.

Yet, Courage had to remain the transcendent being all know him as.

However, he would not mind meeting like this with Asai again if the circumstances were in their favor.

Asai was very glad she met someone like Courage.

He brought an incomparable light to her life that she never saw while under Deathelena's supervision.

Most of her existence included loneliness and attempting to conquer her erratic Staraidus.

Even conversations with Auderesa did little to comfort her.

It was an existence she would never wish for anyone to experience.

It was dreadful.

Moreover, she knew Courage felt alone as well.

However, rather than reject it, he embraced it.

It was not because others misunderstood him.

It was because he was a very private individual.

Not to mention, mostly everyone Courage met liked him.

His trustworthy yet sarcastic personality was welcoming.

Asai learned so much about Courage in the little time they spent together.

Yet, to her, it felt like eons.

She knew she would learn more about him as long as she was around him.

This was a situation she would always admire.

Courage returned to Asai's bedroom.

He held her bridal fashion.

She fell asleep during their excursion.

He gently placed her on the bed.

He noted that she was quite disheveled from their intense love session.

And his Sacred Leikaitas steady leaked from her.

He set his hands inches above her.

Then, her body briefly illuminated green.

Edolia is a process that star beings utilize to cleanse themselves.

Edolia Extere'al is the external cleansing.

Edolia Intere'al is the internal cleansing.

He used Edolia Extere'al to cleanse her.

After he purified her, as well as himself, he wrapped the blanket around her.

He conjured the Sacroncai Armor about himself.

When there was nothing else of note, he vanished from her bedroom.

Then, he vacated Auderesa Universe.

"Create your reality.
You control your destiny."

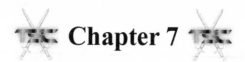 **Chapter 7**

Deathelena's Wrath

Elaimia searched tirelessly for Asai and Courage.

Yet, no matter where she looked, they were nowhere to be seen.

She did not sense their presence, either.

This led to the dreadful conclusion that they were no longer in Hychineira Kingdom, let alone planet Gwempteya.

Should her assumption be correct, she knew Deathelena would be highly upset.

Elaimia feared for the worst should she fail to locate them.

However, after hours of investigating, she relented.

She stood in an empty dark hallway.

Candles with red and purple fire – the *Crolmite* Flames – lined the walls in sconces.

Deathelena... Asai and Courage are gone.

It's alright, love.

What? You're not going to punish me?

No. But I do have something in mind for you.

Like what?

That's for you to find out. Now go rest in your room. You've done enough for today.

Yes, ma'am.

Elaimia retired to her private quarters.

Once she was settled in her room, she dispelled her black robe.

She also dispelled her clothing.

Then, she laid on her bed naked.

She stared at the ceiling.

She was daydreaming about Courage.

That was close. But... he's nicer than he seems. He could've either killed me, had his way with me, or banished me. He's... so powerful. So... domineering. He's very scary, but also... very sexy...

She blushed.

So shameful of me to think this way. He probably has this influence on everyone. Maybe I'll see him again someday...

Then, she felt sleepy.

She slowly closed her eyes.

Suddenly, Deathelena emerged beside her.

She admired Elaimia's slim, appealing physique.

She placed her hand on Elaimia's abdomen.

Elaimia gasped.

She looked toward Deathelena, who grinned.

"G-Goddess Deathelena... is something wrong?"

Deathelena kissed her lips.

Elaimia was shocked.

Deathelena pushed her tongue into Elaimia's mouth.

Elaimia did the same.

They moaned as they tasted each other.

Deathelena slid her hand toward Elaimia's womanhood.

She used her middle finger to stimulate her clitoris.

Elaimia immediately withdrew from the kiss.

She covered her mouth to avoid screaming in bliss.

She laid her head on her pillow, attempting to compose herself.

Deathelena chuckled in her ear.

"You always do great work for me. Though Fesforia carries this nation on her back, being a goddamn star being and all, she doesn't compare to your diligence."

Deathelena inserted two fingers into Elaimia's womanhood.

Elaimia groaned loudly.

She arched her back as Deathelena slowly fingered her.

"I'll put my plans to find Asai and Courage, as well as conquering Rhol'heima and the universe on hold. Tonight, your entire body belongs to me. I hope you're prepared."

"Y-yes… ma'am…"

"Good girl…"

Deathelena inserted a third finger into Elaimia.

Before Elaimia could scream in ecstasy, Deathelena kissed her lips.

Deathelena dispelled her Hychineirian Uniform.

Then, Deathelena laid between Elaimia's legs.

Deathelena conjured a genuine manhood in place of her womanhood.

Next, she slowly entered Elaimia.

Elaimia moaned.

When Deathelena completely entered her, she screamed.

Finally, the only sounds that could be heard were Elaimia's groans, whimpers, and screams, as well as her abundant secretion as Deathelena thrust within her.

"I… I love you, my Goddess Deathelena…"

"And you'll love me more once I'm through ravishing you."

After Deathelena made passionate love to Elaimia numerous times, Elaimia fell asleep.

Deathelena sat at the edge of the bed.

She was contemplating.

I should go see a close friend of mine, a female Azagnorpor who is much smarter than Fesforia. Maybe she has a solution on how to defeat Courage. I've had about enough of this.

Deathelena kissed Elaimia's lips.

They moaned.

Then, Deathelena departed from Elaimia's private quarters.

Deathelena boarded the Mother UFO.

Finally, she headed toward the location of her best friend.

Courage emerged near the Temple of Transcending.

It was sunset.

Then, he observed himself.

He remained in his Kizaloras form.

Then, he reverted to his normal self.

Star beings could change into their Kizaloras form at any time.

In addition, their Kizaloras form is considerably powerful.

The Kizaloras form is their true form.

After careful consideration, Courage no longer assumed his session with Asai was a dream.

She took him to her constellation, her universe, to show him her appreciation, the highest extent of it.

It was unexpected, yet very powerful.

The more I linger the universe, the more I learn. That strange female Melhouna. Asai. That had to be the most... unpredictable thing that's ever happened to me. Yet... she was very genuine. And... I had no idea something like that could feel... beyond comprehension.

Now... there's a score I need to settle with those Hychineirian bastards. They were using Asai to get to me. That's fucking low. That lying bitch Elaimia... all of them will rue the day they crossed me.

Courage placed his fists together.

Then, the Vevolomurus appeared as a black mark on his forehead underneath his headband.

Next, the Vesorai covered his neck and face.

The dark lines connected with the Vevolomurus.

The lines also ceased underneath his eyes, ears, nostrils, and lips.

Courage sealed his Sacred Staraidus.

He wanted to test his capacity.

Then, Courage teleported to planet Gwempteya, Hychineira Kingdom, where he intended to make Elaimia and Deathelena grieve for their underhanded scheme.

Courage emerged in Hychineira Kingdom.

He was quite far from Deathelena's Castle.

He attempted to keep his Selsengra lapse.

There are certain aspects the Vevolomurus Seal could not obstruct.

Yet, he only hoped he would get a decent fight from Deathelena and the Hychineirian Nation before he ended their existence.

At Deathelena's Castle, several Hychineirian Soldiers noted something in the distance.

They saw an enormous green aura beaming from the individual as it approached, as well as a massive apparition of a bull.

"The hell is that?" Hychineirian Soldier A asked.

"Whatever it is, this isn't gonna be pretty..." Hychineirian Soldier B replied.

"That's the legend, you fucking idiots!" Hychineirian Soldier C stated. "This is an emergency! Sound the alarm and find Goddess Deathelena!"

Hychineirian Soldier C pulled the switch on the wall.

The alarm sounded throughout the castle.

All of the Hychineirian Soldiers, Hychineirian Knights, and Hychineirian Summoners gathered before the castle.

The Hychineirian Soldiers are the infantrymen.

The Hychineirian Knights are the elite fighters.

And the Hychineirian Summoners are the magicians and archers.

They watched as the one they thought was a myth approached.

Many of them considered this suicide.

Yet, they honored Deathelena.

They all are half of what Deathelena is.

They are demigods.

Yet, they knew they paled in comparison to the legend, let alone star beings.

They had a difficult choice: either die by the legend for their crimes across the universe or they would die by Deathelena for their cowardice.

"Oh... Deathelena..." Elaimia dreamed. "That... feels so good. Don't... ever stop..."

Upon hearing the alarm, Elaimia startled from her sleep.

She leaped out of bed.

She ran toward her bedroom window.

She gasped.

The one she attempted to mislead had returned.

Lightning flashed across the sky.

The thunder roared.

And Killosogma Plumes sprung forth.

All of this seemingly represented the ire of the one the Hychineirian Nation despised – the Sacred Star of the Cosmos.

The Mother UFO Deathelena piloted returned.

It hovered above her castle.

The door slid upward.

She noted the Hychineirian Nation gathered before her castle.

Then, she noticed the loathsome individual the Hychineirian Nation prepared to fight.

She chuckled.

Oh dear Courage… how I've been waiting to fight you once more. I'm more than ready for you this time, darling. I look forward to licking your "Sacred Livalaquia" off your corpse.

Flowerensia and co. stood before the Temple of Transcending.

They sensed that Courage vacated the vicinity moments ago.

After Courage departed for Ulenar Island, he told Flowerensia he would inform her what he thought of the tropical vista.

He never did.

He was excessively enthralled with being private and becoming much stronger that the thought of visiting his friends did not occupy his conscious.

Courage is the essence of a hermit.

They were worried about him.

"Is… Courage going to be alright, Flowerensia?" Helipak asked. "I haven't seen him in a while. It's like he closed himself off from everything and everyone. There are people who love him."

"…He's fine. But… he requires time to himself. It… isn't easy having the weight of the universe on his shoulders… I assume…"

"Indeed," Ulanahar agreed. "Yet… it feels as if he's been gone much longer than a week. I wouldn't want him to think we're being dependent, but it would be nice to see his presence in the kingdom once in a while. He brings life to this place. No offense, Flowerensia."

"None taken, dear. I feel the same way…"

"Antisocial personality disorder…" Kimiko wondered. "You think our buddy has it?"

"The irony, Kimiko…" Flowerensia said. "If Courage was a psychopath, he would've killed me the moment we met."

"True…" Kimiko stated.

"You all worry too much," Melharina said. "I understand you all are concerned about him. But maybe he has business elsewhere. You know, unfinished business he failed to take care of before he landed here. That ever cross any of your minds?"

"It matters not," Serenity interjected. "We're his friends. He doesn't have to inform us of his every step. Yet, visits would be highly appreciated. We aren't his enemies."

"It does matter," Melharina countered. "It's his life. No one is in control of it but him. Yeah, he should come by once in a while, but damn. You all act like he's been gone for eons. Let the man live and take care of his business."

"Yeah, but…" Velcrimia stated. "It has been rather dull since his departure. You think… maybe he thinks people only want to be associated with him because he's the legend? If so, I can understand why he would choose to be a recluse."

"That's a definite possibility, Velcrimia," Gravulkim said. "Some beings, including our own, can be very shady. Yet, he'd know if we were that disgusting to only use him for what he is. None of us here are like that. At all. It sickens me just talking about this."

"Everyone's hypothesis may be right to a degree," Janeiholm stated. "But I think Flowerensia and Melharina are right out of all of us. Being a major force across the cosmos is a responsibility I wouldn't wish on anyone. Yes, it comes with countless perks. But it also has drawbacks.

"One of the most common perks for being famous is popularity. Obviously, Courage has this. One of the drawbacks is people wanting to fight you because you're popular and they aren't. Envy. They hate you because you possess what they lack. It's rather childish.

"I respect Courage for the simple fact he makes the title rather than the title making him. In fact, he probably couldn't care less about being the legend. He is who he is. And he's proud to be a star being, which is why he spoke highly of us to Feloreigro and many others.

"If he didn't give a rat's ass about us, I highly doubt he would've spoken to us, let alone defended our history.

"Overall, I'm positive Courage has his reasons for being away so long. I'm not going to press him about it. Shit happens. That simple."

"Well... aren't you a sweetheart..." Helipak purred.

"I'll bust your damn head if you talk to me like that again," Janeiholm asserted.

"Alright, alright, I'm sorry. I just like that you're passionate about Sweet Courage, is all..."

"Courage ain't "sweet", femboy. He's a killing machine. But he has more spirit than people realize."

"Your assessment is spot on, Janeiholm," Melharina said. "But do you have a clue as to where he might've gone?"

"Nope. After we left Serenity's domain, that was the last we saw him. Flowerensia was the last one with him."

"You're right, hon..." Flowerensia confirmed. "When he first arrived in my kingdom, he stayed at my temple. After we left Zeinhailurein, he wanted his own residence. He took a liking to one of my islands, so I allowed him to have one. He chose this one..."

Flowerensia placed her hand on her chest.

Tears cascaded down her cheeks.

"After that… I didn't see nor hear from him again. I understand why… Helipak said what he said. It's like he completely… shut us out after he moved here. It's… it's… it is heart-wrenching…"

She could no longer conceal the fact that she loved Courage.

And the fact that it was not apparent to him made it worse.

Helipak embraced Flowerensia.

They silently wept on each other's shoulder.

No one knew what to say.

The atmosphere permeated with uncertainty.

Then, someone emerged from Pareizyma Jungle.

"I know where he might've gone."

Everyone looked toward the mysterious individual.

"Who are you?" Flowerensia asked.

"My name is Asai Rionai. I'm a Melhouna. My constellation is Auderesa, the Celestial Rabbit."

Asai wore her tiara, star amethyst earrings, purple choker, and the Hychineirian Uniform that is similar to Deathelena's.

However, instead of having Scorpreikia on the back of the cape, she has Auderesa.

Flowerensia observed her uniform.

She became suspicious.

"You're not affiliated with Deathelena, are you? That's her uniform design."

"She took me in her care when I was a teenage Acolyte Star. I didn't know how to control my Staraidus. So, she tutored me.

"I never committed violent acts as a result of being under her wing. However, I was put into a coma by a jealous Azagnorpor who's still in league with her.

"Courage... the one you all seek... he's the one who saved me. He's the one who awoke me.

"Three days have passed in my universe since we had our discussion. Yet, it seems that only a few hours have passed in your world."

"Why... was he in your universe...?" Flowerensia questioned.

"I took him to my constellation to show him my appreciation. After I retired, he left."

"You have Courage's powerful vibe about you..." Ulanahar said. "She speaks true."

Even though I'm getting a sense that it's much deeper than she's leading on. Could she and Courage have...?

"How did you know to come here?" Flowerensia queried.

"...The Tauran'creima Aura guided me here."

"...I... I see..." Flowerensia stated.

Then, Flowerensia noticed a bull-shaped emblem on Asai's neck.

"Where... did you get that marking from?"

Asai placed her hand over the design.

"That's... personal..."

Asai sensed disbelief among them.

However, the only ones she felt an affinity for are Ulanahar and Velcrimia.

"I believe her," Velcrimia stated.

"Likewise," Ulanahar said.

"Thank you so much," Asai stated. "May I ask you two your name? Please?"

"Velcrimia Celestia. I'm a Melhouna. My constellation is Teretri'aga, the Celestial Maiden."

"Ulanahar Gekonia. I'm an Azagnorpor. My constellation is Eidomularus, the Celestial Snake.

"…Asai… I know how it feels to be misunderstood. To be on the outside looking in. I've gone damn near my entire life under surveillance because I'm an Azagnorpor who does great deeds instead of the stereotypical brutality Azagnorpors are known for.

"I welcome you with open arms. Pleasure to meet you."

"Thank you… Ulanahar…"

"You said you know where Courage might've gone. You know exactly where?"

"It's very likely he went to engage Deathelena and Elaimia for attempting to murder him by using me as a scapegoat when I was in my unconscious state.

"They didn't get a chance to follow through with their plan because I teleported us out of there after he revived me. That's when I took him to my constellation."

"How did you know about their plan if you were unconscious?" Kimiko asked.

"Courage and I figured it out during our discussion."

"So why did you teleport him away if you were unaware of their devious plan?" Kimiko persisted.

"…I took a liking to him. So I sought to get him away from the Hychineirian Nation. I didn't care for my safety because Deathelena and her army never brought me harm. With the exception of an Azagnorpor..."

"Planet Gwempteya, Hychineira Kingdom, is where he went," Serenity said. "That's Deathelena's main stronghold."

"We'd just get in his way if we went there to stop him, or fight alongside him," Kimiko stated.

"It matters not," Serenity said. "He has our support. And he needs to know he isn't alone."

"If we're going to do this, I say we keep our distance and observe," Gravulkim stated. "If things get nasty, that's when we intervene. Courage is the most capable of us all. There's no denying that.

"However, like Serenity said, he needs to know he isn't alone and doesn't have the weight of the universe on his shoulders.

"He defended us. Now it's high time we did the same."

"I just want to see his precious face again..." Helipak said. "Since I last saw him, my dreams have always been about him. I... I'd rather not get into details about what he does to me. Or what I do to him. All I can say is that... it's beyond my imagination..."

He sighed.

Next, he blushed.

Then, he twirled a lock of his hair around his index finger.

"You're very kind, Helipak..." Flowerensia stated. "We just need to hope for the best."

"We should go now," Velcrimia said. "Asai might be right. Didn't Courage fight Deathelena when he first arrived here, Flowerensia?"

"Yes. He beat her effortlessly. He defended me because she wanted revenge for me and Melharina sealing her away. Although Deathelena is the strongest of the deities, Melharina is the only one able to hold her own against her.

"It's likely he went to her kingdom to put an end to her."

"So let's go see how things are going," Velcrimia stated.

Everyone teleported to planet Gwempteya, Hychineira Kingdom.

They were eager to show Courage their loyal support.

Courage stood before Deathelena's Castle.

Deathelena stood among the Hychineirian Nation.

Fesforia and Elaimia were standing on either side of Deathelena.

The Hychineirian Nation was terrified.

Yet, with Deathelena among them, they had a fair amount of resolve.

Elaimia was petrified.

Fesforia observed Courage.

This is her first encounter with the legend.

Fesforia is an Acolyte Star, as well as an Original Star.

She is powerful enough to operate the Hychineirian Nation.

Yet, she knew she paled in comparison to the splendor of Courage.

Even with his Sacred Staraidus sealed, they could see the Tauran'creima Aura around him, as well as Tauran'creima himself, which appeared as a colossal apparition that glowered upon all of them.

Nevertheless, Deathelena had to protect her people.

And she had to proceed with her diabolical galactic plans.

Even if it cost her life again.

"Tetsu'reidza…" Deathelena said. "Darling, do you notice anything… *different* about me?"

Courage sensed that she is much stronger.

Furthermore, she is a star being.

He was shocked.

"How the hell did you become a star being, you wretch?"

She laughed.

"Yes! Now, I'll *finally* be able to match you, honey! I'm a Dark Azagnorpor. An Original Star. A Dark Master Star. I'm Deathelena Scorpreikia *Recreigialas*. Beware of the Celestial Scorpion."

The Hychineirian Nation gasped.

"And to answer your question, honey, a dear friend of mine assisted me. I've finally "made the transition"."

"What's your friend's name?"

"Aerogym Rexenia. I'm sure you'll meet her *someday*. She's been *dying* to meet you. Maybe we could sleep together and have a little fun, love. Lighten up."

Aerogym was an Azagnorpor, as well as an Original and Master Star.

Her constellation was *Arach'maragia*, the Celestial Black Widow Spider.

Courage scoffed.

"Hell no. Fuck outta here. You're just going to be more of a pain in the ass than usual. How is this even possible?"

"Like the healing compatibility among star beings, the same applies when a star being transmutes someone of another species. The compatibility must be there."

"Damn it..."

"Regardless, love. What brings you to my luxurious vista?"

"You know why I'm here."

"Why is it you're here? Polar Opposites, or Polarity, Scorpreikia and Tauran'creima may be, but there's an incredible... *intensity* between them. *If* you catch my drift, sweetie. I'm an expert in *Astrailaulogy*, the studying of star beings and constellations, after all."

"Ugh. Shut up, already. You sent that lying bitch Elaimia to persuade me to come here so you could kill me. You used Asai's condition as a motivation. Both of you are fucking useless."

Elaimia was shocked.

She looked away out of shame.

I'm so sorry, Courage...

Courage sneered.

You thought you had me, didn't you, bitch? I knew you were full of it. Now, you and everyone here are dead.

No! Please, Courage! I'm sorry!

Shut up...

"I'll show all of you the error in which you fail to see before your goddamn faces."

Courage marched toward Deathelena.

Then, one of the Hychineirian Knights charged toward Courage.

He held his Hychineirian Sword upward.

He prepared to strike Courage.

When he neared Courage, he swung the blade downward.

Suddenly, Courage ceased the Hychineirian Sword with one finger.

Everyone gasped.

"Deathelena..." Courage said. "If this is the best your nation has, then you're as pathetic as them. They're a reflection of you. If I was in my Kizaloras form, this feeble attack would've passed through me."

Swiftly, Courage kicked the Hychineirian Knight's abdomen.

The Hychineirian Knight glided across the vicinity.

He fell off the edge and into the Marligrat'chia Sea.

He screamed.

He raised his hand as he submerged beneath the Killosogma.

The Hychineirian Nation was appalled.

Courage continued marching toward Deathelena.

"I'm sure you'll revive him at some point. I'm not a cookie-cutter being. All who oppose me, or any star being, will meet their end. My wrath knows no bounds, but their life does."

Courage chuckled.

"Forfeit the game before I take you out of your frame and put your name to shame. When I'm through with you and your Slutwalk Kingdom, you'll be nothing but obliterated lames."

"Tetsu'reidza... enough..." Deathelena stated. "If you want to fight me, then I accept. However, leave my people out of this. If I win, I'll rule the entire universe. If you win, well... it's another tally on your chart, you bastard."

Elaimia shook her head.

"Goddess Deathelena... please reconsider..."

"It can't be helped, dear. I'm the ruler of this nation. This very planet. It's my job to fend off people like him. So you and Fesforia stay out of this."

"But…" Fesforia and Elaimia said.

"Damn it, no buts!" Deathelena retorted. "He'll kill you without hesitation should you intervene!"

"Fine…" Fesforia and Elaimia relented.

"Come, Courage," Deathelena called. "We'll go to Relmi'shira for our bout."

"Is that another one of your hellholes?"

"If that's what you want to call it, dear."

Courage approached Deathelena.

"You two, move," Deathelena ordered.

Fesforia and Elaimia obeyed.

They stood among the Hychineirian Nation.

When Courage neared, he stopped several feet from Deathelena.

Then, Deathelena teleported with Courage to Relmi'shira.

Elaimia placed her hand on her chest.

Please be safe… my dearest Goddess Deathelena…

Deathelena and Courage arrived at Relmi'shira.

They stood in the depths of *Groidorfeneir* Valley.

Relmi'shira resembled Hychineira Kingdom.

However, it is extremely sinister.

Massive *Morguitha* Skulls, each with different color glowing eyes, covered the dreadful landscape.

And since Courage is an unwanted guest, the Morguitha Skulls mostly watched him.

The only illumination in Relmi'shira is the Killosogma.

The difference is it gradually faded in and out of existence.

This type of Killosogma is known as Killosogma *Luethos*.

When it faded, the entire realm fell into darkness.

The only aspects of note during this brief dark period are the glow of the inhabitants' malicious eyes, their weapons, and their diabolical Relmi'shirian Glyphs.

The Relmi'shirian Nation were eager for Deathelena to make an example out of Courage.

Just like she did to Flowerensia eons ago.

"We really ought to stop meeting like this, Tetsu'reidza..." Deathelena said. "Surely you don't think our meetings are coincidental, now do you?"

"Don't talk. Just fight."

Deathelena chuckled.

"To the point as always, dear. You're not one for small talk. I guess that's one thing I like about you. Alright. First move's all yours."

"If I attack, it'll be your last time breathing. By the way, ladies first."

"I have a question, dear. Why did you seal your Sacred Staraidus? That's awfully rash."

"Why does it concern you? Use this opportunity to see if you can defeat me."

"...Hon... are you afraid of killing those close to you? Or killing in general? Is that why you sealed your Sacred Staraidus? Or are you testing yourself?"

"What kind of questions are those?"

"It's always been about you, dear. Why do you think I sought you out eons ago? I was curious as to what all the fuss was about with you."

"Yeah, and that curiosity nearly killed the cat. You should've known to stay away from me. Especially with your kind of aura and reputation."

"Opposites attract, like repel, dear..."

"You're disgusting. Now, for the last time, attack me."

Deathelena sighed.

"If you insist, dear. And remember, I'm a star being now. I might still be known as the Death Goddess to some, but that's no longer the case. This should be fun, indeed. The Dark Master Star vs. the Sacred Master Star. Time to rock your world, love. In more ways than one."

Deathelena instantly appeared before Courage.

She threw a punch toward him.

He immediately grasped her fist.

She used her other hand in an attempt to strike him.

He caught that assault as well.

Then, he kicked her abdomen.

She glided backward.

She landed on her back.

Then, she leaped to her feet.

She closed the distance once more.

She attacked Courage with a right high kick.

He matched her kick with his own.

When their assault collided, a lightning bolt struck the ground.

The Relmi'shirian Nation cheered.

Deathelena and Courage attacked each other at very high speeds.

The majority of the time, they parried one another's attacks.

Then, Deathelena created distance between them.

She conjured a black *Veicrelazah* Whip in her hand.

She swung the Veicrelazah Whip at Courage.

He caught it effortlessly.

Then, Courage immediately released the Veicrelazah Whip.

It rejected his righteous presence.

Deathelena laughed.

She slowly licked her lips.

She emitted a slurping sound as she proceeded.

"What's the matter, dear? Did the mean o' scorpion sting *wittle* o' you?"

"Fucking bitch…"

Then, the Veicrelazah Whip wrapped around Courage's shin.

The negative aspect of the Veicrelazah Whip persistently stung him.

He hissed.

Deathelena laughed.

She slowly licked her lips once more.

She gazed at him seductively.

"My. Feeling a little… *numb*, Tetsu'reidza? Hmm?"

Deathelena conjured another Veicrelazah Whip.

She swung it toward Courage.

It struck his cheek.

He hissed.

Sacred Livalaquia, which is green and silver, leaked from his injury.

Angered, Courage released Tauran'creima's Bellow.

Suddenly, Deathelena and the Veicrelazah Whips were pushed very far from Courage.

Then, he felt elated.

He recalled the first time feeling the unspeakable power – the Selsengra – circulating throughout his body the moment Tauran'creima bellowed and after he defeated the Fire, Wind, and Earth deities.

It was inconceivable.

Currently, the Selsengra circulated throughout his body.

However, this time, he did not contain it.

The Vesorai on the Sacroncai Uniform turned from silver to red.

Red sacred flames – the *Selondura* – coursed through the Vesorai.

The Selondura is the most scorching aspect throughout the universe.

It greatly succeeded Killosogma.

Regardless, Selsengra Courage awaited Deathelena.

Within moments, Deathelena appeared before Selsengra Courage.

She swung the Veicrelazah Whips at Selsengra Courage.

He caught them.

Then, Selsengra Courage summoned the Selsengra Aura around his hands.

The Selsengra Aura protected his hands from negative aspects.

Next, he secured part of the Veicrelazah Whips around his hands.

Finally, he released the Selondura along the Veicrelazah Whips.

The Selondura moved very hastily as it approached Deathelena.

The Selondura also incinerated the Veicrelazah Whips.

She was shocked.

She released the Veicrelazah Whips.

Unfortunately for her, when the Selondura reached the tip of the Veicrelazah Whips, the sacred flames leaped toward her.

She was set ablaze.

She released Scorpreikia's Screech in agony.

The yell echoed throughout Relmi'shira.

The Relmi'shirian Nation booed Selsengra Courage.

When the Selondura ebbed, Deathelena was gravely wounded.

Dark Livalaquia, which is black and silver, leaked from her injuries.

Her Hychineirian Uniform was scorched.

Consequently, she was naked.

The *Hychineiriaza*, her Constellation Ascension Glyphs, covered her body.

Deathelena breathed slowly.

She groaned in pain.

Yet, she grinned.

"You… like what you see, dear? Am I appealing to you?"

"Ugh. Don't flatter yourself. Put some clothes on."

Deathelena held her breasts.

"Come off it, Tetsu'reidza. You burned my clothes so you could see what I looked like naked. So perverted. Now here. Feast your eyes on me. All over me."

"Shut the hell up. Stop trolling. I'm not going to entertain your sick thoughts, you depraved bitch. If anyone's perverted, it's you."

"So you don't want me?"

"Shut up and fight."

"Why're you holding back if you can kill me? Do you… pity me? Did you have a change of heart? Is that why you won't kill me? If this is true…"

Deathelena placed an index finger in her shaved womanhood.

She moaned.

Then, she withdrew it.

Next, she slowly licked the secretion off her finger.

She purred.

"Then, you're sweeter than you lead people to believe, my sweet."

She was right.

Courage was not the kind to kill someone who did not possess the caliber to murder him.

However, the only reason he murdered the Fire, Wind, and Earth deities was because he was highly upset that there were gods and goddesses challenging star beings to prove who was superior.

Regardless, he believed what he did to them was overkill.

Even if it was to prove his perspective.

He felt remorse.

Those gods did not do anything personal to him to warrant their murder.

And as horrible as Deathelena is, he did not want to do the same to her.

However, if the situation was extremely dire, and caused by her, or anyone, he would be forced to do the unspeakable.

Then, Deathelena conjured red Relmi'shirian Glyphs.

They slowly circled her entire body.

She clasped her hands before her.

Her hair spread to either side of her head.

Then, it bobbed eerily in the breeze.

"We should go on a little field trip, honey," Deathelena said. "I think you'll love it as much as I."

Then, Deathelena teleported with Selsengra Courage elsewhere.

The Relmi'shirian Nation could still see Deathelena and Selsengra Courage.

Deathelena and Selsengra Courage appeared in Relmi'shira Catacombs.

It was completely dark.

Red Relmi'shirian Glyphs slowly faded in and out of existence about the Relmi'shira Catacombs.

Deathelena summoned two Morguitha Fedmori'ias.

Morguitha Fedmori'ias possessed the appearance of Deathelena.

However, the only difference is that their skull is displayed.

And their eye sockets are vacated.

Occasionally, purple-glowing pupils emerged in the eye sockets.

They changed shape and size depending on their thoughts.

When they were idle, the glowing pupils disappeared.

"First stop, Relmi'shira Catacombs," Deathelena stated. "Enjoy, my love."

Deathelena closed her eyes.

Then, she chanted in Hychineirese.

Her Dark Staraidus started rising.

The Morguitha Fedmori'ias charged toward Selsengra Courage.

Selsengra Courage fended off the Morguitha Fedmori'ias.

Morguitha Fedmori'ia A performed a right high kick.

However, Selsengra Courage caught her delicate foot.

The Selsengra Aura burned her.

Morguitha Fedmori'ia A screamed.

Morguitha Fedmori'ia B attempted to intervene.

Yet, Selsengra Courage held his other Selsengra Aura-covered hand toward her.

She reluctantly withdrew.

Then, Selsengra Courage grabbed Morguitha Fedmori'ia A's leg.

Next, he threw her.

She glided across the vicinity.

She landed on her abdomen.

Selsengra Courage extended his hands toward the Morguitha Fedmori'ias.

He fired one Selondura Sphere toward them from his hands.

When the Selondura Spheres neared, they struck them.

They were engulfed in sacred flames.

They released Scorpreikia's Screech in anguish.

Then, the Morguitha Fedmori'ias disintegrated into purple particles.

Deathelena scowled.

"I always expect the best from you, love."

Suddenly, a large purple circle appeared underneath Selsengra Courage.

It possessed a combination of Hychineirian and Relmi'shirian Glyphs.

This is the *Reidono'monseiya*.

This is similar to Courage's Meidoreha'agreda.

However, the Reidono'monseiya allowed the caster to penetrate the conscious of others and force them to experience what they wish.

Selsengra Courage was paralyzed.

Deathelena summoned two Morguitha Fedmori'ias once more.

The Morguitha Fedmori'ias slowly approached Selsengra Courage.

Then, they each conjured a Ni'egoraga.

Suddenly, Morguitha Fedmori'ia A lunged toward Selsengra Courage.

She thrust the Ni'egoraga toward him.

It penetrated the Sacroncai Armor and his abdomen.

Selsengra Courage yelled.

Then, Morguitha Fedmori'ia A blew Frousanei from her mouth.

It froze the Selondura coursing through the Vesorai.

Selsengra Courage yelled once more.

The Selsengra Aura around his hands gradually faded.

Next, Morguitha Fedmori'ia B emerged behind Selsengra Courage.

She thrust the Ni'egoraga through his back.

He shouted.

Then, each Ni'egoraga was shrouded with the Telti'leigrus.

His Tauran'creima Essence began depleting.

Then, they embraced him.

Morguitha Fedmori'ia A kissed his cheek.

"This ain't over, you cunts!" Selsengra Courage berated.

Morguitha Fedmori'ia A twirled a lock of her hair around her index finger.

"But, we want to fuck you. All three of us. Please, heroic Courage?"

Her voice is soothing yet ethereal.

Selsengra Courage became irate.

"I don't care what you want! Save your wretched cunt for someone else! Away with both of you!"

Deathelena laughed.

She seductively approached Selsengra Courage.

"They like you, dear. Especially with that strong voice you have."

"Yeah right."

"Always the skeptic, aren't you, dear? Alright, girls. Move. It's my turn."

The Morguitha Fedmori'ias obeyed.

They slowly withdrew the Ni'egoragas from him.

He hissed.

Once they removed the Telti'leigrus-covered Ni'egoragas, his Tauran'creima Essence stopped depleting.

Then, they stood on the parameter of the Reidono'monseiya.

Next, Deathelena stood before Selsengra Courage.

She gently placed her hands on his head.

She massaged her fingers through his hair.

Next, she softly grasped his hands.

She placed his hands on her firm buttocks.

She kissed his lips.

She secured her arms around his neck.

She moaned.

Then, her eyes illuminated solid purple.

Finally, Deathelena delved into Selsengra Courage's conscious.

Deathelena and Courage were lovers.

It was difficult for them to be away from each other.

Currently, they were making love.

They were in Kizaloras form.

Deathelena's Kizaloras form was a combination of purple and black.

Courage was atop Deathelena.

He kissed her lips.

He thrust into her moist womanhood.

Deathelena secured her arms and legs around him.

They moaned.

They groaned.

They grunted.

She screamed.

Courage tended to Deathelena from her beautiful face to her pretty toes.

And Deathelena fulfilled most, if not all, of Courage's fantasies.

She never wanted to release him.

She never wanted the passion, the sensuality, to cease.

She loved him very much.

They had a spiritual connection that was very unique.

Then, Deathelena switched positions.

She placed her hands on his taut chest.

Then, she bobbed slowly.

They groaned.

Courage placed his hands on her hips.

Then, he set his hands on her firm buttocks.

He squeezed them.

She giggled.

Then, she leaned down.

She kissed his lips.

They moaned into each other's mouth.

All they knew was ecstasy.

Deathelena slowly withdrew from Selsengra Courage's lips.

Then, she whispered into his ear.

"See how good that feels, sweetie? The more we pull away, the stronger the passion becomes, love."

"Bullshit. If you think I'd do this with you, you're mistaken, goddamn it."

"What? Am I ugly?"

"No. Far from it. But your evil ways are. Now, fuck off."

"No!"

Then, she kissed his lips once more.

She pushed her tongue into his mouth.

She closed her eyes.

She moaned loudly.

Secretion leaked from her womanhood.

Then, she delved into his conscious once more.

Deathelena and Courage were Millennial Stars.

They looked that of teenagers.

They went to a treehouse every morning.

It was a treehouse they built.

Within this treehouse, they mostly made love.

However, at times, they talked about deeper aspects of life.

Courage, though bold and open-minded, wanted nothing to do with Deathelena's darker topics.

Currently, they were concluding their love session.

They were in a seated position.

Deathelena was atop Courage.

Her arms were fastened around his neck.

Courage's back was against the wall.

His Sacred Leikaitas leaked out of her womanhood.

They groaned.

And they panted.

Courage steady thrust into her.

He held her firm buttocks.

Deathelena whimpered.

She bobbed in time with his thrusts.

She screamed.

After some time, they slowed their collision.

Deathelena kissed Courage's lips repeatedly.

Courage reciprocated her love.

"Damn… you're so potent," Deathelena said. "In more ways than one."

"And you're very beautiful. Even though you come from an origin opposite of mine."

Deathelena blushed.

"T-thank you… Courage…"

"You're sexy when you blush. Well, you're sexy all the time. But you get my point."

"I do get it. And you're brave and handsome."

"Yeah thanks, but my only problem with you is when you stick those fangs into my neck and draw Sacred Livalaquia out of me. The hell's your problem? I thought you hated the way it tasted."

"I did despise it. But eventually, I grew accustomed to it. And… I'm just marking who I love most. It's always been you. No one else."

"Yeah, a little warning would help, ya know. Shit. Now I have your glyph on me. The Glyph of Scorpreikia."

Deathelena giggled.

"Sometimes, I like surprising you. And don't forget you marked me as well. The Glyph of Tauran'creima."

"Hmph. I bet you do like surprising me."

Then, Deathelena became somber.

"Honey… what do you think the future holds for us…?"

"The hell if I know. I mean, when we first met, we fought all the time. I kicked your ass. Then, on rare occasions, you bested me. Now that's old news. So my only guess is we continue to grow a stronger bond."

"Thinking about it, I hated the way I treated you. I was such a bitch. Now, I'm glad to be your lover. All of me belongs to you, Courage. Always."

"Damn right you do, delicious. From your pretty face to your tasty little toes. From the inside out."

They kissed once more.

"I love you, Tetsu'reidza Tauran'creima Courage Astrial'len."

"And you're mine, Deathelena Scorpreikia Recreigialas."

They kissed again.

They moaned into each other's mouth.

Courage laid between her legs.

Deathelena secured her arms and legs around him.

Then, they proceeded making love once more.

Deathelena slowly withdrew from Selsengra Courage's lips.

A saliva thread stretched between their lips.

She licked it into her mouth.

"See?" Deathelena stated. "This is what *could've* been. I *hate* the fact that we're on opposite ends."

"It can *never* happen, Deathelena. What you're conjuring is wishful thinking. Just give up and go home. Save yourself the trouble. And the embarrassment."

"Never. I won't give up until aspects I hold valuable are mine. You included."

"Keep dreaming. If I wanted you, I could have you. I'd take you, or whoever, on *my* terms. Understand? It'll *never* happen on *your* terms. Ever."

Deathelena was shocked.

She released Selsengra Courage from her hold.

"...I see, dear. Dominate as always..."

Then, Deathelena conjured a Ni'egoraga.

She prepared to impale Selsengra Courage.

Suddenly, Selsengra Courage released Tauran'creima's Bellow.

Deathelena and the Morguitha Fedmori'ias glided backward.

Selsengra Courage dispelled the Frouzai.

The Selondura scorched through the Vesorai once more.

The Selsengra Aura appeared around his hands as well.

Then, Selsengra Courage conjured the Vevolomurus beneath him.

It overlapped the Reidono'monseiya.

The Selsengra coursed throughout the Vevolomurus.

Then, the Selsengra Vevolomurus dispelled the Reidono'monseiya.

Deathelena and the Morguitha Fedmori'ias approached Selsengra Courage once more.

They had their hands clasped before them.

Their eyes were closed.

Then, Deathelena summoned illuminate purple needles – the *Seitairezes*.

She launched them toward Selsengra Courage.

When the Seitairezes neared, Selsengra Courage telekinetically stopped them.

The Selsengra Vevolomurus converted the Seitairezes into Selsengra Seitairezes.

Then, he summoned a Gwi'denahala.

He telekinetically pushed the Selsengra Seitairezes toward the Gwi'denahala.

Once they passed the Gwi'denahala's threshold, it closed.

Suddenly, a large Gwi'denahala appeared before Deathelena and the Morguitha Fedmori'ias.

They were assaulted by the Selsengra Seitairezes.

They screamed.

The Morguitha Fedmori'ias disintegrated into purple particles.

When the attack concluded, Selsengra Courage dispelled the Gwi'denahala.

Deathelena was seriously injured.

Regardless, she conjured two black and silver *Igarakia* Scythes in her hands.

She outstretched her arms to either side of her body.

Black Astral Tears cascaded from her eyes.

She dispelled the Selsengra Seitairezes from her body.

"Deathelena... stop..."

"Not until I have you, dear."

"You dumbass."

She slowly neared Selsengra Courage.

Then, she summoned a red Relmi'shirian Glyph.

She swung one of the Igarakia Scythes through it.

The Relmi'shirian Glyph appeared near Selsengra Courage.

The Igarakia Scythe slashed his cheek.

He yelled.

Sacred Livalaquia cascaded from the injury.

"Damn you, Deathelena…"

Deathelena summoned another Relmi'shirian Glyph.

She swung an Igarakia Scythe through it once more.

The Relmi'shirian Glyph emerged near Selsengra Courage.

The Igarakia Scythe sliced his other cheek.

He shouted.

"Damn it! Enough!"

She licked the Sacred Livalaquia off the Igarakia Scythes.

She moaned.

"So sweet. Just like I envisioned."

"Envision this, goddamn it!"

Selsengra Courage stomped the ground.

The foundation shook.

A Selsengra Vevolomurus appeared beneath Deathelena.

She screamed.

The bottom of her feet burned.

The Selsengra Vevolomurus appeared on the back of Selsengra Courage's right hand.

It also appeared on his palm.

As she slowly flew upward, he arced his hand.

Then, a flaming, mesh-like barrier surrounded the Selsengra Vevolomurus.

The Selsengra Vevolomurus was now the Selsengra *Vevosancrius*.

Deathelena dispelled the Igarakia Scythes.

Then, Deathelena summoned a Seitairez.

She pricked her wrist.

Dark Livalaquia fell onto the Selsengra Vevosancrius.

Suddenly, the Selsengra Vevosancrius was converted into the Reidono'monseiya.

However, a single sacred glyph was not yet altered.

Selsengra Courage snapped his fingers.

The sacred glyph shot a Selsengra Beam through Deathelena's abdomen.

She released Scorpreikia's Screech in agony.

The Reidono'monseiya vanished.

The Seitairez also disappeared.

Then, Selsengra Courage dispelled the sacred glyph.

Deathelena fell to the ground.

Dark Livalaquia pooled around her.

Selsengra Courage shook his head.

"Poor woman. If only you chose a different path."

Deathelena groaned.

She attempted to stand.

"Deathelena, it's over. Stop."

"N-no. Not yet…"

Suddenly, a black aura framed her body – the Scorpreikia Aura.

Then, the Scorpreikia Mask covered part of her face.

Only her lips and chin were displayed.

Her solid purple eyes shined through the Scorpreikia Mask's eye sockets.

Next, two large black Scorpreikia Pincers emerged about her hands.

Five Seitairezes protruded from the back of her hands.

Moreover, a very long, segmented black Scorpreikia Tail emerged from her lower back.

The venomous Scorpreikia Stinger was at the end of the Scorpreikia Tail.

Furthermore, an apparition of Scorpreikia appeared behind her.

She rose to her feet.

She released Scorpreikia's Screech in excitement.

The Scorpreikia Apparition mimicked her.

She was now *Scorpreitiac* Deathelena.

"Honey…" Scorpreitiac Deathelena said. "It's not over. I'll keep fighting. For my nations. For everything I hold dear. Now, come with me. To *Burialicor* Desert. Don't let the sands devour you before I do."

Scorpreitiac Deathelena teleported with Selsengra Courage to Burialicor Desert.

Asai and co. approached Fesforia and the Hychineirian Nation.

"Hey wait, hold up," Fesforia said. "Who the hell are you guys? I recognize some of you from the war we had years ago. But the rest of you bastards... I haven't a clue. Why are you here? Looking for trouble?"

"No, we came here to buy fucking candy, bitch..." Kimiko mocked. "Of course we came here to kick ass! Where the hell did Courage and Deathelena go?"

"They went to Relmi'shira for their bout," Elaimia informed. "Everyone is forbidden to interfere."

"She took him to one of the most hellish places..." Ulanahar stated. "What could she be planning? Relmi'shira is her territory. So, she'll likely use the terrain to her advantage."

"That's a fair assessment, Ulanahar," Velcrimia said. "Knowing her, she's probably scheming how to cheat him out of victory."

"I'm not worried about Sweet Courage," Helipak stated. "We witnessed him defeat three gods without even trying. Deathelena will be a cakewalk for him."

"Careful, Helipak..." Flowerensia advised. "Though I'm highly confident in Courage as well, Deathelena is not to be underestimated. She nearly took my life numerous times. She's the strongest of the deities. As I told Courage, she may not have achieved her goals, but she's a force."

Then, Flowerensia became depressed.

"...However... I have myself to blame for not being stronger than her. If Courage hadn't come when he did... history would have repeated itself. I hate to admit it, but... she was right.

"I'm not a violent goddess. Yet, I do take precautions to protect my people. But it's never enough against someone like her. Even if she dies… she'll return much stronger than she was before. It's disheartening.

"Melharina… thank you. You saved my ass several times. I wish… I was as strong as you…"

"Don't sweat it, dear," Melharina assured. "Though I have to admit, Deathelena is a handful. There were times when I thought she had me. That weirdo bitch is something else. However, since she's absent, the only one who's actually a threat is the stripper Azagnorpor."

"Hey, kiss my ass, you bitch!" Fesforia retorted. "And FYI, Deathelena is no longer a goddess. She's a star being. So good luck trying to stop her now, you fuckwits."

Everyone gasped.

"What?" Flowerensia queried. "How is that possible?"

"A friend of hers helped her out, dumbass," Fesforia stated. "If you thought you couldn't beat her before, you're *really* fucked now."

Fesforia scoffed.

"Even if you were to "make the transition", you still couldn't beat Deathelena. You're too weak. You don't have a warrior's will. Fucking pathetic. Go back to picking your flowers, bitch."

"Shut the hell up, you stripper whore!" Melharina shouted.

"And you're no different either, cunt," Fesforia demeaned. "You only leveled the playing field when facing Deathelena. Now, you, the deities of Rhol'heima, and all of your bastard friends are screwed.

"She's a Dark Master Star. A Dark Azagnorpor. An Original Star. Beware of the Celestial Scorpion."

Flowerensia became terrified.

"If this is true… then, the next time she attacks my kingdom… and if Courage isn't there… my people and I are dead…"

"Stop being a pessimist, sweetie!" Melharina said. "I'll fight anyone to the death! This wretched bitch is no different! She needs to be taught a lesson! A lesson in respect!"

"That'd be suicide, Melharina," Janeiholm stated. "And, I don't think you'll be the one to teach her that lesson."

"And why is that?" Melharina asked.

"Because she has a bone to pick with her," Gravulkim replied.

Gravulkim pointed toward Asai.

Her eyes reflected disdain toward Fesforia.

Memories of how cruel Fesforia treated her resurfaced.

Asai clenched her fists.

Then, she marched toward Fesforia.

Elaimia gasped.

"A-Asai… is that you?"

Asai stopped halfway from them.

"Yes, Elaimia. It is."

The Hychineirian Nation gasped

"You're… an adult now," Elaimia said. "It's… an honor."

"Thank you, Elaimia. You were the kindest of the lot. I appreciate you immensely. You were like an older sister to me."

"Of course, dear. It… was the least I could do…"

"I have a favor to ask of you."

"Yes. Anything."

"Don't intervene."

"W-what do you mean by that?"

Asai returned her attention to Fesforia.

She proceeded toward her once more.

She stopped when she was several feet from her.

Fesforia scoffed.

"Based on your little conversation, you were the girl Deathelena favored. Now… it seems you're one of the big girls now…"

"Fesforia… I looked up to you like an older sister. But… you spat upon me and my admiration like it was nothing.

"You hurt me. Emotionally and physically. But I never let that stop me from trying to gain favor with you. You fucking abused me. All because of your jealousy. And because of who I am.

"I *never* discriminated against you for being an Azagnorpor. It was your confidence I confided in. But your arrogance toward me was despicable."

"Aw, boo-hoo. So what you want me to do? Huh? By default, we're not *supposed* to like each other. You're a goodie. I'm a baddie. That's how it is. Deal with it."

"So you'd rather abide by a technicality than defy it? You're weak. Ulanahar's stronger than you'll ever be. She doesn't allow being an Azagnorpor prevent her from doing right by people.

"Not to mention, she accepted me with open arms. Unlike you. She's like the older sister I never had."

"Pathetic. Listen, if you got beef, then come at me. We can finally settle this. I can finally do away with you. Like how I tried to do years ago. I would have gotten away with it, too. If it wasn't for Deathelena's interference."

"I wouldn't have allowed you to kill her," Elaimia stated. "I'll never be close to your caliber, Fesforia. But I wouldn't have allowed you to kill someone so kind. Someone who was still trying to find their purpose in life."

"You're too soft, Elaimia," Fesforia said. "You always were. How you're a Lieutenant General is beyond me."

"And if you think you're going to have an easy victory, you're gravely mistaken," Asai stated.

"Is it me, or does Asai have Courage's personality?" Kimiko asked.

"Why would you ask that?" Ulanahar queried. "Anyone in her situation would have a right to be upset. Or are you referring to the vibe she emanates?"

"Yeah that…"

"Yes… she definitely has his vibe. That much I already established…"

"You think they…"

"That's none of our concern. If they did, well… great…"

Asai marched toward Fesforia once more.

Fesforia instantly closed the distance between them.

She swiftly threw a punch at her.

Asai caught it effortlessly.

Fesforia threw another punch.

Asai caught that one as well.

Fesforia snarled.

She attempted to strike Asai's abdomen with her knee.

However, Asai matched her knee with her own.

Asai released Fesforia's fists.

She placed an index finger on Fesforia's forehead.

She lightly pushed against it.

Instantly, Fesforia flew backward.

She fell through the wall on the left side of the steel double doors.

The Hychineirian Nation and Flowerensia and co. gasped.

"Holy shit!" Kimiko said. "D-did you see that, Ulanahar? Asai didn't even try!"

"Of course. She's gifted."

Fesforia charged through the hole in the wall toward Asai.

Fesforia attacked her with a left high kick, followed by an elbow to her abdomen.

Asai blocked them.

Fesforia scoffed.

Then, she threw a punch toward Asai's face.

Asai evaded her attack.

"You still have much to learn."

Asai punched Fesforia's lips.

She glided backward until she fell through the right side of the wall near the steel doors.

"Ouch..." Melharina stated. "This battle's over before it even began. Pitiful. Little bitch is getting her ass handed to her."

Fesforia emerged from the hole.

Livalaquia leaked from her lips.

Suddenly, her eyes illuminated solid red.

The Ramonicos Aura framed her body.

She summoned two flaming *Killokosia* Swords in her hands.

"It seems you were right, Flower," Melharina admitted. "This Azagnorpor, as well as star beings in general, are very exceptional. No wonder they're highly revered. Even more than us.

"I guess that's one of many reasons why other deities, if not all other species, either admire or despise them."

"I told you, Melharina. Yet, with Asai's talent, she's making short work of her."

Ramondei Fesforia wiped the Livalaquia from her lips.

She pointed a Killokosia Sword at Asai.

"I'll cut you to pieces and burn you to cinders!"

"Talk is cheap, actions speak," Asai stated.

Ramondei Fesforia snarled.

She closed the distance between them.

She swung the Killokosia Swords horizontally.

Asai stopped them with her index fingers.

Ramondei Fesforia gasped.

A blue sparkling aura covered Asai's fingertips.

This is the Frouzai Aura.

Then, Asai cast Frouzai from her fingertips.

Next, the Killokosia Swords froze.

Asai struck the Killokosia Swords with her index fingers.

The Killokosia Swords shattered.

Asai dispelled the Frouzai.

Then, she struck Ramondei Fesforia once more.

Ramondei Fesforia glided backward.

She struck the steel doors.

The steel doors were knocked off their hinges.

Ramondei Fesforia landed on her back in the foyer.

Suddenly, the Vesorai covered the right side of Asai's face.

The Tauran'creima Aura coursed through the Vesorai.

Then, the Tauran'creima Aura faded in and out of existence at intermediate intervals.

Her right purple eye changed to green.

It strongly resembled Courage's eye.

Her Staraidus is inconceivable.

It is a combination of her Staraidus and Courage's.

Xydeivioria is the process of giving another star being part of their power sexually or otherwise.

Vesorai and *Velidocia*.

Tauran'creima Aura and Auderesa Aura.

Auder'creima Asai marched toward the fallen Ramondei Fesforia.

When she neared, she grabbed Ramondei Fesforia by her neck.

Then, Auder'creima Asai struck both of Ramondei Fesforia's eyes.

Next, she struck her nose.

Moreover, she struck her lips.

As a result, both of Ramondei Fesforia's eyes were blackened.

Furthermore, her nose and lips leaked Livalaquia.

And her front teeth were loose.

Ramondei Fesforia weakly raised her hand toward her own face.

She tried to hasten *Malaidoria,* which is a regeneration ability that restores missing limbs, teeth, and all aspects star beings utilize.

However, Auder'creima Asai punched her, thus nullifying her attempt.

Then, Auder'creima Asai lifted her.

Next, she released Tauran'creima's Bellow.

Ramondei Fesforia glided across the foyer.

She struck the wall at the end of a hallway.

She was embedded within it.

She was unconscious.

The Ramonicos Aura gradually faded.

Auder'creima Asai pursued her once more.

However, Ulanahar appeared before Auder'creima Asai.

"Asai... enough..."

"...Ulanahar... I didn't mean to overdo it. But... the pain... the anger. It took over..."

"I know. I understand. Really I do. But now, it's over. I don't think she'll challenge you ever again."

"I think she will. I wouldn't put it past fools like her."

"If I may ask... how did you gain some of Courage's Sacred Staraidus? No one has his indescribable power, let alone his bellow."

"He... gave it to me..."

"It's more than that. Isn't it?"

"Yes, it is. But, I'd like to talk with you about this later. We have to find Courage."

"Alright. Agreed."

Flowerensia and co. and the Hychineirian Nation approached.

"Last time I checked, rabbits didn't bellow," Kimiko said. "There's something strange going on. Like, how is it possible for you to possess Courage's power? You'd think she'd overload and explode."

"Excuse me?" Auder'creima Asai questioned. "Can you cut the asinine remarks? What's your deal? Are you always so, for the lack of a better word, annoying?"

"Whoa, whoa, chill!" Kimiko conceded. "Don't go all Courage on me, alright? We all know something's going on between you and him. He wouldn't just outright give you his power without a damn good reason."

"And what's it to you or anyone who he decides to give his power to? You think I'd be alive if I tried stealing it from him? And who's to say if I managed to take it from him, that it would accept me? His power is *sacred*, so it would be very likely it would reject me and kill me.

"Anything that is sacred, especially in Courage's case, is of the utmost importance. It can't be matched. Anything that is sacred chooses its wielder. Not vice versa. However, in Courage's case, he always had it.

"What he decides to do with his power is solely his choice. Not mine. Nor anyone's. So fuck off. I don't care who doesn't believe me.

"Talk is cheap. Actions speak."

Everyone remained silent.

However, after watching Asai, Helipak had an inspiration.

Maybe I'll ask Sweet Courage to train me someday. It'll be an opportunity for me to become stronger. And... I can also become closer to him.

"I'm going to see how Courage is faring against Deathelena," Auder'creima Asai said. "I've dealt with enough bullshit for one day."

Then, Elaimia stepped forward.

"I'm coming with you."

"Of course, Elaimia."

"Hey, can one of you pry Fesforia out the wall?" Elaimia asked one of the Hychineirian Soldiers.

"On it!" two Hychineirian Soldiers obeyed.

After the Hychineirian Soldiers retrieved Fesforia, they, the Hychineirian Nation, and Auder'creima Asai and co. teleported to Relmi'shira.

Scorpreitiac Deathelena and Selsengra Courage stood on a respective *Sandai'siala* Tower of Burialicor Desert.

The Sandai'siala Towers are of a high altitude.

They extended beyond the clouds.

Scorpreitiac Deathelena and Selsengra Courage leapt from countless Sandai'siala Towers during their intense bout.

Scorpreitiac Deathelena was very erratic.

However, Selsengra Courage managed against her.

They leaped toward each other.

They clashed with many physical attacks.

However, every assault they threw was countered.

Then, the left Scorpreikia Pincer opened.

She shot the Seitairezes at Selsengra Courage.

He summoned a Gwi'denahala.

The Seitairezes passed the threshold of the Gwi'denahala.

Another Gwi'denahala appeared before Scorpreitiac Deathelena.

The Seitairezes headed toward her.

She summoned the Pronzeimius.

When the Seitairezes neared, they disintegrated upon impact with the Pronzeimius.

Selsengra Courage performed a right high kick.

Yet, Scorpreitiac Deathelena blocked it with the back of the Scorpreikia Pincer.

Then, she struck him with the Scorpreikia Tail.

He plummeted toward the sands.

He landed on his back.

Scorpreitiac Deathelena slowly descended upon the sands.

She landed on her feet.

She folded her arms.

She occasionally shifted the Scorpreikia Tail.

Then, she seductively chuckled.

Selsengra Courage rose to his feet.

He faced Scorpreitiac Deathelena.

She knelt.

Then, she rapidly dug below the sand.

She burrowed toward Selsengra Courage.

When she neared, she thrust one of her Scorpreikia Pincers above the surface.

She attempted to grab his shin with the Scorpreikia Pincer.

Fortunately, he eluded.

Then, she burrowed around in an attempt to keep him unaware of her next attack.

When she neared once more, she thrust the Scorpreikia Tail above the surface.

She attempted to impale him with the Scorpreikia Stinger.

Its red venom – the *Ikrameia* – leaked from the Scorpreikia Stinger.

Selsengra Courage evaded her attacks once more.

He kicked the Scorpreikia Tail away from him.

She growled.

She burrowed away from him.

Then, she emerged halfway above the sand.

The right Scorpreikia Pincer opened.

She shot the Seitairezes at him.

Then, she submerged beneath the sand once more.

Selsengra Courage avoided the Seitairezes.

However, he was struck by the Seitairezes she launched toward him while he evaded the other Seitairezes.

The Seitairezes penetrated the Sacroncai Armor and struck his chest.

He yelled.

She laughed beneath the sand.

Then, she broke the surface of the sand.

She leaped toward him.

While in flight, she aimed the Scorpreikia Stinger at him.

When she neared, she thrust it into his head.

He yelled.

Then, she thrust the Scorpreikia Stinger into his neck.

He choked.

Then, she struck him with the Scorpreikia Tail.

He glided across Burialicor Desert.

He landed on his abdomen.

He landed near Burialicor Ruins, which is surrounded by quicksand.

Then, he knelt on one knee.

He looked toward the approaching Scorpreitiac Deathelena.

The heat wave distorted her image.

When she neared, she stopped before him.

She chuckled.

That's right. Kneel before me, my sweet. It's the perfect position for you, love.

She dispelled the Scorpreikia Pincers.

Next, the Frouzai Aura shrouded her hand.

Then, she cast Frouzai.

The Selondura within the Vesorai froze.

Selsengra Courage yelled.

The Selsengra Aura around his hands slowly faded.

She dispelled the Frouzai Aura.

Then, she placed her hands on the back of his head.

She intertwined her fingers.

She held his head against the mound of her womanhood.

He tried to pull away.

But she did not allow him.

She pulled his head closer to her womanhood.

Tsk-tsk-tsk. You're not going anywhere. Go on and lick my pussy, honey. This is what we've been waiting for.

She slowly swayed her hips.

"It's sad that it's come to this, my honey. That Ikrameia will end you soon. However, nothing's stopping me from joining you… in *death*."

She laughed.

"Yet, before we go, how about a little fun? Just between you and I. I know you're a kinky bastard, you know, with the foot fetish and other areas of the female form."

Selsengra Courage chuckled.

"And that's a bad thing?"

Scorpreitiac Deathelena grinned.

"Perfect. So how about you kiss and suck the pretty toes of me, your new lover? I know you fucked Asai. I know you did very kinky things to her.

"Now, fulfill our fantasies by doing the same to me. Those visions I showed you are real in one way or another. Deny it, if you want. It matters not."

"Hang on. I have one condition."

She sighed.

"What now? What's this condition you have? Let's not ruin the fun."

"Here's my condition…"

He clenched his fists.

The Selsengra Vevolomurus beamed on the back of his right hand, as well as his palm.

Then, he delivered the Selsengra Vevolomurus Uppercut to her chin.

She glided upward.

Next, she plummeted toward the sand.

She landed on her back.

She was unconscious.

Suddenly, the Vevolomurus appeared on her forehead.

Then, Selsengra Courage rose to his feet.

Fucking depraved cunt.

Fortunately, he is impervious to the Ikrameia.

The Selsengra, along with his sacred nature, prevented him from being affected by various celestial ailments.

He dispelled the Seitairezes in his chest, as well as the Frouzai.

The Selondura beamed throughout the Vesorai once more.

The Selsengra Aura shrouded his hands as well.

Suddenly, the Hychineiriaza briefly illuminated purple.

Scorpreitiac Deathelena groaned.

She slowly opened her eyes.

She shook her head to fend off the dizziness.

Then, she rose to her feet.

She looked toward Selsengra Courage.

She chuckled.

"Oh, you're a tricky bastard! I like how you keep it spicy! Similar to how we'd be if we were fucking each other!"

She laughed.

"Final stop! *Curseiruna* Island! It lies among the foreboding clouds of Relmi'shira!"

Then, Scorpreitiac Deathelena and Selsengra Courage teleported from Burialicor Desert.

Scorpreitiac Deathelena and Selsengra Courage emerged at *Curseiruna* Island.

Lightning flashed across the sky.

Then, black Scorpreikia Armor covered Scorpreitiac Deathelena's body.

The Scorpreikia Armor possessed shoulder armor and small spikes.

Suddenly, the left Scorpreikia Pincer opened.

She aimed at Selsengra Courage.

The mouth of the Scorpreikia Pincer illuminated purple.

Then, she launched a Scorpreikia Beam toward him.

When it neared, he evaded it.

Then, the right Scorpreikia Pincer opened.

She fired another Scorpreikia Beam at him.

He avoided it once more.

Suddenly, the Glyph of Scorpreikia appeared on her back.

It illuminated purple and black.

Then, she floated backward.

She stopped.

She brightened between purple and black.

Next, she flew toward Selsengra Courage at an inconceivable speed.

A large field of Scorpreikia Aura surrounded her.

This is the *Scorpreirailot.*

She released Scorpreikia's Screech.

Selsengra Courage looked behind him.

The Scorpreikia Beams were headed toward him as well.

Then, Selsengra Courage summoned two Gwi'denahalas.

He summoned one before the incoming Scorpreikia Beams and one beneath himself.

Selsengra Courage and the Scorpreikia Beams entered their respective Gwi'denahala.

Then, the Gwi'denahalas closed.

Scorpreitiac Deathelena nearly struck Selsengra Courage.

She stopped.

"Where the hell did he get off to?"

Then, one of the Gwi'denahalas emerged before her.

Suddenly, Frousanei expelled from the Gwi'denahala.

She gasped.

She became frozen.

Then, the second Gwi'denahala appeared.

Selsengra Courage flew from its cavity.

He kicked Scorpreitiac Deathelena.

The Frouzai shattered, as well as the Scorpreikia Armor.

She landed on her back on Curseiruna Island.

She was shocked.

Then, Selsengra Courage snapped his fingers.

The Selondura coursed through the Vevolomurus on her forehead.

She released Scorpreikia's Screech in agony.

When the Selondura ebbed, the Vevolomurus was red.

This is the Selsengra Vevolomurus Seal.

The Selsengra Vevolomurus Seal prevented adversaries from utilizing any of their powers.

If she attempted to override the seal, she would die.

The Scorpreikia Tail was dispelled, in addition to the Scorpreikia Aura.

Then, Selsengra Courage flew toward Curseiruna Island.

He landed next to the fallen Deathelena.

Her eyes were closed.

He knelt next to her.

He dispelled the Selsengra Aura around his hands.

He also dispelled the Gwi'denahalas.

He calmed the Selondura within the Vesorai.

Then, he cradled her in his arms.

She moaned.

She slowly opened her eyes.

She gave him a seductive gaze.

"Just what I always wanted from you."

"Are you kidding me? You tried to kill me. Who are you trying to fool here, Deathelena?"

"No one. I'm grateful for the time we spent together. Even when we fought long ago."

"…Yeah. This was a fight I wasn't expecting from you. But… you brought the fight, nevertheless."

Selsengra Courage sighed.

"Thank… you…"

"Oh honey, say it like you mean it."

"Shut up. I'm just glad I met another strong opponent."

Deathelena chuckled.

"Likewise. You know I'll be back for you, love."

"No shit. I kinda guessed that. And you're going to get your ass whooped again. Change your path."

"I don't think I'll change it anytime soon, sweetheart. I'm having too much fun. At least you'll have someone keeping you busy. Spank me some more. I look forward to it."

"You're a bother."

"And you're sweet."

Deathelena weakly placed her hand on the back of his head.

She drew her face close to his.

Then, their lips lightly touched.

"I love you… Tetsu'reidza Tauran'creima Courage Astrial'len. The ties that forever bind."

She kissed his lips.

She moaned.

After some time, she reluctantly withdrew.

"…Rest Deathelena."

"Of course, darling."

Deathelena closed her eyes.

She fell asleep.

Then, he held Deathelena bridal fashion.

Next, Selsengra Courage stood.

He utilized *Kekritas* to heal all of his and Deathelena's injuries.

Then, he used *Oraishai* to instantly repair his and Deathelena's clothing.

Kekritas and Oraishai are common abilities among star beings.

Then, he teleported with Deathelena to Groidorfeneir Valley.

When he arrived, the Relmi'shirian Nation noticed them.

They grew irate upon noticing the unconscious Deathelena.

Then, the Relmi'shirian Nation rushed toward Selsengra Courage.

"Stop!" a voice shouted.

Selsengra Courage and the Relmi'shirian Nation looked toward the source of the voice.

The Hychineirian Nation along with Auder'creima Asai and co. arrived.

The one who called out was Elaimia, who was ahead of the Hychineirian Nation.

She walked toward the fallen Deathelena in Selsengra Courage's arms.

She extended her arms toward Deathelena.

He gently placed Deathelena in her arms.

Elaimia knelt on one knee.

She cradled Deathelena in her arms.

Tears welled in Elaimia's eyes.

The tears fell onto Deathelena's face.

She stroked Deathelena's hair.

"Hey, Courage..." Elaimia called. "Do me... a favor..."

"Hmph. What is it, you lying wretch?"

"Kill me. I want to join her. In death."

"She's not dead."

Elaimia gasped.

"W-what?"

"I didn't kill her. She wasn't worth it. Now stop the waterworks and move along."

Elaimia wiped her tears.

"...T-thank you..."

"Hmph. I don't need your thanks. You and your nations will be back to cause more mayhem. I guarantee it. So save it."

"I know you hate us. But… I still appreciate you for sparing her. Thank you…"

"She's *death*. She was going to come back, regardless. You know this, right?"

"Yes…"

"Alright, then. Now move it."

"…You've changed. You could've killed the most notorious goddess in the universe. But you didn't. You've killed before. But now… you abstain from it. You're nicer than I thought…"

"Piss off, woman. Don't misjudge my character. You're not innocent with me. You lied to me, remember? And had I been a feeble-minded weakling, I would've been killed because of you.

"You're only being nice to me because I spared your lover. So stop the false sentimentality. And if it is genuine, it's only temporary. Remember, you and your nations hate me, goddamn it."

"I'm so sorry, Courage. Maybe things'll change. Perhaps this was a humbling experience for Deathelena."

"Bullshit. She said she wants to fight me in the future, so I highly doubt Deathelena will stop her nonsense."

Elaimia noticed the Selsengra Vevolomurus Seal on Deathelena's forehead.

"How can she fend for herself with this… seal on her…?"

"That's to stop her from being an idiot. If she tries to override it, she'll die."

"Is this seal temporary?"

"Maybe. Either I can dispel it, or she'll have to find a way to overcome it without dying."

"What? But..."

"Listen, woman. Enough questions. You're pissing me off. Tend to your precious Deathelena and your nations. I'm going home."

May we meet again... Sacred Star of the Cosmos.

Then, Selsengra Courage ambled toward the Hychineirian Nation.

They scurried away from him.

He looked upon the unconscious Fesforia in one of the Hychineirian Soldier's arms.

She groaned.

She slowly opened her eyes.

Yet, they remained half open.

She was exhausted and in great pain.

She gradually looked at Selsengra Courage.

Looking into his fierce eyes unnerved her.

It reminded her of Asai's righteous anger.

He scoffed.

"You had it coming, girl. Hopefully, this taught you a lesson."

Then, Selsengra Courage walked toward Auder'creima Asai and co.

"We're glad you're alright, Sweet Courage..." Helipak blushed. "But... what's with the... seal...?"

"To test myself. I'll remove it soon. Regardless, why are you all here? Did you follow me?"

Helipak giggled.

"Sure did, honey. I'd follow you anywhere. Forever."

"Yes, we did follow you," Melharina confirmed. "You've been distant lately. But like I tried to tell them, you merely had business to handle, am I right?"

"Correct, Melharina. I refuse to become idle when there's always an opportunity to become much stronger than I am."

"Yes... but..." Flowerensia said. "Would it kill ya to come see us sometime? I mean, we aren't around you just to piss you off, or because you're the legend. We like you because you're a cool and edgy individual.

"We discussed this when we found out you weren't on the island. Everyone here is of accordance. Yet, if it wasn't for Asai, we wouldn't have found you."

Selsengra Courage observed Auder'creima Asai.

She blushed.

"...I see..." Selsengra Courage stated. "Use it wisely."

"Y-yes... s-sir..."

Everyone gasped.

However, Ulanahar chuckled.

She just defeated an Azagnorpor who's a General of a dark army. Asai carried herself with authority. Yet, in the face of Courage, she turns to mush.

It's already been confirmed that some type of connection lies between those two. I'm willing to bet the lovemaking was beyond anything conceivable.

"My apologies, everyone," Selsengra Courage said. "We can talk more about this when we return to Velmelkia Kingdom."

"Hold on, Courage," Auder'creima Asai stated. "I wish to speak with Deathelena one last time."

She approached Deathelena.

She knelt next to her.

Deathelena groaned.

She slowly opened her eyes.

Yet, they remained half open.

Deathelena looked at Auder'creima Asai.

Deathelena smiled.

"You've made me a proud surrogate mother."

A green sparkling Sacred Tear fell from Auder'creima Asai's right eye while an Astral Tear cascaded from her left eye.

"I know you've decided to go along with that damn Tetsu'reidza. But I'll always love you. The Hychineirian and the Relmi'shirian Nations will always accept you."

"Thank you... Mother Deathelena..."

Deathelena chuckled.

"That damn Tetsu'reidza's Sacred Staraidus flows through you. ... At least you know what love feels like. I bet he made you feel extreme ecstasy. I bet he made you scream, didn't he?"

Auder'creima Asai blushed.

Yes, he did, Mother Deathelena. Very, very, very much.

You lucky bitch.

Deathelena laughed weakly.

Then, Deathelena stroked Auder'creima Asai's hair.

Next, the Glyph of Scorpreikia briefly appeared on Auder'creima Asai's forehead before it faded.

"That's my gift to you, love. Now go. You no longer need my help. You're a big girl now. Take care."

"Again, thank you, Mother Deathelena."

She kissed Deathelena's cheek.

"Big Sister Elaimia," Auder'creima Asai called. "Take care of everyone. And I thank you for always being there for me."

"You're welcome. And be sure to visit us sometime."

And by the way, Courage is very sweet. And very handsome. Just don't tell him I said that, or he'll kill me.

Auder'creima Asai chuckled.

I think he already knows you think that, big sis. Take care, love.

Auder'creima Asai rejoined Selsengra Courage and co.

Then, Selsengra Courage and co. teleported to Velmelkia Kingdom.

Once Elaimia quelled the Relmi'shirian Nation and established order in Relmi'shira once more, she and the Hychineirian Nation returned to Hychineira Kingdom.

"Always transcend."

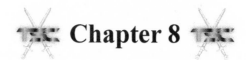 **Chapter 8**

Grandmaster Showdown

One month later.

Courage participated in the Velmelkia Tournament hosted by Flowerensia at the Velmelkia Colosseum.

It was afternoon.

He was the main attraction.

He was also the favorite of the crowd.

The more he progressed, the louder the Velmelkian Nation cheered for him.

He defeated Helipak, Gravulkim, Janeiholm, Kimiko, Melharina, Serenity, Asai, Velcrimia, and Ulanahar with ease.

At some point during the month, Ulanahar and Velcrimia became Master Stars.

Nevertheless, Courage was about to duel the Velmelkia Undisputed Champion, Sadon Frendumar, for the title.

Sadon is very tall and muscular.

He is bald.

He has dark thick eyebrows.

He has solid white eyes.

And he has brown skin.

He wore black combat pants that has red decoration.

And he wore red martial art tape around his hands and shins.

Sadon is a Melhouna and a Master Star, as well as an Original Star.

His constellation is *Leodycreus*, the Celestial Lion.

Sadon defended the Velmelkia Undisputed Championship for over a millennium.

He is one of the strongest star beings to ever grace Velmelkia Kingdom, let alone planet Venusia.

He is also one of the longest-reigning champions Flowerensia ever had.

Regardless, the Velmelkian Nation cheered as Flowerensia prepared to speak into the wireless microphone she held in her hand.

She stood in the center of the colosseum.

The Velmelkia Championship match was about to commence.

"Well, it's finally come! Two of Velmelkia's best fighters are about to come face to face! Are you all excited?"

The Velmelkian Nation shouted.

"Damn… he didn't even try…" Kimiko stated. "He was right. I wasn't ready for him. Hell, we all gave our best and he maneuvered around us like we weren't shit. He didn't even use any of his powerful attacks. He just used basic martial arts against us.

"Damn it… how powerful are you, Courage…?"

Kimiko was disappointed that she failed to meet Courage's expectations.

However, Melharina and co. did not take their defeat as personal as Kimiko.

"Sweet Courage could've handled me more roughly," Helipak said. "I would've *loved* his masculine touch *all* over me. Goodness… I'm getting butterflies just *thinking* about it…"

"Helipak… stop…" Gravulkim intervened. "Like Kimiko said, we all put great effort in our bout against Courage. However, he proved the legend right. He's incredibly powerful."

"I even changed into Helinara, my feminine half," Helipak stated. "Hell, he could've had his way with me in front of everyone here! A live porno, indeed. So exquisite."

Helipak blushed and giggled.

"Rape fantasies of Courage and your utter submissiveness to him…" Janeiholm said. "You're depraved, man. You already look and sound very girlie. Even without changing into Helinara.

"And if he would've handled you roughly, he would've broken you. I know he thinks you're a fucking weirdo."

Helipak shivered with glee.

"If he *ever* broke me, it would be a dream come true. And he likes weirdos. It keeps things interesting. Where's the balance if there's no one to offset anything? Huh? Yeah, I thought so. Go me!"

"Well... at least you have fans, Helipak," Serenity stated. "You have an artistic fighting style. It's admirable."

"Tell me about it..." Melharina agreed. "You were all over the place. It's like you were dancing. Your speed was insane. And those *Melordias* Claws of yours aren't a joke, either.

"*But...* your efforts weren't enough to put the legend out of business. He just pushed you beyond one of the borderlines and called it a day. In fact, he pretty much did that to all of us. He didn't want to hurt us.

"If he wanted to, he could've shut us down the moment the match started. He wanted to give us a fighting chance. He also wanted to give the audience a spectacle. Damn... we must be weak as shit compared to that stud."

"Yeah... you're right..." Serenity said.

"Damn," Helipak stated. "I wanted to taste his sweet Sacred Livalaquia on my claws, but I couldn't get him. I bet it taste beyond anything imaginable. *Mmm...* I'm getting hot. Hotter than any star..."

"Man, you're fucking sick," Janeiholm ridiculed. "Your obsession with Courage is beyond creepy. I bet your dreams about him are lewd as fuck."

Helipak giggled.

"Yes. Yes they are. My dreams about my beloved Courage are very... graphic. It's orgasmic. A true work of art."

He conjured an Ovele'mulus.

Then, he placed it in his hair.

"In my universe, my dreams, I always spread my legs, ass, and mouth *only* for Courage. He can have either Helinara. Or me. Helipak.

My warmth always welcomes him. From my face to my toes, all of me is his. My essence belongs to him.

"Nevertheless, my love for him is eternal. He and I are the epitome of poetry. The very arts of existence."

Disturbed by Helipak's explicit fantasy, Melharina and co. gasped.

Then, they blushed.

They looked away out of shame.

However, Janeiholm snarled.

"Damn it, Helipak! We did *not* need to hear your immoral thoughts of how much you worship Courage!"

Helipak chuckled.

"Jealous, love? Are you jealous that my love for him exceeds all? My flair, my very *lifestyle* is beyond all imagination! *Nothing* compares to my beauty! Well, with the exception of Courage, of course."

Janeiholm sneered.

"You flamboyant son of a…"

"By the way," Velcrimia interrupted. "Don't take the loss so hard, Serenity and Kimiko. We gain new fans every time we enter this tournament. We display our prowess and attempt to obtain the championship.

"Yet, Sadon is a major player. It's hard wresting the Velmelkia Championship belt away from him."

"Indeed…" Ulanahar said. "This match will be quite interesting. However, I believe the majority have their bets on Courage. Yet, I'm certain other wagers are in favor of Sadon. All I can say is this will be unlike any match in history.

"The Celestial Bull vs. the Celestial Lion. The Legendary Tauran'creima vs. the Majestic Leodycreus. It all comes down to this."

"I believe in Courage," Asai said. "He'll win. I know it."

"I'm sure he believes *in* you as well," Helipak teased. "Catch my drift, Miss Asai? *Hmm?*"

"H-Helipak, don't say such things," Asai stated. "At least not here. Damn."

"What's wrong, dear? Scared of a little... *passion?* Especially the kind of *passion* between the sheets between two star beings? *Hmm?*"

"No. Never."

Helipak chuckled.

"I like your fortitude."

"And I admire your zest for life. You're one of the coolest stars I've ever met."

"My sentiments, Graceful Asai."

"Likewise. I appreciate all of you. Thank you."

Flowerensia pointed toward one of the combatant entryways.

"Coming from this entrance, we have the long-reigning champion! The one who's bested every opponent brought before him!

"He even held his own against dark forces who plagued my planet at very crucial times in history!

"You know him! You love him! Velmelkia's Champion, the Majestic Leodycreus... Sadon *Frendumar!*"

The Velmelkian Nation cheered as Sadon's upbeat entry music played.

It was called 'Domain'.

Sadon emerged from the entrance.

He marched toward the center of the colosseum.

The Velmelkia Championship belt was secured around his waist.

The Velmelkia Championship belt is light blue.

It has emeralds around its parameters.

It has a holographic Swa'reikei in the center.

In gold letters, it stated 'Velmelkia Champion' underneath the Swa'reikei.

As Sadon ambled toward the center of the colosseum, the monitor high above displayed his image.

And the Velmelkian Cameras flying around the colosseum recorded him.

When Sadon reached Flowerensia, the volume of his theme was turned down mildly.

Then, Flowerensia spoke.

"So, champ! Do you have anything you'd like to say to your challenger?"

She gave him the microphone.

"Well, it's been long overdue. I need a reason to keep defending this title. So far, the challengers that faced me were talented. Yet, they didn't give me the thrill I was looking for.

"It was a great pleasure earning this title. When I first held it, I was extremely happy. Yet, as time proceeded, I became bored. Very bored.

"There wasn't anyone who could match me. It was as if defending this title became nothing more than a game, which it isn't.

"So, to my challenger... I have a feeling you're the one I sought. You're the one people count on. You're the one who's spoken very highly of. You're the one the universe calls upon. Your very name echoes throughout time.

"To you, I say please… see if you can relinquish me of my title. Only then will I deem you the adversary worthy of the praise you receive."

The Velmelkian Nation yelled.

Sadon returned the microphone to Flowerensia.

"So there you have it! Sadon expects nothing but the best from here on! To those who face him, make sure you're on your A-game! Otherwise, your defeat is imminent!"

She pointed toward the other combatant entryway.

"Now… this man is the one who was foretold throughout the cosmos. The one most of us hold in very high regard. He's defeated the Death Goddess three times, and he's killed several gods. All without any effort.

"And… he would've eliminated an entire evil nation. But… he withheld…

"Regardless, without further delay, here is the one and only legend! The Legendary Tauran'creima… Tetsu'reidza *Courage!*"

The Velmelkian Nation cheered as Courage's hyper entry music played.

It was called 'Transcendence'.

Everyone, including Helipak and co., rose from their seat.

They clapped to the rhythm.

Courage emerged from the entrance.

His expression was one of extreme determination.

He ambled to the beat.

The Velmelkian Cameras recorded him.

And the monitor displayed his image.

He reached the center of the colosseum.

He raised both of his hands.

Then, he waved to the Velmelkian Nation.

They screamed their approval.

Afterward, he observed Sadon.

Both men smile.

They respectfully recognized each other as a worthy fighter.

Sadon chuckled.

That look in his eyes… yeah. He's the one, alright. Relieve me of this belt. And I'll recognize him as the one all praise.

Courage extended his hand toward the microphone Flowerensia held.

She handed it to him.

His theme was turned down.

"Alright, who's ready to see a match of a lifetime?"

The Velmelkian Nation yelled.

"Say what? You need to scream louder than that if you want a match between me and Champion Sadon to happen! Now let me hear you!"

The Velmelkian Nation screeched.

"Alright! That's what I thought! Now, Champion Sadon. I can tell you're going to give me a hell of a match.

"However, I feel the same way you feel. I have yet to meet someone who can give me the thrill of battle. I feel... like I was made to do this. I feel... like I was made to do battle with those worthy of my fists.

"Upon first receiving your championship, you expected to meet others of the same caliber as you. Yet, you're still unfulfilled because the opponents you faced lacked the substance you crave.

"Your boredom grew to the point you felt as if it isn't worth defending the title anymore. You defend it in hopes of meeting someone worthy. Well... that's where I step in.

"Champion Sadon... from your perspective, should I not meet your expectations. Should I fall below the caliber you set. Should I fail to uphold my expectations of a legend... then I don't deserve a shot at the Velmelkia Championship title..."

Everyone, including Sadon, was shocked.

Regardless, Courage continued.

"Yes. I'm setting the standard that high. For the simple fact that it isn't an excuse why you had to wait for a worthy opponent. The best fighters deserve the best challenge.

"Though I'm certain the opponents you faced are credible, if they failed to take the belt from you, then that's telling of your fortitude.

"Champion Sadon, and the Velmelkian Nation, I've rambled on long enough. I just wanted to make my point clear.

"Now, let's get this party started!"

The Velmelkian Nation screamed.

Courage returned the microphone to Flowerensia.

"Hot damn! What a promo! Yet, I feel all Courage had said has incredible depth to it! Now... this is the moment we've all been waiting for! The Legendary Tauran'creima vs. the Majestic Leodycreus! Tetsu'reidza Courage vs. Sadon Frendumar!

"Let the Velmelkia Championship match... begin!"

The Velmelkian Nation yelled.

Before the match commenced, Courage raised his hands.

He dispelled his Sacroncai Armor.

All he wore were light green fighting trunks, green martial art tape around his hands and shins, and his red headband.

Everyone gasped at the Vesorai upon his body.

The Velmelkian Cameras zoomed in on Courage's body to obtain further details.

Helipak, and many others, blushed.

As usual, Helipak giggled.

My word... such a sexy hunk. So delicious you are, Courage. The things I'd love to do to you. Or... the things I'd love for you to do to me... for days on end...

He sighed.

Narosasei aront... (Delectable honey...)

Hesitantly, Flowerensia spoke.

"C-Courage... may I ask why you removed your armor?"

"Champion Sadon isn't armed, nor wearing any protective gear. I want to make this match as fair as possible. Besides, this is all I need to fend for myself. Don't worry."

"So... your Constellation Ascension Glyphs are always present..." Sadon said. "You grow more intriguing by the second. May the best man win."

"Likewise. Champion Sadon."

Sadon removed the Velmelkia Championship belt from his waist.

He handed it to Flowerensia.

She gently took it from him.

Then, she vanished from the center of the colosseum.

She emerged near Helipak and co.

Courage and Sadon marched toward one another.

Then, they instantly closed the distance.

They threw a punch.

Both assaults collided.

Suddenly, an enormous wind erupted about Velmelkia Colosseum.

The Velmelkian Nation screamed.

Courage crouched.

He swiftly struck Sadon's waists multiple times.

Then, he attacked Sadon's abdomen three times.

Sadon grunted.

Next, Courage followed up with an uppercut to Sadon's chin.

The uppercut lifted Sadon off the ground.

Everyone gawked as Sadon glided upward.

Courage glided upward as well, with his fist extended.

Then, Courage landed on his feet.

Sadon regained focus.

He realized he was almost beyond the borderline.

He stopped.

He flew back to the center of the colosseum.

The Velmelkian Nation cheered.

"Damn, that was close…" Kimiko said.

"Hell yeah," Melharina agreed. "This match would've been over had he passed that borderline."

Sadon closed the distance once more.

He threw a right punch toward Courage.

Courage parried the assault.

He followed up by forcing his palm into Sadon's abdomen.

Sadon was pushed back considerably.

When he neared the borderline, he punched a hole in the ground.

However, he continued going backward.

A fissure was created as a result.

Sadon teleported.

Sadon emerged beside Courage in mid-air.

Sadon threw a punch toward Courage.

The blow struck his face.

Courage staggered.

Everyone gasped.

He struck Courage again.

Then, he struck Courage relentlessly.

Next, he lunged toward Courage with his knee lifted.

The assault struck the center of his chest.

Courage grunted.

He fell onto his back.

Sadon waited for Courage to stand.

"Hot damn!" Janeiholm said. "That… look like it hurt. A lot. Sadon's a big dude, so I know his hits hurt like hell."

"Yes," Serenity agreed. "Sadon packs a wallop. But so does Courage. And he can take incredible pain. This is just the beginning. Two Master Stars of their caliber should be one we'll remember for quite some time."

Courage leaped to his feet.

Then, he raised his hands.

Sadon and everyone gasped.

They looked at him in confusion.

"I have a request, Flowerensia."

Flowerensia floated toward Courage.

"Yes? What is it, dear?"

"I'd like to take this battle elsewhere. As powerful as Sadon and I are, it'd be too easy for either one of us to get a ring out. Not to mention, things could get pretty unsafe for these people should the battle heat up.

"So I think the last man standing should be declared the winner. Is that alright with you, Champion Sadon?"

"Definitely."

"What location do you have in mind, Courage?" Flowerensia asked.

"I'll let Sadon choose. He's the champion, after all."

"*Orgrechi* Canyon. We'll fight there."

"Alright," Flowerensia agreed. "I'll have my cameras watching the fight so everyone can see. And please. Try to keep the battle clean."

"Of course we will," Courage said. "Alright, Sadon. Take us to Orgrechi Canyon."

"Got it."

Sadon teleported with Courage to Orgrechi Canyon.

Sadon and Courage emerged at Orgrechi Canyon.

They stood near the *A'yasakai* River.

The Velmelkian Cameras recorded them from above.

Courage flew toward Sadon.

He threw a punch.

Sadon grasped his fist.

He lifted Courage.

Then, he threw Courage over the A'yasakai River.

Courage struck a cliff.

He grunted.

Sadon slowly approached.

Courage refocused.

Sadon closed the distance.

He threw a left hook.

Courage parried.

Yet, Sadon did the same when Courage attempted a counterattack.

They parried each other's attacks for quite some time.

The more they countered one another, the more determined they grew.

It was a test of true skill.

Then, Sadon went for a headbutt.

Courage did the same.

Their heads collided.

They grunted from the mild pain.

However, Courage swiftly crouched.

He struck Sadon's abdomen.

Sadon yelled.

He glided backward.

He fell into the A'yasakai River.

Courage awaited him near the edge of the cliff.

Within moments, Sadon emerged from the A'yasakai River.

He slowly flew into the air until he was level with Courage.

Yet, they remained at a distance.

Sadon utilized Edolia Extere'al to evaporate the water off himself.

Sadon went on the defensive.

He set both of his arms frontward.

His left hand was clenched.

And his right hand was arched.

He slowly approached Courage.

When he neared, Courage threw a right hook.

Sadon instantly parried.

He struck both of Courage's eyes.

Courage grunted.

His eyes were blackened.

Courage ignored the pain.

Then, Courage performed a roundhouse kick.

Again, Sadon parried.

He struck Courage's nose.

Courage hissed.

He staggered backward.

His back struck the cliff.

He held his nose to alleviate the pain.

However, he proceeded toward Sadon once more.

Courage threw jabs and mid-level kicks.

Once more, Sadon parried all of his attacks.

He struck Courage's lips.

He staggered backward once more.

His lips leaked Sacred Livalaquia.

Yet again, he ignored the pain.

He marched toward Sadon once more.

When he neared, Sadon immediately secured his arm around the back of Courage's neck.

He held him in a headlock.

Courage was surprised.

Yet, he realized Sadon broke his defensive stance.

Consequently, he was open for attacks.

Courage ruthlessly struck Sadon's waist and abdomen.

Sadon released Leodycreus' Roar in anguish.

It shook the foundation of Orgrechi Canyon.

Sadon kneed Courage's abdomen in an attempt to quell his relentless attacks.

It was successful, yet only briefly.

Sadon kept his hold on Courage's head.

Then, Courage placed a small amount of Sacred Staraidus in his fist.

He struck Sadon's abdomen with the Sacroncai Punch.

Sadon choked.

He nearly released Courage.

However, he managed to keep him restrained.

Sadon grabbed the waistband of Courage's fighting trunks.

Then, he suplexed him.

Courage landed on his back with a loud thud.

Then, Sadon looked upon him.

Courage was unconscious.

Everyone at the Velmelkia Colosseum gawked at the monitor.

They were appalled.

Both fighters were holding back tremendously.

Had they decided to use their powers, the fight would have been exceedingly destructive.

However, destructive powers were forbidden in the Velmelkia Tournament.

Only the use of martial arts was allowed.

Regardless, Flowerensia and co. were completely shocked.

She wanted to refrain from crying, let alone starting the countdown.

However, she could not make exceptions, even for the legend.

If an opponent was incapacitated, they had ten seconds to stand.

Otherwise, they would forfeit the match.

The Velmelkian Cameras have speakers and a microphone built into them, so Sadon, and possibly Courage, could hear the countdown.

"Come on, Courage!" Kimiko cheered. "Get your ass up! You're so fucking close to having the title! Don't bail now!"

"One…" Flowerensia began.

"My gracious…" Serenity said. "This was unforeseen…"

"Two…"

"Hey, don't doubt the man, alright?" Kimiko stated. "Courage even said this would be a good match! It's not over yet! Courage would rather die than admit defeat! That's how stubborn he is! I know it!"

"Three…"

"I agree, Kimiko," Melharina said. "That hunk has way too much resilience to call it quits. He gave Sadon a run for his money. And should Courage get his ass up, Sadon's definitely in for it."

"Four…"

"My darling…" Helipak whispered. "You can't lose. You just can't…"

"Helipak…" Velcrimia called. "It isn't over yet. He wouldn't come this far just to be knocked out."

"Five…"

"Precisely," Ulanahar agreed. "The stronger Courage's opponent is, the stronger he'll become. This battle only serves to push him further. Quite honestly, I think he's holding back. Even without the use of his powers, Courage is extremely lethal.

"Sadon wanted a challenge. He's got it. He's got Courage to deal with now."

"Though I agree with you, Lana…" Janeiholm stated. "Big Man Sadon isn't a joke, either. None of us could take the belt from him. And when Deathelena's forces invaded this kingdom, he killed the majority of them. That dude is a *beast*!"

"Are you against Courage?" Ulanahar questioned.

"No," Janeiholm replied. "Just putting things into perspective as to not be biased."

"Janeiholm's right," Gravulkim said. "We all tried our hand at obtaining the championship. But it didn't end in our favor."

"You're right, Gravulkim," Ulanahar acknowledged. "The only ones who lasted the longest against him were you and Janeiholm.

"And though he credits every opponent he faces, he gave you two the most recognition by stating that you have a lot of fortitude. And to further improve yourselves."

Asai was upset.

She rose from her seat.

She walked down the stairs.

Then, she stood at the railing.

She gazed at the monitor.

Everyone noticed her.

Asai gestured a Velmelkian Camera toward her.

The Velmelkian Camera approached her.

Asai began chanting Courage's name.

Then, Helipak and co. chimed in.

Next, those of the Velmelkian Nation who were cheering for Courage chanted as well.

Yet, those who were for Sadon chanted his name.

"So… are you just going to lie there and admit defeat? Or are you going to rise and conclude this bout?"

Courage emerged before Tauran'creima in Kizaloras form.

He looked about his surroundings.

They were floating in outer space.

Courage snarled.

"Are you serious right now? I'd *never* admit defeat! What's this all about?"

"Your adversary, and those in favor of you grow impatient. You lie there as if you are conceding the fight. Your time grows short. Arise."

"I was just biding time! It's fair to at least see what my opponent is capable of before I decide it's best to end it. Come on, now. You should know me. We're one in the same."

"Indeed. But it is best not to dawdle any further. Go and claim victory. Now… arise!"

Tauran'creima bellowed.

Suddenly, the entire vicinity changed to white.

"Damn it, Courage!" Sadon protested. "Get up! She's already at seven!"

"Eight…"

"Alright, make that eight! There's no way a suplex could've done you in! I refuse to believe that! Get up!"

Abruptly, Courage sprung to his feet.

Sadon was relieved.

Then, they heard the ecstatic cheers from the Velmelkian Nation through the speakers from the Velmelkian Cameras.

"It's about time!" Sadon said. "You had me worried. I doubt a suplex would've put you out."

"You're right. Sorry about the delay. A bullshit tactic on my part."

"Odds forgiven. Now, come on! Take the belt from me! Put me out of the competition!"

Sadon conjured the red Leodycreus Barrier around himself.

Each star being has a nigh-impenetrable barrier that protects them from almost anything.

Sadon took his defensive stance once more.

Courage approached him.

He clenched his fists.

He prepared a Sacroncai Punch in his fists.

Sadon gauged him.

Courage threw a right punch.

The Sacroncai Punch shattered the Leodycreus Barrier.

As the Leodycreus Barrier dissipated, Sadon immediately threw a right elbow at Courage.

Courage crouched beneath his assault.

Courage threw a left punch toward Sadon's abdomen.

The Sacroncai Punch connected.

Sadon choked.

Before Courage could barrage him with ruthless attacks, he teleported.

Sadon emerged a few feet away from Courage.

Sadon took his defensive stance once more.

Both fighters approached each other.

When they neared, Courage threw a low right kick toward Sadon's left shin.

Sadon pivoted.

He struck Courage's face twice in rapid succession.

Courage yelled.

In addition, he was dazed.

Sadon grasped Courage's head with his massive hand.

Then, he threw Courage toward the escarpment.

Courage struck the cliff.

He shook his head to regain his focus.

Sadon charged toward him.

When Sadon neared, he threw a right punch toward Courage.

Courage evaded.

Sadon struck the cliff.

The assault placed a large hole in the cliff.

The foundation shook as well.

Suddenly, boulders began falling.

Sadon effortlessly broke three boulders.

Several boulders fell toward Courage.

He kicked one boulder toward Sadon.

Sadon shattered his fifth boulder.

However, when the boulder Courage kicked toward him neared, it struck him.

The boulder shattered upon impact.

Sadon yelled.

A second boulder headed toward him.

Sadon released Leodycreus' Roar as he struck the boulder.

The boulder crumbled.

Courage caught the incoming third boulder with one hand.

He pointed toward it with a grin as he looked at Sadon.

Sadon gestured Courage to throw it.

However, Courage teleported.

Sadon was surprised.

He looked about his vicinity.

Courage was nowhere to be seen.

Sadon could not feel his Sacred Staraidus, either.

He was perplexed.

Then, he hunted for Courage.

Suddenly, Courage emerged with the boulder several inches away from his feet in mid-air.

He telekinetically held the boulder in place.

Courage prepared the Sacroncai Kick.

Then, he struck the boulder toward Sadon at an incredible speed.

Before Sadon could react, the boulder struck him.

Sadon released Leodycreus' Roar in agony.

He glided rapidly until he struck a cliff.

He was embedded within it.

Before Sadon could pry himself out of the cliff, Courage quickly flew toward him.

Courage flew into Sadon with his fists extended.

Both fighters broke through the cliff.

They emerged on the other side.

Courage landed on his feet.

Sadon landed roughly.

He rolled to a stop.

Courage waited for Sadon to stand.

Sadon groaned.

He slowly stood.

He staggered as he attempted to keep his balance.

He placed his hand on his head.

He shook his head to regain his focus.

His vision cleared.

He took his defensive stance once more.

A breeze blew across Orgrechi Canyon.

The tails of Courage's headband danced wherever the wind drifted.

Courage smiled.

Then, Courage walked toward Sadon.

Sadon stood firm.

When Courage neared, both fighters began parrying each other's attacks.

The Velmelkian Nation cheered.

Flowerensia and co. shouted as well.

However, as fast as Courage and Sadon were moving, most were unable to keep track of them.

Star beings are the fastest, strongest, extraordinary entities throughout the universe.

Nevertheless, Flowerensia and co. and the Velmelkian Nation only saw flashes of light from their attacks.

Courage threw a right punch toward Sadon.

When Sadon attempted to grasp the incoming attack, Courage immediately pulled his fist away.

Courage feigned his attack.

Then, he struck Sadon's abdomen with his left fist.

Sadon yelled.

He doubled over.

Courage crouched.

He readied a Sacroncai Punch in his right fist.

He sprung upward with his fist extended.

The Sacroncai Uppercut struck Sadon's chin.

Sadon drifted high into the air.

Courage glided midway into the air.

Then, he landed on his feet.

Sadon descended rapidly.

He landed on his back.

Courage approached him.

The Velmelkian Cameras hovered above them.

When Courage neared, he stooped next to Sadon.

He observed him.

He was unconscious.

Courage lifted Sadon's arm three times.

His arm fell limp every time.

Helipak and co., as well as the Velmelkian Nation, roared their acclamation.

Flowerensia commenced the countdown.

Sadon was counted out.

He could no longer continue the fight.

As a result, he was dethroned as the Velmelkia Champion.

Courage teleported with Sadon to Velmelkia Colosseum.

Courage and Sadon appeared at Velmelkia Colosseum.

Everyone rose from their seats.

They cheered.

Those who lost their wager paid what they owed and departed.

The Velmelkian currency are different color coins called *Heleidia*.

"Courage won!" Kimiko praised. "He won!"

"I had no doubts in Courage," Melharina said. "However, Sadon has my respect for holding that title down for so long. He's the real MVP."

"I'm glad Courage pulled through," Serenity stated. "Things seemed quite bleak when Sadon embraced the defensive route. Yet, he has my respect, nevertheless."

"I'm so happy for you, dear..." Helipak whispered. "There's no way you can fail. Ever."

"He's the only one who took the belt from him," Ulanahar stated. "This is monumental."

"Yes," Velcrimia agreed. "Now, there's no one who'll be able to take the belt from Courage. Unless..."

"Unless what?" Ulanahar queried.

"Unless Transidyus and Leiku were to participate..." Velcrimia clarified. "Those two... my gracious. So powerful. Their presence alone is overwhelming. Courage would definitely have a *very* difficult time against those two."

"Indeed," Gravulkim said. "If we thought facing Sadon was bad, Transidyus and Leiku are in a league of their own. Those two, the only Grandmaster Stars, are not to be underestimated. That's a mistake anyone would surely regret."

"A sparring match wouldn't be so much of a sparring match with those two powerhouses…" Janeiholm stated.

"Even if Courage doesn't defeat them…" Asai said. "He'll always have the will to fight those who're stronger than him. Anyone else would run for the hills. That's not Courage. He'll always transcend above all odds."

"Graceful Asai is right," Helipak stated. "Sweet Courage is one in a billion. So even if he meets powerhouses, Courage won't *ever* give up! It'd… it'd have to be *extremely* dire for him to… *retreat*…"

"I don't think that'll ever be an issue," Ulanahar said. "Courage has us. He doesn't have the universe strictly on his shoulders. Yes, he's a great deal stronger than all of us. When things become excessive, yes, I'm sure he can handle it. But he has us to relieve him of that pressure."

"But he'd just say we're in his way," Kimiko stated. "I'm with you, Lana. But disobeying someone like Courage won't end well for those on the receiving end. Bulls are stubborn for a reason."

"Doesn't matter," Ulanahar countered. "If we're *truly* his friends, then we'll do what we must to ensure his safety. Not just our own."

Melharina and co. agreed with Ulanahar.

Nevertheless, Flowerensia floated toward Courage.

She held the Velmelkia Championship belt.

She hovered before Courage.

Tears of elation fell from her eyes.

She handed him the belt.

He gently took it from her.

He placed the belt over his shoulder.

Then, Flowerensia spoke.

"Congratulations! You're Velmelkia's new champion!"

Everyone screamed their approval.

"Is there something you'd like to say to everyone, Champion Courage?" Flowerensia asked.

"Yes."

He extended his hand toward the microphone.

She handed it to him.

"There's one thing I need to ask… is there a doctor in the house? Like, for real."

Courage pointed to his black eyes and injured lips.

Everyone laughed.

"Nah, I'll be alright. But it's a shame I look like a damn raccoon."

Everyone laughed hysterically.

"Hey, but listen. This man gave me a hell of a fight. Let's give Sadon Leodycreus Frendumar some love!"

Everyone cheered.

Then, Courage extended his hand toward the fallen Sadon.

"Speaking of which…"

He utilized Kekritas to mend Sadon's injuries.

He also used Harminagias to awaken him.

Sadon groaned.

He slowly awoke.

He gradually sat up.

He looked around.

He realized he was returned to Velmelkia Colosseum.

Then, he noticed Courage, who offered him his hand.

Sadon took it.

Then, he pulled himself up.

"Only thing I have to say is…" Courage said.

Courage shook Sadon's hand.

"…Thank you."

Everyone applauded.

"Oh, and thank you."

Courage pointed to his black eyes and injured lips once more.

Everyone, including Sadon, laughed.

"Out of any opponent I've fought so far, you're the only one who was able to give me a fantastic fight. And without the use of our powers made it much more thrilling. And for that, I thank you once more."

Everyone clapped.

Courage offered the microphone to Sadon.

He kindly took it.

"Truth be told, I'm more grateful than you'll ever imagine. I finally found someone worthy of trading fists with. Someone who possesses a caliber that can push me to become greater. A caliber that can push me to my limit.

"You live up to your reputation well, Champion Courage. The Velmelkia Championship lies in your hands now."

Everyone cheered.

Sadon spoke once more.

"Not only have you earned the Velmelkia Championship..."

He placed his hand upon Courage's shoulder.

"You've also earned my respect. Thank you."

Everyone praised Courage and Sadon by chanting their names.

Sadon handed the microphone to Flowerensia.

She gently took it.

"That's right, everyone! Chant for both of these incredible fighters! Trust me, we'll all remember this match for years to come! This one's going in the history books, for sure!"

Then, Courage felt a remarkable power nearby.

He looked above.

Standing atop of the colosseum was Transidyus and Leiku.

They smiled upon Courage.

Courage reciprocated the gesture.

Just the two men I need to see. You two are next.

Leiku chuckled.

If that is what you wish, meet us at Aereshia Meadow at sunset.

Transidyus agreed.

After all, I did promise you a match. I intend to keep it. See you then.

Transidyus and Leiku teleported from Velmelkia Colosseum.

After the festivities, Courage and co. arrived at Aereshia Meadow at sunset.

Transidyus and Leiku had their back to them.

They were watching the sunset.

"He's definitely the one, Leiku. No question. He has what it takes to be a Grandmaster Star. Or in his case, a *Sacred* Grandmaster Star. Other stars have tried to become a Grandmaster. But they failed. They weren't ready."

"Lofty Courage is not ready, either. He requires time. He is one of the most talented of the stars, without question. He even defeated Master Sadon. However, before we consider testing him further, we must see how he fairs against us.

"There are those who cannot lay a finger on him. However, his winning streak stops here, as in he will have extreme difficulty against us. Even without the use of our powers. He will likely use this as a learning experience."

"You sound cynical, Leiku. I understand you're cautious. But his gifts speak for themselves. The man is beyond all comprehension."

"I am not cynical. Far from it. I am merely stating the way things are, as well as the outcome of this bout. Even if he can't hit us, he may have a surprise for us one day. Until that day dawns, we will see how he fairs."

"Is that right?" Courage intervened.

"Ah!" Leiku said. "You've finally arrived."

Transidyus and Leiku turned toward Courage and co.

"Like everyone else, it sounds like even you and Transidyus have a massive bet on me."

"Indeed," Leiku confirmed. "You are the Sacred Star of the Cosmos. Everyone places a high wager on you. Take it as a compliment from those who have faith in you. That includes us."

"Yeah, so I've gathered," Courage stated.

"We can commence whenever you're ready, Courage," Transidyus said. "I'll go first, Leiku."

"Of course," Leiku agreed.

Courage marched toward a cherry blossom tree.

He placed the Velmelkia Championship on the ground against the base of the tree.

Then, Courage and Transidyus marched toward each other.

They stopped several feet from one another in the center of Aereshia Meadow.

Flowerensia grasped the Velmelkia Championship.

She placed it on her shoulder.

Helipak sniffed the championship.

It possessed Courage's irresistible scent.

Helipak moaned.

Narosasei aront! (Delectable honey!) Such exquisiteness! I can just imagine him on top of me, thrusting every inch of himself into me over and over again until he's satisfied. Whatever makes him happy, then I'm happy.

Flowerensia laughed.

Kimiko sneered.

"Really, man? You're that desperate for Courage? How low can you go…?"

"As low as Sweet Courage'll ever want me to go, my dear…"

Kimiko placed her hand against her face.

She sighed.

"Why the hell did I even ask…?"

Transidyus closed his eyes.

Then, he pulled his headband over his eyes.

Flowerensia and co. gasped.

"What the hell are you doing, Transidyus?" Courage questioned. "Why're you blindfolding yourself?"

"I don't need to see my adversaries. Attack me whenever you're ready."

"Uh, does anyone know anyone who's ever fought blindfolded?" Kimiko asked.

"Nope," Melharina said.

Everyone else shook their head.

They were uneasy.

Courage immediately closed the distance.

He threw a punch toward Transidyus.

Transidyus caught the assault.

Everyone gasped.

Courage used his other hand to throw a punch toward Transidyus' abdomen.

Transidyus caught that attack as well.

Then, Courage went for a headbutt.

Yet, it was futile.

Courage was instantly immobilized.

He released Courage's fists.

Courage was shocked.

What the hell? I can't move! Damn it!

"Holy shit!" Kimiko said "W-what the hell did Transidyus just do? Courage can't even move!"

"He compressed the natural air around Courage," Gravulkim replied. "Had he used *Sanei*, which is celestial wind, Courage would be in serious trouble. Transidyus is taking it easy. I'm serious. He hasn't moved at all during the course of Courage's attacks."

"That's scary as hell..." Kimiko stated. "I'd hate to imagine if Transidyus and Leiku weren't on our side. *Everyone* would be screwed. Even still, I'm not counting Courage out."

Then, Transidyus telekinetically tossed Courage.

He glided through the air.

He landed on his back.

Courage tried moving his limbs.

The natural air no longer hindered him.

He leaped to his feet.

"You're more than welcome to transform, or ascend your Sacred Staraidus," Transidyus offered.

"...I don't think it would make a difference," Courage replied. "Besides, I'm not desperate to prove anything. I'm just noting how powerful you really are. And so far, I'm very impressed."

"Alright, come forth once more," Transidyus said.

Courage closed the distance between them.

He threw a punch.

Transidyus caught it.

Before Courage could counter, Transidyus lightly pushed his fist with his index finger.

Courage slid backward considerably.

He slowed to a stop.

Then, he teleported.

He emerged behind Transidyus in mid-air.

He performed an aerial kick.

The natural air compressed around Courage.

He was restrained once more.

Goddamn it! Again? How powerful is he, for fuck's sake!

"If you can't outmaneuver me, then you have no hope of defeating me," Transidyus stated. "You have a long road ahead. You'll defeat many adversaries. You'll encounter many aspects. You'll grow stronger.

"I look forward to our next encounter, Courage. Until then, always transcend."

Transidyus dispelled the natural air around Courage.

He landed on his feet.

Damn. Guess I have my work cut out dealing with these two, after all.

Transidyus lifted his headband from over his eyes.

"Leiku, don't overdo it."

Velcrimia blushed.

Transidyus is really cool. My gracious… I need to calm myself…

"Do not mind me, Transidyus," Leiku groused. "You are very formal about everything."

Leiku approached Courage.

He stopped several feet before him.

"After being unable to strike Transidyus, are you certain you wish to face me?"

"You should already know the answer to that. Come on, now."

"Very well. However, unlike Transidyus, I will not give you the benefit of attacking me, for I will be the one delivering the assaults."

"Right. Try your luck."

"Courage, don't underestimate the Grandmaster Stars!" Gravulkim warned. "Transidyus already proved he surpasses you. Leiku isn't any different. Take heed to the lessons being taught. Remain modest."

"Alright, alright, fine," Courage conceded.

Leiku telekinetically plucked a single blade of grass from the ground.

He *Celestialized* it.

Then, he launched it toward Courage.

Celestialization is the process of making any object have the capacity to harm star beings or other extraterrestrial lifeforms.

Leiku and Transidyus were the only ones who could track the incomprehensible speed of the Celestial Grass Blade.

The Celestial Grass Blade struck the trunk of a cherry blossom tree.

"You missed," Courage said.

"You should touch your right cheek, Courage," Kimiko stated. "I think he missed you intentionally. Yet, it still managed to connect with you."

Courage touched his cheek.

Kimiko was right.

The Celestial Grass Blade struck him as it passed.

Sacred Livalaquia leaked from the injury.

If he was serious, he could've killed me with a blade of grass. That would've been beyond embarrassing. Even still, Gravulkim was right. These Grandmasters are in another league.

Instantly, Leiku closed the distance between them.

He rapidly struck numerous Staraidus *Hy'diagus* in Courage's chest through his Sacroncai Armor.

He used his index and middle fingers of both hands to accomplish this.

Staraidus Hy'diagus' are sensitive zones on the body of star beings.

They could assist, or hinder, the star being.

Courage yelled.

Then, Leiku pushed him.

Courage glided through the air.

He landed on his back.

He was quite far from everyone.

Transidyus frowned.

"I told you don't overdo it."

"If I had overdid it, he would be dead."

"It doesn't matter. Did you really have to go on the offensive? You know we're much stronger than him. You could've gotten your point across without laying a finger on him. Damn it."

"Oh, stop neighing, Transidyus. If I overdid it, fine. My apologies."

Courage slowly approached the group.

He had his arm across his chest.

"Do you still wish to continue, Lofty Courage?" Leiku asked.

Courage chuckled.

"Either until I pass out... or die."

Everyone gasped.

"Leiku, stop!" Transidyus protested. "There's no need to proceed. Courage. My friend. You did well."

"Did well? Are you kidding me? I didn't do shit. Both of you kicked my ass without any effort. That's humiliating."

"Courage..." Kimiko said. "No disrespect, but now you know how we felt when you owned our asses."

"Speak for yourself, Kimiko," Melharina stated. "Take it as a learning experience. Even if you never surpass Courage, take it as a means to grow stronger. One step at a time. Strive to become a Master Star someday. Sadon, Ulanahar, Asai, and Velcrimia are way ahead of you.

"The same goes for you, gentlemen."

"Right," Gravulkim agreed.

"Got it," Janeiholm concurred.

Helipak placed his hands on his hips.

He closed his eyes.

Then, he stroked his hand through his hair.

He moaned.

Then, he slowly licked his lips.

He emitted a slurping sound as he proceeded.

Finally, he gazed at Melharina seductively.

"You can count on me!"

"You're a fucking perv, dude," Janeiholm said. "Goddamn…"

"Yeah," Gravulkim stated. "It took you that long to agree to become stronger? Gracious…"

"Oh, don't be jealous, you studs," Helipak said. "I'm only a "perv" for my beloved Courage. *Mmm-hmm!*"

"There's always next time, Courage," Transidyus stated. "For now, we part ways."

"You are not the Transcendent One for no reason, Lofty Courage," Leiku said. "Remember that."

Damn it. I lost. Kimiko's right. The sting of defeat is annoying. But anyone who's stronger than me will eventually see what I can do.

"This isn't over, Transidyus and Leiku. I don't give a damn if I have to face both of you a thousand times, I don't accept losses."

"Learn from those losses," Transidyus stated. "Continue to improve. And perhaps one day, you'll outshine us."

"Indeed," Leiku agreed.

"Of course…" Courage said.

Courage teleported elsewhere.

"Take care, all of you," Transidyus stated.

"Likewise," Flowerensia and co. said.

Transidyus and Leiku vanished.

Then, Flowerensia realized Courage forgot his championship.

Helipak noted her expression.

We should see if he's alright, Flowerensia. His ego is bruised.

Yeah… but where could he have gone?

He probably returned to Ulenar Island.

Right!

"Everyone," Flowerensia stated. "I think Courage probably returned to his island. I want to return his championship. If he's there, please stay silent. He's most likely reflecting on this occurrence."

Everyone agreed.

Then, Flowerensia and co. teleported to Ulenar Island.

Flowerensia and co. searched the Temple of Transcending for Courage.

He was nowhere to be seen.

Flowerensia placed the Velmelkia Championship upon an altar.

Then, they felt his Sacred Staraidus on the other side of Ulenar Island.

They teleported to where they sensed him.

When they arrived, they saw Courage floating inches above Crozeni Ocean.

Four pillars of water was around him.

The water columns spun moderately from their stationary position.

Courage was gazing at the sunset.

He was in deep contemplation.

Flowerensia and co. remained silent.

They admired the splendiferous scene before Flowerensia signaled that they should depart and leave Courage to his privacy.

You'll be alright, dear Courage. That I promise. The moment you entered my kingdom, I knew you were the one. Like Gravulkim said, "Without struggle, there's no learning experience." Try not to take it too hard, love.

"Look deep within for your true power resonates in the unknown."

 **Chapter 9**

Oblivionu'crei, The Cosmos Destroyer

Two weeks later.

Courage was in the Temple of Transcending.

He was meditating within the Vevolomurus.

Courage was disappointed in his performance against Transidyus and Leiku.

Yet, he expected defeat.

But for him not being able to strike them, let alone last a fair amount of time against them, was truly upsetting.

Regardless, he overcame his frustration.

And although he preferred his privacy, he visited Flowerensia and co. occasionally.

Sometimes, he spent quality time with Asai.

Some occasions were very passionate.

Other times were very spiritual.

It was an amalgamation of everything awe-inspiring.

The passion Courage brought to her every time only multiplied.

The ecstasy he made her feel was indescribable.

Courage was very enigmatic.

Asai loved his mystery and intensity.

Sometimes, they merely sat in silence with their backs against each other.

No words needed to be exchanged.

Asai was very grateful Courage was spending time with her.

She knew he preferred to be by his lonesome.

Yet, whenever they engaged, it was never inconvenient.

It was sublime.

Suddenly, he felt a foreboding presence.

It pervaded the entire vicinity.

Courage opened his eyes.

A reflection of red pierced through the stain glass windows.

It also managed to shine through the walls.

The hell is going on? Why has the atmosphere changed all of a sudden? Wait... could it be... him...? If so, it's about time he showed up.

Then, there were frantic knocks on the temple doors.

"Courage!" Flowerensia called. "Please! This is dire!"

Courage rushed toward the temple doors.

He swung them open.

"What's the matter, Flowerensia? What seems to be –?"

Courage looked about his surroundings.

It reflected Zeinhailurein when the one Serenity called a devil emerged.

Killoswi'is flickered about the entire area.

However, the ominous scenery pervaded the entirety of planet Venusia.

Crozeni Ocean was a sea of Killosogma.

Red and black clouds shifted across the sky.

There were also three *Zeigramonalaus* in the menacing sky.

Zeigramonalaus were celestial suns.

The difference between the regular sun and the Zeigramonalau was that a Zeigramonalau was far more dangerous.

Its heat was extraordinary.

And, should it explode, it could engulf multiple universes.

Flowerensia and co. were distraught.

They remembered the malignant scene from Zeinhailurein as well.

But they did not know who, or what, was behind it.

Only Courage and Serenity knew.

However, Courage wanted to enlighten them.

"Remember when I told you all that an Altreigromian wanted to face me? Well, I think he's back. You know who I'm referring to. Right, Serenity?"

"Indeed. Oblivionu'crei was his name. You may be right, Courage. The sinister atmosphere we witness now is much like the one I remember when that devil first showed up."

"Well, what the hell does it want?" Kimiko questioned.

"He wants to right the wrongs of the universe," Courage replied. "Basically, he wants to ruin all universes and create new ones. With him as the sole ruler."

"Wow..." Kimiko said. "Psycho much?"

"I don't know all the details, Kimiko," Courage stated. "However, I admire the ferocity he has. I know he'll be one of my greatest challenges yet.

"Regardless of his perspective of how the universe should be governed, I want to see if he has the strength to support his campaign by defeating me."

"Damn..." Janeiholm said. "Again, Courage...? Man, you got me worried about you, for real. How much can you fight? Let us help you, for fuck's sake..."

"Janeiholm. I appreciate your concern. I really do. But I'm a solo fighter. He and I agreed to fight one-on-one. Winner takes all. Besides, I don't want any of you harmed."

"See?" Kimiko stated. "I told you all Courage wouldn't let us help."

"I ever live to test my capacity," Courage said. "I refuse to believe there isn't anything I can't accomplish. And defeating this Altreigromian is one of them."

"Sweet Courage..." Helipak stated. "If you're dead set on this, be careful. The universe needs you more than we do. As much as I love you, I know... a man's gotta do what a man's gotta do..."

"Thank you... Helipak..." Courage replied. "You're the kindest of the lot."

"Wait, I've been meaning to ask," Kimiko said. "What the hell is an Altreigromian? I've *never* heard of such a species."

"Oblivionu'crei said that he's an amalgamation of countless matter," Courage replied. "Which stands to reason he may be as rare as me. If not more. He also said he's the only one of his species."

"Are there any legends of this type of being?" Gravulkim asked.

"I don't think so," Serenity replied. "This is the first time I've ever met something so... evil. Oblivionu'crei makes Deathelena seem benign by comparison."

"Courage..." Melharina said "Like Helipak said, be careful. This... Altreigromian sounds like a piece of work, for real. Be on your A game. And I know you're against it, but if you *ever* need back up, let us know! Don't let your pride be the death of you! We got you!"

"No wonder you and Flowerensia outshine most of the deities," Courage said. "Your genuine nature is most appreciated."

"Real recognize real," Melharina stated.

Then, a gargantuan shadow figure emerged among the Zeigramonalaus.

It stood in the sea of Killosogma.

"W-what the hell is that thing?" Kimiko queried.

"Your worst nightmare, you wretched star being," the character said.

"That metallic, demonic voice..." Courage stated. "Yeah, you're Oblivionu'crei. I haven't forgotten the sound of that grating voice."

Oblivionu'crei chuckled.

"Your memory serves you well, Tauran'creima."

"What the hell's your problem, man?" Kimiko questioned. "What makes you think you have the right to recreate something you never manufactured?"

"Rinaigora... As Tauran'creima told you, I believe there are countless flaws with the way the universe is programmed. Humans are the lowest of any species. Deities seek worship. And star beings despise one another for being different. Animals are no different than you, either.

"It is kill or be killed. Or who is more relevant than who. I seek to change all of that."

"Man, how mental can you be?" Kimiko questioned. "Yes. There are flaws everywhere. Nothing is perfect. I know you're smart enough to know that. Each universe and everything within them are a certain way for a reason. Who are you to change that?"

"Well said, Kimiko," Courage said. "Oblivionu'crei, what she means is that it's alright to have a difference of opinion. But when you take the route of an extremist, that's when your ideals come into question."

"And as far as deities seeking worship, that's where you're wrong," Melharina stated. "I can't speak for other deities, but Flowerensia and I don't need validation. We merely want to give those created in our image a chance at happiness."

"And animals need to survive in the wilderness," Gravulkim said. "Yes, it's quite sad that they must kill one another to sustain themselves. However, that's how the ecosystem operates.

"If Flowerensia and Melharina programmed humans and animals to not require sustenance like us, then they would have. Yet, there's a reason why they didn't."

"And though there is a wedge between Melhounas and Azagnorpors, the same can be said about any species," Ulanahar stated. "There is good and bad in everything. There are good and bad humans. There are good and bad deities. And there are good and bad star beings.

"That's just the way things are. Those who are bad can always change for the better. But it's their choice. Just like you have a choice to reevaluate your perspective of the universe. Trillions of lives are at stake because of you."

Oblivionu'crei respected each of their perspectives.

However, his vision of universal control was ingrained in his conscious.

"Rinaigora. Light Goddess. Doncil'doras. Eidomularus. And Tauran'creima. All of you speak true. However, I will not steer from that which I have set. The universe requires a grand ruler. And that ruler... is me."

"Damn it!" Kimiko shouted. "For fuck's sake! We just told you why that's not going to work! Yet you're still set on this psychotic perception! What the hell's the matter with you? Maybe if you had a decent role model in your life, you'd think different!"

"Rinaigora. There may be some truth to what you say. Yet, I know what is best for these flawed universes. You do not."

"Yes the hell I do! Life's been this way since the beginning! Who the fuck are you to believe you're entitled to change that? You're thinking about committing multi-universal genocide all for your sick assessment, you fucking bastard!"

"So you would prefer to live in a flawed universe than a perfected one, Rinaigora?"

"Damn straight! I don't need perfection! I am who I am! We are who we are! And ain't jackshit's gonna change that! And if you think

I'd be happy living in a perfected universe with you as its ruler, you're gravely mistaken! I don't need a ruler, because I rule my own fucking life!"

"Kimiko, calm down," Courage said. "I'll handle this."

"Damn it, Courage!" Kimiko protested. "How the hell can you be calm knowing what this bastard's capable of? He's pissing me off! Either you get him or I'll get him for you!"

"*Calm* down," Courage reiterated. "I know you're upset. But lashing out won't help anything."

"Fine… I'm sorry…"

"You don't have to apologize for being passionate. I said I understood."

"You better not fail. Or I'll have you and that bastard's head."

"Careful. I might come back to haunt you."

Kimiko chuckled.

"If you still wish to challenge me, Tauran'creima, then come," Oblivionu'crei said. "As I said before, these universes lie upon your shoulders."

"You're about to get your ass kicked, you fucker!" Kimiko said. "Maybe after that, you'll realize what an ass you were for believing in your crazy concept!"

"Still your tongue, Rinaigora. You have said quite enough. One more word and I will obliterate you and your constellation."

"Never gonna happen!"

Kimiko rushed toward Oblivionu'crei.

Then, Courage grasped her shoulder.

She looked back toward him.

He shook his head.

She relented.

"Fine... Alright, Courage..."

Courage flew skyward.

Then, he and Oblivionu'crei teleported elsewhere.

However, when Oblivionu'crei and Courage emerged at their location, Flowerensia and co. could see their image in the foreboding sky.

Courage appeared on Oblivion Island above a Zeigramonalau in outer space.

Oblivionu'crei stood in the Killosogma of the Zeigramonalau.

His arms were folded.

His profile was toward Courage.

He patiently waited for Courage to approach the island's edge.

Courage ambled toward a flight of stairs.

He walked up the stairs.

When he reached the top, he stopped at the edge of the island.

Oblivionu'crei was staring in the distance.

"Interesting, is it not? How all of this came into existence. The Great *Exclo'leishia*... The creation of the universe..."

"So we all came from a source? What is this Exclo'leishia?"

"You are an Original Star. The First People. You should know this."

"True. Yet, there are things that are an enigma to us. Like how we didn't know what an Altreigromian was."

"The Great Exclo'leishia was how these universes and everything within them were created."

"I'm having a difficult time believing that."

"Foolish. Why do you think star beings are regarded as the most powerful? Each constellation is regarded with high esteem among countless beings. Especially yours. The universe is the only powerful force. And those created by it consequently reflect that greatness.

"However, you are an enigma."

"Likewise."

"Indeed. Before we commence, I should inform you that all of the cosmos can see us. They can look skyward and witness us. Even those who sleep will see this in their dream."

Oblivionu'crei chuckled.

"The only drawback for those who sleep is that they will not awaken until our bout concludes."

"W-what the hell? You mean you put some type of curse over everything?"

"If that is what you want to call it. It is not of my will. However, I will call it… *Astrocomasala.*"

"How the hell is it not of your will when you just named it?"

"Everything requires an identity. I have no need to lie to you, Tauran'creima. It is up to you to dispel the Astrocomasala by defeating me. Only then will those who sleep awaken. However, if you fail to defeat me, those affected by the Astrocomasala will die.

"And all of existence will be under my government."

"You sick bastard…"

289

"Any place I arrive, that is a sign. A symbol. A site for new beginnings. My arrival is the end of the beginning. And the beginning of the end. Which simply means all of what has been created... will be astronomically improved under my rule. True perfection.

"Overall, I am the alpha and the omega."

"I admire your charisma, but I think you're taking this to excessive lengths."

"It must be done, Tauran'creima. Our perspectives differ. As a result, it has come to this."

"Yes. We differ because I allow freedom of choice. You want absolute ownership. You want ownership over what you haven't established. You want ownership over what cannot be tamed. The universe knows no bounds. It's perpetual.

"You're not allowing freedom. You're encroaching upon every living creatures' right to live as they please. That... I cannot accept."

Oblivionu'crei looked upon Courage from his peripheral.

"So it shall be."

"Two questions: how did you get so big? And how can you stand in Killosogma without dying?"

"Size alteration. I can grow as big as the universe. Or I can shrink to the size of an atom. And Killosogma does not affect me like it does other beings."

"Interesting."

Oblivionu'crei raised his left hand.

"We have said enough. Are there any other inquiries before you and all of existence are ended?"

"Well damn. Since you put it that way. No, I don't."

"Then allow me to display to you why I am known as the Cosmos Destroyer."

Oblivionu'crei extended his index finger.

He pointed toward the horizon.

Then, red and black celestial electricity – the *Electraheil* – shrouded his finger.

Next, a large energy beam – the *Hellihil'ailian* – was launched toward his target.

An incredible explosion erupted in the distance.

A red and black sphere of Electraheil was of note.

Courage was very appalled.

What the hell did he just do? This is insanity!

When the sphere of Electraheil ebbed, a *Zeigramon'stralia* emerged.

A Zeigramon'stralia was a supermassive black hole.

The event horizon was red and yellow.

It rapidly spun counterclockwise.

Rinaigora and the other Melhouna Constellations went to investigate the Zeigramon'stralia.

Rinaigora proceeded flapping her wings toward the Zeigramon'stralia in an attempt to close it.

"Universe E1-*Angeilatus* has been eradicated," Oblivionu'crei confirmed. "In that universe, many creatures lived. Among them were the powerful *Angelasi*. Think of them like the deities of Rhol'heima, but of a lesser caliber."

Courage's shock instantly changed to immense hostility.

He felt the Selsengra rapidly coursing throughout his body.

He unleashed the Selsengra, thus becoming Selsengra Courage.

His eyes changed to solid fiery red.

Selsengra Courage released Tauran'creima's Bellow.

He stomped the ground once.

The foundation shook.

Then, he took a fighting stance.

"Why so upset, Tauran'creima? You did not know those beings. For all you know, they could have despised the likes of star beings."

"It matters not! You killed an *entire* solar system of beings who did nothing to you!"

Selsengra Courage stomped the ground once more.

The foundation quaked again.

He expelled steam from his nostrils.

"Hypocritical..." Oblivionu'crei countered. "I have been observing you since our meeting. And if you had not possessed any restraint... it is likely *you* would have exterminated the Hychineirian and Relmi'shirian Nations. Mass genocide.

"Though our perspectives differ, our motives correspond. Eternal peace."

"I refuse to believe any of that! I'm nothing like you!"

"You are in denial. I will reiterate. Though our perspectives differ, our motives correspond. Eternal peace. What you perceive as *evil* might not be as it seem. And what you perceive as *good* might not be as it seem. Only those who are experiencing their ordeal truly know the answer.

"All others are merely spectators."

Selsengra Courage admitted that Oblivionu'crei's logic was flawless.

There were different ideals, different angles to view every situation.

Yet, Selsengra Courage knew he was fighting for the right reasons.

"As stated, Universe E1-Angeilatus is obliterated," Oblivionu'crei repeated. "This universe, which is Universe A11-*Mayethikaya*, is next, should your defeat occur. Try not to fail your race… the *Mayethikayians*. Or better known as star beings."

Selsengra Courage slowly flew toward Oblivionu'crei.

Oblivionu'crei raised his fist.

He swung it toward Selsengra Courage.

Selsengra Courage sprung upward.

The assault missed.

Selsengra Courage landed on Oblivionu'crei's forearm.

Oblivionu'crei raised his other hand.

He swung his hand toward Selsengra Courage in an attempt to crush him.

Selsengra Courage vanished.

Oblivionu'crei struck his own forearm.

Selsengra Courage emerged before him.

He struck one of Oblivionu'crei's eyes through his Helligaiyon Helmet.

Oblivionu'crei yelled.

Selsengra Courage teleported.

Oblivionu'crei brought his hand to the eye hole of his helmet in an attempt to quell the pain.

When the anguish declined, he used his other hand to swiftly throw another punch toward Selsengra Courage.

He avoided the attack.

He quickly appeared before the Kreseirumana Crystal on the Helligaiyon Helmet.

He struck it.

Unfortunately, it did not shatter.

Oblivionu'crei growled.

Selsengra Courage prepared the Selsengra Sacroncai Punch.

He struck the Kreseirumana Crystal once more.

This time, it shattered.

Oblivionu'crei released Kreseirumana's Howl in agony.

Selsengra Courage was repelled backward.

Then, he landed safely on Oblivion Island.

The Kreseirumana Crystal commenced gradually regenerating.

"Just as I expected," Oblivionu'crei said. "You are living up to the legend, as well as my expectations. However, this is far from over."

Three purple *Seqi'lia* portals emerged.

Two Seqi'lias were on either side of Oblivionu'crei.

And the last one was at the other end of the island.

Then, a fierce amethyst eye – the Eye of Kreseirumana – appeared in the recuperating Kreseirumana Crystal.

Oblivionu'crei held his hands forward.

The Eye of Kreseirumana commenced glowing.

Oblivionu'crei attempted to backhand Selsengra Courage.

He teleported.

Yet, that was what he was expecting.

The Eye of Kreseirumana instantly tracked Selsengra Courage.

Oblivionu'crei swiftly thrust his fist into one of the Seqi'lias on either side of him.

Another Seqi'lia emerged immediately where Selsengra Courage appeared.

Oblivionu'crei's fist struck Selsengra Courage.

Selsengra Courage yelled.

Selsengra Courage glided rapidly across outer space from the devastating impact.

Rinaigora was making progress in closing the Zeigramon'stralia.

She knew she could accomplish this, which was why she denied the other Melhouna Constellations' assistance.

The Melhouna Constellations observed.

Likewise with the Azagnorpor Constellations.

The Azagnorpor Constellations – with the exception of Eidomularus – scoffed at Rinaigora's progress.

Tauran'creima sat nearby.

If Rinaigora failed, he would vanquish the Zeigramon'stralia.

Selsengra Courage returned to Oblivion Island.

Oblivionu'crei tried to grab him.

Selsengra Courage teleported.

Oblivionu'crei chuckled.

The Eye of Kreseirumana tracked Selsengra Courage once more.

Oblivionu'crei thrust his fist into one of the Seqi'lias.

A Seqi'lia appeared where Selsengra Courage emerged.

Oblivionu'crei's fist struck Selsengra Courage.

Selsengra Courage shouted.

"You cannot hope to strike me," Oblivionu'crei stated. "I can track your whereabouts instantly. Teleportation will do you no good."

Selsengra Courage confronted Oblivionu'crei once more.

Selsengra Courage raised his hand.

Then, a Selondura Sphere emerged inches above his palm.

He threw the Selondura Sphere at Oblivionu'crei.

Oblivionu'crei struck the Selondura Sphere away.

With the same hand, Selsengra Courage launched a large flaming beam of energy – the *Selondu'heiyada* – toward the Eye of Kreseirumana.

Oblivionu'crei shielded the Eye of Kreseirumana with his forearm.

However, the intensity of the Selondu'heiyada penetrated Oblivionu'crei's forearm guard.

The Selondu'heiyada injured Oblivionu'crei's forearm.

Then, the Selondu'heiyada emerged on the other side of his forearm.

Oblivionu'crei released Kreseirumana's Howl in anguish.

The Selondu'heiyada struck the Eye of Kreseirumana and the recuperating Kreseirumana Crystal.

The Eye of Kreseirumana and the Kreseirumana Crystal disintegrated.

Moreover, the Selondu'heiyada pierced the Helligaiyon Helmet.

It penetrated his forehead.

Oblivionu'crei yelled.

The Selondu'heiyada drifted into the depths of space.

During Oblivionu'crei's throes of anguish, he launched himself toward Selsengra Courage.

He swiftly grabbed him with one hand.

He squeezed Selsengra Courage.

He yelled.

Then, he shrouded his hand with yellow and black celestial electricity – the *Electragaul*.

Selsengra Courage released Tauran'creima's Bellow in agony.

The Electragaul proceeded withdrawing Tauran'creima Essence from him.

"Is that it?" Selsengra Courage said. "Give me more voltage, you ingrate! Stop being stingy!"

"This is your end, Tauran'creima. You have fought well."

Oblivionu'crei began submerging beneath the Zeigramonalau.

However, when Oblivionu'crei was halfway into the Zeigramonalau, he yelled in pain.

Selsengra Courage converted the Electragaul into Selsengra Electragaul, which was red, yellow, and black.

The Selsengra Electragaul shrouded Oblivionu'crei's arm.

He released Selsengra Courage.

Selsengra Courage flew toward Oblivion Island.

He landed on the edge.

During his anguish, Oblivionu'crei slowly rose from the Zeigramonalau.

He threw a punch toward Selsengra Courage.

Selsengra Courage summoned a Gwi'denahala before him.

Oblivionu'crei's fist entered the Gwi'denahala.

Another Gwi'denahala emerged before Oblivionu'crei.

Consequently, his own fist struck his face.

Oblivionu'crei glided backward.

Then, he slowed to a stop.

He reverted to his normal height.

He teleported.

He appeared before Selsengra Courage.

He landed on the edge next to Selsengra Courage.

"Sacred Star… the interesting one of the lot."

Oblivionu'crei healed all of his injuries by using the *Regalishi'on* spell.

The Regalishi'on also reconstructed his forearm guard, his Helligaiyon Helmet, and the Kreseirumana Crystal.

"Let us take this battle elsewhere. Let us see how versatile you truly are."

Oblivionu'crei teleported with Selsengra Courage elsewhere.

Oblivionu'crei and Selsengra Courage appeared at Dismal Falls.

They were standing upon *Deadenai'creya* River.

A waterfall was a few feet from them.

Moreover, the scenery was surprisingly serene.

"You impress me, Tauran'creima. I only hope you can keep up your momentum."

"Don't worry about me, you bastard. Be concerned with keeping your life intact."

Oblivionu'crei chuckled.

"Very well. Let the thrilling fight continue."

They walked toward each other.

Then, they instantly closed the distance.

Their fist collided.

Next, Selsengra Courage crouched.

He rapidly struck Oblivionu'crei's abdomen.

Each assault was stronger than the last.

Oblivionu'crei yelled.

During Selsengra Courage's onslaught, Oblivionu'crei prepared his attack.

Then, he struck the side of Selsengra Courage's face with the spikes on his forearm guard.

Selsengra Courage yelled.

The assault sent Selsengra Courage gliding away.

Yet, Selsengra Courage pivoted in mid-air.

He landed on his feet on the water.

He slowed to a stop.

He touched the side of his face.

Sacred Livalaquia leaked from the wounds.

Oblivionu'crei closed the distance.

He threw a right hook.

Selsengra Courage crouched.

He grabbed his upper arm.

Then, he threw Oblivionu'crei.

However, he quickly recovered while in mid-flight.

He landed on the water.

Oblivionu'crei prepared another strike.

Yet, Selsengra Courage was already before him in mid-air.

He performed an aerial kick.

It connected.

Oblivionu'crei staggered backward.

Then, Selsengra Courage appeared above him.

He struck the top of his head with both of his feet.

As a result, Oblivionu'crei plummeted underwater.

Selsengra Courage followed.

Oblivionu'crei recuperated.

Then, they proceeded fighting underwater.

Oblivionu'crei struck Selsengra Courage's abdomen with his elbow.

The spike penetrated the Sacroncai Armor.

However, Selsengra Courage recovered.

Selsengra Courage grabbed his arm.

Then, he kicked him in his abdomen several times.

As Selsengra Courage tried to kick him once more, Oblivionu'crei struck him away with his other fist.

The spikes on Oblivionu'crei's knuckles left lacerations on Selsengra Courage's cheek.

The Kreseirumana Aura, which was red and purple, briefly framed Oblivionu'crei before fading from existence.

Consequently, his power – the *Ultrimi'i* – rose slightly.

It was possible for some entities to possess more than one aura.

Oblivionu'crei swiftly closed the distance.

Oblivionu'crei delivered an uppercut to Selsengra Courage's chin.

Selsengra Courage rapidly glided upward.

He broke the surface of the water.

He glided into the air.

Then, Oblivionu'crei appeared above him.

He grabbed Selsengra Courage by his neck with one hand.

He electrocuted Selsengra Courage with Electragaul.

He screamed.

Then, Oblivionu'crei punched him.

Selsengra Courage fell toward the water.

Suddenly, the Glyph of Tauran'creima appeared below Selsengra Courage.

It was large and glowing red.

Selsengra Courage recuperated in mid-air.

He landed on the Glyph of Tauran'creima.

Oblivionu'crei was perplexed.

What the hell are you up to, Tauran'creima…?

He floated down toward the water.

He stood upon it.

Suddenly, the water secured itself around Oblivionu'crei's shins.

Oblivionu'crei was shocked.

He attempted to free himself.

But it was futile.

Selsengra Courage extended his hands toward the water.

He telekinetically brought the water to him.

The water secured itself around his hands.

The water linked Selsengra Courage and Oblivionu'crei.

Selsengra Courage released Selsengra Electragaul toward him.

Noting this, Oblivionu'crei tried to expedite his escape.

Yet, the water remained secured.

The Selsengra Electragaul reached him.

He was electrocuted.

Oblivionu'crei released Kreseirumana's Howl in incredible agony.

Selsengra Courage kept electrocuting him for some time.

Oblivionu'crei was gravely wounded.

Selsengra Courage dispelled the Selsengra Electragaul.

Then, he launched the Selondu'heiyada toward him.

When the Selondu'heiyada reached him, he was engulfed in its splendid flames.

Oblivionu'crei yelled.

Then, he fell to his knees.

His head was bowed.

The Selondu'heiyada gradually ebbed.

Suddenly, Oblivionu'crei laughed.

"I am glad I finally met you, Tauran'creima! The more you fight, the fascinating you become! You are indeed the toughest of them all! Come! Let us journey elsewhere!"

Oblivionu'crei teleported with Selsengra Courage to another location.

Oblivionu'crei and Selsengra Courage appeared in Kreseirumana's Chamber.

Kreseirumana's Chamber was a large, very dark room.

E'valandura permeated the vicinity.

E'valandura was celestial darkness.

The only illumination was from the Killoseigas burning in two large elaborate lamps.

A massive portrait of Oblivionu'crei with Kreseirumana behind him adorned the wall.

Normally, dark places would not be an issue for star beings.

However, anything of celestial nature proved bothersome, darkness included.

The only star beings the E'valandura did not affect were Azagnorpors.

As a result, Selsengra Courage had to rely on his exceptional senses.

Suddenly, Kreseirumana emerged on Selsengra Courage's left.

He was a massive, purple glowing apparition.

His amethyst eyes were bloodthirsty.

He growled.

He slowly paced forward.

Then, he suddenly vanished.

What the hell is Oblivionu'crei and this mutt trying to prove? Get on with it, already!

The Kreseirumana Apparition emerged once more.

This time on Selsengra Courage's right.

He growled.

He slowly paced forward.

Then, he vanished once more.

Selsengra Courage sensed that the Kreseirumana Apparition would attack soon.

He also sensed Oblivionu'crei nearby.

He was observing.

The Kreseirumana Apparition appeared before Selsengra Courage.

The Kreseirumana Apparition slowly paced toward him.

He barked once.

It sounded metallic and demonic.

Then, he lunged toward Selsengra Courage.

He opened his maw.

He prepared for the kill.

Selsengra Courage sidestepped the attack.

He struck the Kreseirumana Apparition.

The Kreseirumana Apparition yelped.

Next, Selsengra Courage unleashed the Selsengra Solar Prominence.

The Selsengra Solar Prominence was a wave of Selondura.

The Selsengra Solar Prominence rapidly expanded from around Selsengra Courage.

The Selsengra Solar Prominence struck the Kreseirumana Apparition.

The Kreseirumana Apparition howled in anguish.

His throes of pain lasted for some time.

Then, he toppled onto his side.

The Selsengra Solar Prominence extended across Kreseirumana's Chamber.

Oblivionu'crei teleported before he was struck.

The Selsengra Solar Prominence drifted up the walls.

Then, the Selondura merged on the ceiling.

Oblivionu'crei appeared before Selsengra Courage.

He released Kreseirumana's War Cry.

He tried to punch Selsengra Courage.

Yet, Selsengra Courage parried.

He kicked Oblivionu'crei toward the Selondura-scorched Kreseirumana Apparition.

Oblivionu'crei stumbled backward.

His back struck the Kreseirumana Apparition.

As a result, the Selondura surrounded him.

Oblivionu'crei released Kreseirumana's Howl in agony.

However, regardless of his pain, he closed the distance between him and Selsengra Courage.

He ruthlessly struck Selsengra Courage.

Selsengra Courage was injured.

Oblivionu'crei struck him once more.

Selsengra Courage glided backward until he struck a wall.

He was embedded within it.

Oblivionu'crei kicked him.

Selsengra Courage fell through the wall.

He landed on his back.

Then, he slowly sat up.

Oblivionu'crei stood near the cavity.

Oblivionu'crei dispelled the Selondura from around him.

Suddenly, the Kreseirumana Aura framed him, thus becoming *Kreseiru* Oblivionu'crei.

He was becoming serious.

"Damn it, Tauran'creima. How dare you make Kreseirumana seem worthless? How the hell is that possible?"

"How dare you make justifications for your vision? Only someone with severe mental issues could rationalize your way of thinking."

"Nonsense, Tauran'creima. You know, as well as I, that things could be better if these ingrates knew better. That is where I step in."

"No. This is where you step out. Kimiko and everyone told you why it isn't your place to change what already exists! What drives this asinine motive of yours?"

"I should be asking you the same thing. I already told you my answer: Perfection. The universe would be greater if better creatures such as myself existed. Not the disgusting wretches that plague it."

"And I already told you mine: Freedom of choice!"

Selsengra Courage quickly rose from the crevice.

He went for an uppercut.

Kreseiru Oblivionu'crei evaded.

Kreseiru Oblivionu'crei kicked Selsengra Courage toward another wall.

He struck the wall.

He placed his hand against the wall to maintain his balance.

Kreseiru Oblivionu'crei slowly approached.

When he neared, he lifted Selsengra Courage by his neck.

Then, he slammed him on the ground.

He lifted Selsengra Courage by his neck once more.

He threw him through the wall.

The rubble piled atop him.

He released Tauran'creima's Bellow.

The stones disintegrated.

Kreseiru Oblivionu'crei telekinetically pulled Selsengra Courage from the hollow.

When Selsengra Courage neared, Kreseiru Oblivionu'crei kneed him in his abdomen.

He choked.

The spikes on his knee penetrated the Sacroncai Armor.

He fell to his knees.

Sacred Livalaquia poured from him.

He placed his hands over the injuries.

Then, he fell on his side.

"Pitiful," Kreseiru Oblivionu'crei condescended. "Surely this is not all you have?"

"Far from it... asswipe. Yet, you hit harder than... anyone I've fought thus far. For that, I'm grateful. But... can you hit me harder...? Don't let a Millennial Star's... striking power surpass yours."

Selsengra Courage chuckled.

"So... freedom of choice is why you fight," Kreseiru Oblivionu'crei said. "Yet, what about those who commit atrocities? Do you have an explanation for that?"

"Without cause... there is no effect. Someone wouldn't just... wake up one day and decide "Hey, I think I'll rob a bank, and kill many people". Just like there's a reason why... you choose your ridiculous path. Perfection is your motive. There is no... such thing.

"The good cannot exist... without the bad. Sadly, this is... the way it is."

"And yet you are foolish enough to accept such conditions?"

"Yes! That is only because in some cases, people can have a genuine change of heart! Carnivorous animals need to kill to survive! Some deities like Melharina and Flowerensia don't need worship! And star beings have thrived for eons!

"Those who *choose* the corrupt path *willingly* don't have my sympathy! And you speak of atrocities, when you murdered an entire solar system! Literally over a trillion beings! Dead! Extinct! All because of you! Argh! You fucking bastard!"

The Glyph of Tauran'creima emerged on the back of his right hand.

It shined red.

Instantly, Selsengra Courage delivered the Selsengra *Tauran* Uppercut to Kreseiru Oblivionu'crei.

Kreseiru Oblivionu'crei rapidly glided upward.

He broke through the ceiling.

The Selondura that remained on the ceiling pursued Kreseiru Oblivionu'crei.

The Selondura followed Kreseiru Oblivionu'crei into outer space.

All of the places Oblivionu'crei took Courage were within his subconscious.

When the Selondura neared him, it shrouded him.

Kreseiru Oblivionu'crei yelled.

The Selsengra Aura framed Selsengra Courage.

He was now Selsengra *Aleitor* Courage.

This was the first stage of the Selsengra transformations.

Every star being had four transformations.

When a star being's Constellation Ascension Glyphs emerge, this was the initial stage.

Any transformations that follow would astronomically increase the star being's Staraidus.

Kreseiru Oblivionu'crei returned.

He was battered.

"Alright, Tauran'creima. You are indeed a crafty bastard."

"Yeah, so are you. You think I did these annoying injuries to myself? Yeah, I truly appreciate your hard work in beating the shit out of me, asshole."

"Bah. One of us will remain standing. Come!"

Kreseiru Oblivionu'crei teleported with Selsengra Aleitor Courage to someplace else.

Kreseiru Oblivionu'crei and Selsengra Aleitor Courage emerged in Bleak Forest.

Bleak Forest had a mild fog, and an eerie atmosphere.

The trunk of the trees posed awkwardly.

Then, Kreseiru Oblivionu'crei released Kreseirumana's Bark five times.

He conjured five small Killoseiga Spheres.

Next, he stomped the ground once.

The foundation shook.

Suddenly, four large holes appeared in the ground.

Each hole was filled with Killosogma.

Moreover, he summoned three large spheres of blue celestial electricity – the *Electria'ala*.

The Electria'ala Spheres moved back and forth along a fixed path.

Kreseiru Oblivionu'crei telekinetically directed a Killoseiga Sphere at Selsengra Aleitor Courage.

When the Killoseiga Sphere neared, Selsengra Aleitor Courage raised his right fist.

He turned the back of his right fist toward the incoming Killoseiga Sphere.

Then, a flat, illuminate head of Tauran'creima emerged.

This was called a *Taurylyph*.

The Killoseiga Sphere was repelled by the Taurylyph.

Then, the Taurylyph faded.

Kreseiru Oblivionu'crei telekinetically returned the Killoseiga Sphere to Selsengra Aleitor Courage.

Moreover, he sent two Killoseiga Spheres toward him.

One Killoseiga Sphere was ahead of Selsengra Aleitor Courage.

Another was above him.

And the last one was behind him.

The three Killoseiga Spheres charged toward him simultaneously.

When they neared, all three were reflected.

The Taurylyphs emerged once more.

Then, they faded.

The Killoseiga Spheres rapidly headed toward Kreseiru Oblivionu'crei.

Kreseiru Oblivionu'crei prepared to rebound them.

Selsengra Aleitor Courage thrust his arms forward.

He utilized the natural air to keep the Killoseiga Spheres on their path.

Kreseiru Oblivionu'crei telekinetically pushed against the Killoseiga Spheres.

It was a stalemate.

However, Selsengra Aleitor Courage increased the natural air pressure.

The Killoseiga Spheres progressed toward Kreseiru Oblivionu'crei.

Kreseiru Oblivionu'crei growled.

His eyes briefly glowed solid red.

The Killoseiga Spheres were pushed toward the center.

Selsengra Aleitor Courage scoffed.

That does it, you Galactic Devil. You're pissing me off. ...Yet, I can't complain too much. At least he puts up a hell of a fight.

Selsengra Aleitor Courage used Sanei.

The sparkling celestial wind blew the Killoseiga Spheres toward Kreseiru Oblivionu'crei once more.

Kreseiru Oblivionu'crei increased the intensity of his telekinesis.

313

Yet, it was futile.

Selsengra Aleitor Courage increased the intensity of the Sanei.

The Killoseiga Spheres rapidly approached Kreseiru Oblivionu'crei.

The Killoseiga Spheres, or the Selsengra Killoseiga Spheres, penetrated Kreseiru Oblivionu'crei's abdomen.

When the Killoseiga Spheres struck the Taurylyphs, the Selsengra on each Taurylyph combined with the Killoseiga Spheres.

As a result, they became the Selsengra Killoseiga Spheres.

Kreseiru Oblivionu'crei yelled.

Selsengra Aleitor Courage telekinetically pulled the last two Killoseiga Spheres toward him.

When they neared, he shrouded them with the Selsengra Aura.

Then, he punched both of the Selsengra Killoseiga Spheres toward Kreseiru Oblivionu'crei.

The Selsengra Killoseiga Spheres penetrated his chest.

They emerged on the other side of his body.

Kreseiru Oblivionu'crei released Kreseirumana's Howl in pain.

Selsengra Aleitor Courage instantly closed the distance.

He delivered the Selsengra Tauran Uppercut to Kreseiru Oblivionu'crei.

Kreseiru Oblivionu'crei glided upward.

Selsengra Aleitor Courage appeared behind him.

He kicked Kreseiru Oblivionu'crei toward one of the Killosogma holes.

He landed in one of them.

Then, Selsengra Aleitor Courage telekinetically threw one of the Electria'ala Spheres at Kreseiru Oblivionu'crei.

The Electria'ala Sphere electrocuted him.

Kreseiru Oblivionu'crei shouted.

The Electria'ala prevented those struck by it from accelerated restoration.

There were countless types of celestial elements.

And depending on the user, they could create multiple possibilities.

Selsengra Aleitor Courage threw the second Electria'ala Sphere toward him.

Kreseiru Oblivionu'crei was electrocuted once more.

Selsengra Aleitor Courage threw the last Electria'ala Sphere at him.

Kreseiru Oblivionu'crei was electrocuted again.

Selsengra Aleitor Courage landed several feet from Kreseiru Oblivionu'crei.

He gazed toward the Killosogma.

His eyes briefly illuminated solid blue – the *Felloselondu.*

He changed the Killosogma into Selsengra Killosogma.

As a result, Kreseiru Oblivionu'crei began to boil.

The three Selsengra Killoseiga Spheres that were stuck in his abdomen increased the intensity of the Selsengra Killosogma.

Kreseiru Oblivionu'crei yelled.

He quickly crawled out of the Selsengra Killosogma.

He lied on the ground.

His Helligaiyon Armor was completely damaged.

Parts of his legs were shown through a series of holes in the Helligaiyon Armor.

It looked that of a red crystal.

If what I see isn't an illusion, then it's no wonder he's so tough. This guy… is unbelievable. And… is this what Serenity meant by him hiding his "true" self? She saw past his disguise.

Selsengra Aleitor Courage summoned a Selsengra Orb.

The Selsengra Orb morphed into Selsengra Tauran'creima.

Selsengra Aleitor Courage and Selsengra Tauran'creima charged toward the incapacitated Kreseiru Oblivionu'crei.

As they neared, Selsengra Aleitor Courage morphed into the head of Tauran'creima – the *Tauran'crei'ion.*

Selsengra Tauran'crei'ion Courage released Tauran'creima's Bellow in fury.

Selsengra Tauran'crei'ion Courage and Selsengra Tauran'creima struck Kreseiru Oblivionu'crei in unison.

He was launched very far into Bleak Forest.

Many trees toppled as he collided with them.

Bleak Forest echoed with the sound of collapsing tree.

Selsengra Tauran'crei'ion Courage reverted to Selsengra Aleitor Courage.

Selsengra Tauran'creima bellowed in respect.

Then, he vanished.

Suddenly, Bleak Forest gradually disappeared in a ripple effect.

Selsengra Aleitor Courage appeared on Oblivion Island once more.

He looked toward the Melhouna Constellations.

Rinaigora remained steadfast in her duty in closing the Zeigramon'stralia.

However, the fortunate aspect was that as Oblivionu'crei weakened, so did the Zeigramon'stralia.

Then, Selsengra Aleitor Courage looked toward Kreseiru Oblivionu'crei.

He struggled to stand.

Yet, when he managed to keep his balance, he slightly staggered as he very slowly approached Selsengra Aleitor Courage.

"Tauran'creima, that does it. You are the only one who has forced me to go to great lengths. Now, this will be the end of you all."

"Less talking, more fighting. Let your actions speak. Not your annoying mouth. Besides, you're trying to kill us, anyway. So there's no need to repeat yourself like an imbecile."

Kreseiru Oblivionu'crei dispelled his Helligaiyon Armor.

His body was that of a red crystal.

He possessed illuminate horns.

He had a perpetual scowl.

He had a long pointed nose.

He had three rows of sharp teeth.

He had a pointed chin.

And he had a pitchfork tail that had a Killoseiga on its end.

The Kreseirumana Crystal resided on his forehead.

And like the Helligaiyon Armor, he possessed spikes in the corresponding locations.

"My gracious. You can put your armor back on now."

"To hell with you, Tauran'creima. You have pushed me too far. Universe A11-Mayethekaya will soon be extinct."

Kreseiru Oblivionu'crei flew upward.

Then, he released Kreseirumana's War Cry.

The shrinking Zeigramon'stralia suddenly grew larger.

"Damn it!" Rinaigora shouted. "How is that evil creature able to control this thing?"

"He is an incredible being, to be sure," Leodycreus said. "However, Tauran'creima's Embodiment, the Transcendent One, can handle him. He does not require the likes of us."

Tauran'creima stepped forth.

"Step aside, Rinaigora. I am taking over."

"No, Tauran'creima. I can handle it. Please!"

"No. You have done enough. This is an order."

"Alright. Fine."

Rinaigora retired from her duty.

Tauran'creima began telekinetically closing the Zeigramon'stralia.

Courage sensed a major difference in Oblivionu'crei.

As such, he changed from Selsengra Aleitor Courage into *Tauran'orsai Vecoraigus* Courage.

His eyes were solid fiery green.

The Tauran'creima Aura coursed through the Vesorai.

The Tauran'creima Aura also shrouded him.

The Glyph of Tauran'creima turned green.

Tauran'orsai Vecoraigus was the first stage of the Tauran'orsai transformations.

The initial stage was Tauran'orsai.

However, the Tauran'orsai transformation series was the only one able to reach the fourth transformation.

All of Courage's other transformations could only reach the third.

If Courage were to go beyond any of his transformation's boundary, he would risk grave injury.

The same applies to all star beings.

Tauran'orsai Vecoraigus Courage flew toward Kreseiru Oblivionu'crei.

He went for a Tauran'orsai Tauran Uppercut.

Yet, Kreseiru Oblivionu'crei grabbed his fist.

Tauran'orsai Vecoraigus Courage kicked Kreseiru Oblivionu'crei's waist several times.

Then, he followed up with a punch to his abdomen.

Kreseiru Oblivionu'crei choked.

Small pieces of himself fell as Tauran'orsai Vecoraigus Courage struck him.

Kreseiru Oblivionu'crei threw him toward Oblivion Island.

Tauran'orsai Vecoraigus Courage landed on his feet.

Kreseiru Oblivionu'crei emerged.

He summoned two Kreseirumana Apparitions.

The Kreseirumana Apparitions charged toward Tauran'orsai Vecoraigus Courage.

Tauran'orsai Vecoraigus Courage summoned two Tauran'orsai Tauran'creimas.

The Tauran'orsai Tauran'creimas charged toward the Kreseirumana Apparitions.

When they neared, they collided.

A cloud of smoke permeated the vicinity.

It was a standstill.

Tauran'orsai Vecoraigus Courage flew into the smoke.

Kreseiru Oblivionu'crei did the same.

They parried each other's vicious attacks more than connecting them.

The smoke cleared.

Tauran'orsai Vecoraigus Courage created distance between them.

However, Kreseiru Oblivionu'crei charged toward him.

Suddenly, Kreseiru Oblivionu'crei was struck off course.

A Fedmori'ia of Tauran'orsai Vecoraigus Courage emerged.

Kreseiru Oblivionu'crei recovered.

Then, he looked perplexed at the Tauran'orsai Vecoraigus Courages.

He could not tell them apart.

Suddenly, he was struck with a Tauran'orsai Tauran Uppercut.

He glided upward.

Another Fedmori'ia emerged.

The Fedmori'ia joined the other two on Oblivion Island.

When Tauran'orsai Vecoraigus Courage entered the smoke, he summoned two Fedmori'ias and isolated them.

Kreseiru Oblivionu'crei returned.

He conjured a red and purple shield around himself.

This was the Kreseirumana Barrier.

The Tauran'orsai Vecoraigus Courages scoffed.

Time to end this. This battle's dawdled on long enough. Just have to push him a little further.

Tauran'orsai Vecoraigus Courage conjured his Sacroncai Helmet.

He placed it over his head.

Suddenly, his Sacred Staraidus increased astronomically.

Large waves of Tauran'creima Aura sprung upward.

He was now *Knightolas* Staraidus Courage.

This transformation increased Courage's Sacred Staraidus by one thousand percent.

However, he could only reach five thousand percent.

If he were to increase it beyond five thousand percent, he would be at risk for dire circumstances.

Transidyus watched the fight from Fireiya Tower.

Fascinating. I knew you were the one, Courage. I know potential when I see it. Though we all would love to join you, you're capable on your own. Not to mention, this is a task that falls to you. Not for a Grandmaster like myself. Everyone has a path. I will do my best to guide you.

But the rest is for you to forge. Always transcend... Tetsu'reidza Courage.

Sadon observed the melee from Orgrechi Canyon.

You've grown in such a short time, Courage. You're giving someone like him a way to go. I knew you were something special when we fought. The universe is very fortunate to have someone like you. However, the next time we fight, I assure you it'll be more thrilling.

Leiku viewed the confrontation at the edge of *Ryodan* Forest.

Hmm... Transidyus was right. Though I always believed in you, Courage, I cannot help but be cautious. Being too receptive or overconfident can lead to disappointment. However, what I see from you is far from dissatisfaction. You do the star beings proud.

Deathelena, the Hychineirian, and Relmi'shirian Nations beheld the conflict from her castle.

Deathelena refused to admit that she admired Courage before her nations.

She never thought she would meet someone who completely outclassed her.

It was shameful.

Especially since she ruled two nations that respected her.

"Goddess Deathelena..." Elaimia said. "I knew he was extremely powerful when I first met him."

"Indeed..."

"Shit," Fesforia stated. "If Courage could push this eerie guy's buttons, imagine what he *could've* done if he chose not to hold back on any of us. That shit's too scary to think about. Even still... this Cosmos Destroyer isn't a joke. He shits all over us."

The Hychineirian and Relmi'shirian Nations remained silent.

Their future lied on Courage's shoulders, whether any of them wanted to admit it or not.

It was the truth.

And each of them, Deathelena included, knew it was a fact.

Feloreigro and the deities regarded the battle from Hyrenal Summit.

Transcendent One, you have outdone yourself. I know we seemed to be at odds before. I understand how passionate you are about protecting not just the star beings, but everyone. Hopefully in the future, we can put our differences aside.

Flowerensia and co. continued watching the clash from Ulenar Island.

"My dear..." Helipak whispered. "Such a hunk. So sexy. He's giving that brute what for."

Helipak placed the tip of his index finger between his teeth.

His gaze was seductive.

"*Mmm...*"

And his thoughts were very perverted.

"Again, dude?" Janeiholm questioned. "I bet you're horny as fuck even though all of existence is on the line."

"*Mmm-hmm.*"

"I knew it."

"Courage has him on the defensive," Gravulkim said. "He's pushing him to his limit, I believe."

"You're right," Ulanahar stated. "However, knowing Oblivionu'crei, he may have something planned. He's probably biding time for another attack."

"It won't matter in the end," Kimiko said. "Courage's come too far to let everything be under the government of that bastard."

"Right," Velcrimia stated. "I just want everything to go back to normal."

"Yeah right," Kimiko joked. "You just wanna go back to daydreaming about Transidyus, don'tcha?"

Velcrimia blushed.

"Shut up, Kimiko. That's none of your damn business."

Kimiko chuckled.

"I thought so, lover girl."

"What about you and Janeiholm, hmm?" Velcrimia countered. "Been thinking about him lately?"

"Shh!" Kimiko hissed. "He's standing right *there*, you fucking idiot!"

Velcrimia chuckled.

"I thought so, lover girl."

"He was hiding his true self beneath that armor," Serenity said. "I knew it."

"Courage is picking that dude apart," Melharina stated. "He has no choice but to go on the defensive. Yet, Courage is smart enough to know this dude isn't gonna give up just yet."

"He doesn't have to give up yet," Flowerensia said. "Courage'll make him give up once he's pushed him far enough."

Asai remained silent.

She internalized her acclamation.

She gazed at Courage's image with immense fondness.

I'm grateful for all you've done, Master. The intense spiritual love making. The wisdom you divulge. Your trustworthy yet sarcastic personality. You're one of a kind. Defeat Oblivionu'crei and free everyone's conscious of despair.

Knightolas Staraidus Courage conjured the *Transdeiru* Sword and the *Vydoran* Shield.

The Transdeiru Sword is a resplendent green blade.

And the Vydoran Shield is a blue, shining, elaborate kite shield with the Glyph of Tauran'creima in the center.

One of the Fedmori'ias conjured a dazzling green *Heavetia* Kunai Knife.

He threw the Heavetia Kunai Knife at Kreseiru Oblivionu'crei.

The Heavetia Kunai Knife shattered the Kreseirumana Barrier.

Then, it pierced his chest.

Kreseiru Oblivionu'crei yelled.

Next, Knightolas Staraidus Courage flew toward Kreseiru Oblivionu'crei.

He began slashing him at different angles at an incredible speed.

Kreseiru Oblivionu'crei shouted.

Pieces of himself fell into the void of space.

Then, Kreseiru Oblivionu'crei conjured the Electraheil around his fist.

The Electraheil would electrocute and detonate any individual on the receiving end.

He swung toward Knightolas Staraidus Courage.

He raised the Vydoran Shield.

His Electraheil-covered fist struck the Vydoran Shield.

Knightolas Staraidus Courage repelled him.

Then, he swiftly pierced his abdomen with the Transdeiru Sword.

The sacredness of the Transdeiru Sword combined with the three Selsengra Killoseiga Spheres in his abdomen.

Kreseiru Oblivionu'crei yelled.

Tauran'creima was making significant progress in closing the Zeigramon'stralia.

And due to Oblivionu'crei faltering, the Zeigramon'stralia shrunk tremendously.

Tauran'creima began playing a melody from his conscious:

'Staraidus Museala Extere'al: The Light Returns'.

It was a very powerful, sacred melody.

The instruments that played were a piano, a flute, and a violin.

The Melhouna Constellations rocked back and forth to the harmony.

The sacred tune echoed throughout outer space.

Kreseiru Oblivionu'crei held his abdomen.

Then, he heard music.

He looked toward the Melhouna Constellations.

He sneered.

"You see that, you wretch?" Knightolas Staraidus Courage said. "That's harmony! It matters not where you come from! It matters not what you look like! All that matters is what you stand for!"

Knightolas Staraidus Courage joined his Fedmori'ias on Oblivion Island.

The Fedmori'ias had their eyes closed and their arms extended to either side of themselves.

A magnificent silver light shrouded them.

They were absorbing energy from the stars.

They were absorbing energy from the universe, a process was known as *Egraman'heilia*.

Knightolas Staraidus Courage placed the Transdeiru Sword on its tip.

Then, he spun it.

Like the Fedmori'ias, the Transdeiru Sword began absorbing energy from the universe.

Knightolas Staraidus Courage closed his eyes.

Then, he outstretched his arms to either side of himself.

He commenced attracting energy from the universe.

The sacred melody was also of great assistance.

Kreseiru Oblivionu'crei scoffed.

He conjured several large, flaming spikes beneath Knightolas Staraidus Courage and the Fedmori'ias.

These are called the *Stalagmaluses*.

However, Knightolas Staraidus Courage summoned the Gwi'denahala beneath himself.

The Stalagmaluses were reversed.

Another Gwi'denahala emerged before Kreseiru Oblivionu'crei.

The Stalagmaluses erupted from the Gwi'denahala.

Yet, Kreseiru Oblivionu'crei evaded.

He dispelled the Stalagmaluses.

And Knightolas Staraidus Courage dispelled the Gwi'denahala.

Then, he summoned three meteors.

Each have a different color.

Red, blue, and purple.

These are *Meteorykias*.

Kreseiru Oblivionu'crei telekinetically threw the Meteorykias toward Knightolas Staraidus Courage and the Fedmori'ias.

When the Meteorykias neared, the impact shook Oblivion Island.

When the smoke cleared, they were unscathed.

Kreseiru Oblivionu'crei became irate.

He descended upon Oblivion Island.

Then, he exhaled a stream of Killoseiga toward Knightolas Staraidus Courage and the Fedmori'ias.

The Killoseiga shrouded them.

When the Killoseiga ebbed, they were unharmed.

Kreseiru Oblivionu'crei snarled.

Then, he flew toward Knightolas Staraidus Courage and the Fedmori'ias.

He threw a punch at Knightolas Staraidus Courage.

It connected with his face.

However, he did not flinch.

"Damn it, man," Knightolas Staraidus Courage stated. "Just when I was losing myself in my thoughts, here you come. Goddamn it, Oblivionu'crei. Really? Have you no class?"

"Do not make light of me, you bastard! Die!"

"Oblivionu'crei. It's over. You lost."

"Impossible!"

Kreseiru Oblivionu'crei threw another punch toward Knightolas Staraidus Courage.

However, he was telekinetically pushed away.

He glided backward.

He landed on his feet.

He slid to a stop.

Then, the Fedmori'ias disappeared.

Knightolas Staraidus Courage dispelled the Transdeiru Sword and the Vydoran Shield.

He dispelled the Heavetia Kunai Knife in Kreseiru Oblivionu'crei's chest.

Moreover, he dispelled his Sacroncai Helmet.

The silver light shrouded Courage.

Then, the light gradually faded.

Courage's Sacroncai Armor and his headband are sparkling silver.

His eyes are dazzling silver.

The iridescent Astrial'len Aura coursed throughout the Vesorai.

The Glyph of Tauran'creima also reflected the Astrial'len Aura.

He is now Astrial'len Courage.

Astrial'len was the initial stage of the Astrial'len transformations.

"Oblivionu'crei. I think it's time for you to go. Your fifteen minutes of fame is over."

"Shut up, Tauran'creima! My reign is just beginning! Once I deal with you, all will know the meaning of true omnipotence!"

Kreseiru Oblivionu'crei charged toward Astrial'len Courage.

Astrial'len Courage nearly struck him with silver lightning – the *Eleivora*.

Kreseiru Oblivionu'crei leapt away.

"Leave," Astrial'len Courage said.

"Never!"

Kreseiru Oblivionu'crei charged toward him once more.

He covered his entire body with Electraheil.

Astrial'len Courage telekinetically stopped him.

"Oblivionu'crei. Like I mentioned earlier, you're one of the greatest challengers I've ever had. And for that, I thank you. However, I will not, nor will I ever, accept your philosophy. It is far too cruel for the likes of me.

"Everyone has a right to choose what they decide to do with their life. Those who choose stupidity will suffer the consequences of their actions, while those who know better will reap the fruits of their labor. Shame some beings are still playing checkers while others are playing chess.

"Your New Universe Regulation stops here."

"Curses! Tauran'creima, I just wanted to fulfill my vision! Damn it all!"

"Your "vision" killed over trillions of innocent beings. Your asinine judgment caused their untimely demise. Regardless, I won't kill you. However, I know you'll be back. And I'll be waiting. This is only the beginning.

"Farewell."

Astrial'len Courage's eyes turned solid fiery silver – the *Fellosairaga*.

Kreseiru Oblivionu'crei released Kreseirumana's Howl as he was banished from existence in a swirling effect.

Then, Astrial'len Courage walked up the stairs.

He stood on Oblivion Island's edge.

The Zeigramon'stralia completely closed.

The Melhouna Constellations cheered Tauran'creima.

The Azagnorpor Constellations retreated.

Then, the Melhouna Constellations looked at Astrial'len Courage.

The Melhouna Constellations made their respective animal sound of joy as they flew around Astrial'len Courage.

Tauran'creima played the sacred melody: 'Staraidus Museala Extere'al: Destiny'.

Auderesa hopped toward Astrial'len Courage.

She pecked his cheek.

He chuckled.

"Thank you, Embodiment of Tauran'creima," Auderesa said. "Oh, and I'm certain Asai would love another round, if you know what I mean…?"

She giggled.

"We'll have to see," Astrial'len Courage stated.

"Of course, dear. You're welcome here anytime! Ta-ta for now!"

Auderesa rejoined the Melhouna Constellations.

Then, Leodycreus approached Astrial'len Courage.

"Embodiment of Tauran'creima, you have my eternal respect. Not only did you give my representation, Sadon, an excellent match, but you also saved the entire universe. You are a blessing to all you encounter."

"Thank you, Leodycreus. Besides Oblivionu'crei, Sadon was the toughest being I ever faced. I know we'll have a rivalry until I surpass him and the Grandmasters. Regardless, I learned a lot about Sadon through the passionate exchange of our fists."

Leodycreus laughed.

"Very well, Embodiment of Tauran'creima. Take care of yourself and those around you. Farewell."

Leodycreus rejoined the Melhouna Constellations.

Next, Eidomularus slithered toward Astrial'len Courage.

"Embodiment of Tauran'creima, my thanks for saving the universe, as well as accepting my personification, Ulanahar."

"Of course. It's best not to judge a book by its cover. Ulanahar is definitely invaluable. She completely upstages any Azagnorpor. She's strong because she overcame the stereotype of what an Azagnorpor represents. For that, she has my respect."

"Thank you, Embodiment of Tauran'creima. Farewell."

Eidomularus rejoined the Melhouna Constellations.

Then, Wyen'deishia pranced toward Astrial'len Courage.

He kissed Astrial'len Courage's cheek.

Astrial'len Courage staggered.

Wyen'deishia giggled.

"My, you proved to be the hero I anticipated. Such *handsomeness.* Such *flair*. Such... *everything*!"

The Melhouna Constellations shook their head in disbelief.

"Helipak... is that you...?" Astrial'len Courage asked.

"Why, yes. Helipak, or Helinara, is my representative, love. If you're ever feeling lonely, give Helinara or Helipak a holler, 'k? *She'll* or *he'll* make *certain* you're tended to. They'll soothe you. *Every* part of you."

"Yeah... I guess. That sounds... nice..."

Wyen'deishia laughed.

"Feel free to visit me anytime, dear! Farewell for now!"

Wyen'deishia rejoined the Melhouna Constellations.

Finally, Tauran'creima approached Astrial'len Courage.

The Melhouna Constellations observed in awe.

"I am proud of you. Tauran'creima's Pride... lives on..."

For the first time, Courage shed Astral Tears.

Tauran'creima licked the silver Astral Tears away.

"You have done the cosmos a grand favor. You will only become stronger as time proceeds."

"O-of course..."

"Now, where is that Tauran'creima's Bellow? Cheer up. You have accomplished a great feat this day."

Astrial'len Courage released Tauran'creima's Bellow in reverence.

Likewise with Tauran'creima.

Then, Tauran'creima laughed.

"You should go home and rest. I am certain a spectacular celebration awaits you. Farewell."

Tauran'creima and co. departed together.

Their respective aura created a magnificent spectrum across the universe.

Then, Astrial'len Courage summoned the Gwi'denahala.

The essence of the Fire, Wind, and Earth deities emerged from it.

They headed toward Rhol'heima.

"It's over," Astrial'len Courage said. "It's finally over."

"Gaze toward the sky. Believe in your own being. Forevermore."

 **Chapter 10**

A True Legend

One week later.

Flowerensia and co. and the Velmelkian Nation held a victory rendezvous for Courage in the Velmelkia Town Square early in the morning.

"Courage," Flowerensia said. "Thank you for saving my planet. You've done so much for the universe in such a short amount of time. You truly live up to the legend."

"Right," Melharina agreed. "He's definitely what the universe needs. I had no idea someone like Oblivionu'crei could exist. He was capable of destroying universes. Beyond incredible."

"Courage," Serenity stated. "If it wasn't for you... all of existence as we know it may very well be in ruin. I'm so glad you arrived. I don't think any of us would have been able to defeat him."

"First and foremost," Courage said. "You and Flowerensia already knew something was amiss long before Oblivionu'crei made his presence known. Regardless, he's one of the strongest opponents I've ever fought.

"And regardless of his evil nature, I gave credit where it was due. I appreciated the fight he brought. I anticipate his return. He'll likely be much stronger. I'm also certain there are other worthy adversaries out in the cosmos. It excites me. Very much.

"And... I appreciate you all for having my best interest at heart. Now can we cut the sentimentality short?"

"Not gonna happen, bub," Melharina asserted. "I know emotions aren't your forte, but we got your back. Through and through. You've proved on several occasions that you mean what you say, and say what you mean.

"You don't talk the talk, but you walk the walk as well. If that ain't a real man, then I don't know what is."

"Your assertion is genuine, Melharina," Courage said. "Everything you stated applies to all the women here as well. It takes those of like mind to accomplish many things. However, different perspectives matter as well.

"Even though Oblivionu'crei took the wrong approach in his vision, I understood what he meant. Yet, perhaps from his point of view, he was doing the right thing. The same applies to Deathelena. No one knows for certain.

"Regardless, I choose freewill. People can do as they please. They have a right to their choices. Yet, when those choices have harsh results on the lives of others, I think it's best to find another way."

"That's an interesting way to look at life, Courage," Ulanahar agreed. "I've often thought about that as well. Especially considering what I've experienced. Yet, when I fought against my evil nature, I felt great. I overcame what I was supposed to be.

"And thanks to someone of your caliber, you've given me more reason to remain the way I am. My eternal blessings, Legendary Tauran'creima, Tetsu'reidza Courage."

"You make me proud, Ulanahar," Courage stated. "Your intellect is very sharp. And you're the only Azagnorpor I know that overcame their malignant nature. You're an invaluable member of this team."

Ulanahar blushed.

"...Thank you... Tetsu'reidza Courage..."

"Traqua tesa bwela lu, Pelicea Ulanahar," (Peace be upon you, Sincere Ulanahar.) Courage said.

Her blush deepened.

"S-sies... Tetsu'reidza Courage..." (Y-yes... Tetsu'reidza Courage...)

Goodness! He's making me hot in the nether region! The effect he has on people is unbelievable!

"Feeling a little... *bothered*, dear Ulanahar?" Helipak teased. "*Hmm?*"

"Don't start with me, Helipak..."

"Of course, sweetie. You lucked out. For today."

"Transcendent One," Feloreigro said. "I hope there is no ill will between us."

"Old Timer?" Courage queried. "No, I mean, Feloreigro... I harbor no hatred toward you and those of Rhol'heima. I took my passion too far, I'll admit.

"I had no right to act the way I did. Taking the lives of the Fire, Wind, and Earth deities was uncalled for. My sincere apologies."

"All is forgiven, Transcendent One. At least you found the kindness to return them. You even spared Deathelena. Three times. Your change of heart is apparent. It suits you.

"Should you need anything from me, or those of Rhol'heima, feel free to stop by. And who knows, you might learn a thing or two from this "Old Timer"."

Courage laughed.

It was the first time he felt genuinely happy.

"Thank you, Feloreigro of Rhol'heima. I won't forget."

Then, Helipak approached Courage.

"I don't want to give a typical "thank you" speech. So…"

Helipak placed his hand on Courage's cheek.

Courage raised an eyebrow.

Helipak licked his lips.

In a flash of light, Helipak changed into Helinara.

Seixomorphesis is the ability to change one's gender.

This was exclusive to Helipak.

Though Helinara had all of the female body parts, she did not possess Keileimia.

Helinara wore a yellow blouse, a green miniskirt, and blue sandals.

"Why don't we go someplace… *private*, where I can *really* show you my appreciation for saving all our asses?"

Courage gently grasped Helinara's hand.

"Still at it, eh?"

"Of course. You know I can never get enough of you. *Never*. I meant what I said when I said I'd take care of you, Sweet Courage."

"If I didn't know any better..."

"Oh? Are you insinuating something, Sweet Courage? Why wait when you can ravish me now?"

"I could be insinuating something. But it's inconsequential."

Helinara grasped her ample breasts.

"Every part of me is yours."

"Man, sit your flamboyant ass down somewhere!" Janeiholm protested. "He doesn't want to fuck you! Hard or otherwise! Leave him be!"

"Not gonna happen, Cranky Jaguar," Helinara rebutted. "Why don't you... tell Kimiko how much you love her? You need some lovin' in your life. Really. Life's too excellent to be such a dull."

Janeiholm seethed.

You fucking bitch...!

He hated when Helinara outsmarted him.

Janeiholm and Kimiko blushed.

Then, Janeiholm snarled.

"You Fruity Deer..."

Helinara giggled.

"That's what I thought, Cranky Jaguar."

Kimiko gently grasped Janeiholm's hand.

"Janeiholm... is Helinara right?"

"You can't believe anything that fruit basket says…"

"Janeiholm… we've known each other for a very long time. I noticed the hints you were giving me. I wasn't ignoring them. I just believe timing is everything. If you ever want to talk about that, we can."

"We can talk now."

"Of course."

Janeiholm and Kimiko approached Courage.

"Thank you, Courage," Kimiko said. "For everything. We'll be back soon."

"Of course, friends. Take all the time you need. You're very much appreciated."

Janeiholm and Kimiko embraced Courage.

Then, they departed from Velmelkia Town Square.

They headed toward Purity Lake.

"Lofty Courage," Leiku said. "You have done the universe a great service. Your power ever grows. You are unlike any star. I am proud of you."

"I learned so much from you and Transidyus. I lost to both of you. But from that loss, new knowledge was gained. Thank you. I look forward to the day I can lay a strike on both of you, if not outright defeat you."

"I look forward to that day as well. Until then, never stop growing stronger."

"You don't have to worry about that. Trust me."

"That I most certainly believe," Transidyus stated. "Your potential speaks volumes. Trust us. We know power when we sense it."

"My respect, Transidyus," Courage said. "I'll always look forward to sparring and learning from both of you."

Courage shook Transidyus and Leiku's hand.

"Pardon my interruption, dear men," Helinara stated. "But I believe that dearest over there seems quite lonely."

Helinara pointed toward Velcrimia.

Courage, Transidyus, and Leiku looked toward her.

She had her back against the wall of the Velmelkia Dance Hall.

Her hands were clasped behind her.

She was staring toward them, specifically Transidyus.

Her gaze was doting, yet wistful.

Transidyus pointed toward himself.

Velcrimia smiled.

"Yes..."

"You should go see what she wants, handsome," Helinara urged. "I bet it's something really sweet."

"Of course, Wyen'deishia," Transidyus said. "I'll return momentarily."

"Please, Grandmaster Transidyus..." Helinara stated. "*Helipak* or *Helinara* will do nicely."

"Of course. Thank you."

Transidyus ambled toward Velcrimia.

"Yes, Teretri'aga? Is something the matter?"

Velcrimia giggled.

"Please, Transidyus. Just call me Velcrimia."

"Oh… well, of course."

"I just… wanted to know if you wanted to hang out with me for the remainder of Courage's party. Is… that alright…?"

"Why, yes. We can."

"Thank you, Transidyus."

Transidyus and Velcrimia approached Courage.

"I appreciate all you've done for all of us star beings, Courage," Velcrimia said. "The great deeds you've done will always be remembered."

"Your gratitude is much appreciated, Velcrimia," Courage stated. "Like Ulanahar, your intellect is also very sharp."

"Yes," Velcrimia said. "I spent the majority of my time trying to get her out of her metaphorical shell. She hated everyone."

"I can understand why," Courage stated. "Nevertheless, Ulanahar appreciates you for sticking by her. The best of friends you two are."

"Thank you, Courage. Well, Transidyus and I should be going. We'll be back soon."

"Of course," Courage said. "See you later."

Transidyus and Velcrimia departed Velmelkia Town Square.

They headed toward *Eiyana* Forest.

Helinara approached Gravulkim, who was sitting on a metal bench by his lonesome.

She sat next to him.

"Hey there, Big Bear Boy. What's wrong?"

"Nothing. I'm ever grateful Courage risked his life for everyone across the cosmos. But now… I feel bored…"

"Hmm… not bored. Lonely. You feel left out."

Gravulkim did not want to admit it, but she was right.

Gravulkim was not attempting to be selfish in any fashion.

He valued Courage's valor.

And he felt Courage deserved the recognition he received.

But yes, he felt alone.

Even with his friends nearby.

"Courage would say this is a gathering for all of us," Helinara said. "Not just for himself. He's just that humble. And even if the majority are paying attention to him, it wouldn't matter to him.

"See, look at it like this. Say if you traveled someplace else and saved that particular sector. Those people would praise you."

"Yeah… but this is different. Courage is the legend, which was foretold across the galaxy. That kind of popularity cannot be matched.

"Make no mistake. This isn't about who can outmaneuver who. Or about jealousy. Far from it. Like I said, I'm just bored. I'm just taking in the atmosphere."

"…Where's Maria?"

"She's out of town. We talk every now and then telepathically."

Maria Zeyle'ago was Gravulkim's significant other.

Maria was a Melhouna and an Acolyte Star.

She was also an Original Star.

Her constellation was *Kelkreita*, the Celestial Tigress.

Then, some of Gravulkim and Helinara's fans approached them.

Gravulkim's somber mood suddenly brightened.

"We'll talk soon, Big Bear Boy," Helinara stated. "For now, have fun with your admirers."

Sadon was having a conversation with Courage.

"You're more than the champion, Courage. You're the role model people need."

"Truly?"

"Yes. Definitely. I'm glad I met someone like you. Not only did you relieve me of the championship, but you gave me a fight I'll never forget. And you saved the universe from a major calamity. You exceeded my expectations. You're the definition of a legend.

"You're a true role model for everyone."

"...Thank you. That means a lot."

"No problem. Should you ever want to spar, let me know."

"I'll definitely remember that. Hell yeah."

"Well, look at the Celestial Bull and the Celestial Lion get along," Helinara teased. "Alright, Mr. Lion. Miss Snake might have some words for you."

Helinara lightly pushed Sadon toward Ulanahar, who looked just as confused as Courage and Sadon.

"Hey, what the hell do you think you're doing?" Sadon questioned. "I was talking with Courage. Get your hands off me."

Most of the Velmelkian Nation turned toward the minor incident.

Helinara immediately withdrew.

"Oh gracious me! I'm so sorry. I… thought she might've wanted to talk with you about something important."

"Well, if that was the case, she would've approached me about the issue, bub. She doesn't need the likes of you speaking on her behalf."

Then, Sadon raised an eyebrow.

"…Wait a minute. I recognize you. You're that happy-go-lucky opponent I fought years ago. You held your own, but you weren't enough to take the belt from me. Improve yourself instead of minding people's business."

Helinara was emotionally devastated.

She was on the verge of crying.

Courage sighed.

"Sadon… it's alright. Uh… *he*… gets like this sometimes. He gets too excited for his own good and likes to mingle often. Not his fault. Just his nature. Forgive him."

"Of course, Champion Courage. I'll take your word for it."

Helinara secured her arms around Courage's neck from the right.

She whispered into his ear.

"Thank you, dear…"

She laid her head on his shoulder.

"Ugh… Helinara. This isn't right. Let go of me."

"In a minute."

Mildly irritated by Helinara, Sadon ambled toward Ulanahar.

"Pardon. You were another one of my opponents years ago. Ulanahar was your name, correct?"

"Yes."

"You did a great job holding your own."

"No. You're the real champion. Though I appreciate your sportsmanship, if I didn't beat you, what does it matter?"

"It matters because you fought someone much stronger than you. You wanted to prove that you had what it took to become champion. And even though you lost, you still picked yourself up and gotten much stronger. You're a Master Star now."

"Thank you, Sadon. But you and Courage are still light years ahead of me."

"We're men, Ulanahar. That's what we do. We compete and become stronger. It's in our nature to improve ourselves. Females can do the same, but not of the caliber as men. These are facts. That's just the way it is. Doesn't matter the species."

Ulanahar laughed.

"That's very true."

"Say, if you want, we can talk about what's interesting. Or go someplace intriguing."

"Is that a date?"

"It can be whatever you want."

"Of course. Sounds nice."

Then, she became depressed.

"But… why would you want to be around an Azagnorpor?"

"The same reason Courage and your friends are around you. Because of *who* you are. Not *what* you are."

Ulanahar smiled.

"Of course, Sadon. Thank you."

Sadon and Ulanahar walked toward Courage.

Helinara released Courage.

She went and sat next to Gravulkim.

"Thank you, Courage, for accepting me," Ulanahar said. "And thank you for putting a stop to Oblivionu'crei. Sadon and I will return later."

"Of course," Courage stated. "I appreciate all of you. Good luck. Both of you."

Sadon and Ulanahar departed Velmelkia Town Square.

They headed toward Velmelkia Park.

Asai approached Courage.

She stood before him.

They looked into each other's eyes.

Then, she embraced him.

He reciprocated her affection.

"You're welcome, Asai."

The Velmelkian Nation cheered.

When the praises settled, Flowerensia spoke.

"Everyone! I'd like you all to report to Lofty Plains at sunset! I have an additional surprise for Courage! For now, let's enjoy some music in the Velmelkia Dance Hall!"

Then, Helinara approached Courage.

"Sweet Courage... may I have a word with you? In private?"

"Is this a serious matter?"

"Yes. I assure you."

"Then come. Let us go. We'll return shortly, Flowerensia."

"Of course, dear."

Helinara and Courage teleported from Velmelkia Town Square.

Helinara and Courage stood at the edge of Aereshia Meadow.

"How do you do it, dear?" Helinara asked. "How do you defy such odds?"

"I can't explain it. I just do what I must. If it seems right, then that's all the reason I need."

"You're amazing, dear. You're admirable. That's one of the reasons I love you so much. You're capable of doing things I couldn't fathom undertaking…"

"False. You're a star being like I am, which means you're beyond countless species. Raise your self-esteem. Don't settle for less. Ever."

"…Honey, when you told me the universe would provide for me… and that I should grow stronger… I thought it was impossible. But witnessing you best evil, as well as maintaining your equilibrium at all times… you're more than just my muse, dear…"

"Well, utilize that muse, that inspiration, to ever grow into a better, stronger star being, Helinara. No exceptions."

"Yes, sweetie. I'll try. For you."

"Not for me. For yourself. You're the one that's going to benefit from your improvements."

"Yes, love…"

Helinara embraced Courage.

She held him close.

She closed her eyes.

His scent intoxicated her.

And she admired his powerful presence.

This man is all I "ever" think about. He smells so good. And he's so dominant. I'm getting wet. And I feel like I'm about to pass out. Gracious…

Then, she looked into his eyes.

Next, she kissed his lips.

She moaned.

He was shocked.

H-Helinara…

I couldn't help it, Courage. I love you so very much.

After a while, she slowly withdrew from his lips.

So sweet. Just like I expected from you, my Sacred Star.

She secured her arms around his neck.

She massaged the back of his neck.

She gazed at him seductively.

Come with me to my constellation, sweetie. Make love to me. As much as you want.

Very tempting. But maybe… next time…

Of course, honey. You know what's best.

Courage regain his composure.

"Helinara, we should attend the Velmelkia Dance Hall at once. Flowerensia and the others expect us."

"Yes, honey. Anything you want. Always."

Helinara and Courage vanished from Aereshia Meadow.

A variety of music was played at the Velmelkia Dance Hall.

Sometimes by a DJ.

Other times by different bands.

Courage displayed his unrivaled talent in musicianship.

He usually played Staraidus Museala melodies from his conscious.

However, he played a variety of instruments, as well as participated in orchestras.

He created numerous symphonies with them.

Velmelkian Jazz, Rock, Metal, Techno, Rap, and music of many genres were conducted.

Melharina and co. sat at a large roundtable.

"Damn, Courage is so talented!" Melharina said. "The music he plays is beyond excellent! He's incredible!"

"Agreed," Sadon stated. "Not only is he an exceptional fighter, but he's a remarkable musician as well."

"Yes…" Helinara and Asai blushed.

"I have a feeling this is going to be an interesting day," Melharina said.

"Alright, who's ready for the Velmelkia Slow Dance?" Flowerensia queried.

The Velmelkian Nation cheered.

"Great! Now everyone knows how this works. For one minute, you have to dance with someone. Then, you have to switch partners. Use this time to get acquainted with everyone."

Flowerensia played the official Velmelkia Slow Dance melody from the DJ turntable.

The tune consisted of a violin, a harp, a flute, and a piano.

Periodically, a xylophone would commence a solo.

The Velmelkia Slow Dance theme was called 'Eternal Bonding'.

The Velmelkian Nation started dancing with someone special.

Likewise with Melharina and co.

Courage and Velcrimia were standing near each other.

Then, Velcrimia looked at Courage.

She blushed.

Oh dear, it's Courage. Would he want to dance with me?

Next, Courage looked at her.

"Hey, care to dance, Velcrimia?"

"Y-yes. Very much."

Courage held her waist with his left hand.

And he gently held her hand with his right hand.

Velcrimia placed her right hand on his shoulder.

They intertwined their fingers.

Then, Velcrimia slowly swayed her hips to the rhythm.

Courage stepped to the tempo.

They held each other close.

This was the formation of the Velmelkia Slow Dance.

As Velcrimia and Courage gazed into each other's eyes, her blush intensified.

"You're good at this slow dance, Velcrimia."

"Thank you... So are you."

Courage chuckled.

Velcrimia giggled.

"Oh Courage..."

"Velcrimia..."

Asai danced with Gravulkim.

"Wow, Gravulkim. You're a gentle bear."

"And you're a cuddly bunny."

They laughed.

Ulanahar danced with Janeiholm.

"Lana... this makes me feel weird..."

"That's because you have some maturing to do, Janeiholm. You can't always be a hyperactive ass all the time."

"Well, *excuse* me, beautiful. I never thought this romantic thing could happen to me... Cut the music, cut the torture, please..."

Ulanahar squeezed his shoulder.

She held him closer.

Then, she purred.

"Shut up... and deal with it."

"Yes, ma'am..."

Helinara danced with Sadon.

"Hey uh... Helinara. If it means anything, I apologize about before. I didn't mean to yell at you."

"No, you were right. I got carried away. And I should become stronger. You and Courage told me this."

"I promise you will."

"Thank you, Mr. Lion!"

They chuckled.

Transidyus danced with Melharina.

"Well, look who I have here. The Celestial Horse himself. An honor. And a pleasure."

"Likewise, Melharina. The Goddess of Light... the exceptional one among the deities."

Melharina chuckled.

"If we had a room, I'd show you what's *really* exceptional."

"You're amusing, Melharina."

"I'm dead serious, love. The possibilities are endless."

"I know they are endless. Just like the universe."

"You have a way with words, dear. Almost poetic."

Melharina blew a kiss at Transidyus.

Serenity danced with Leiku.

"Grandmaster Leiku, it's an honor dancing with you."

"Likewise, Serenity. You have the moves of a Millennial Star."

Serenity giggled.

"As do you."

And Kimiko danced with Flowerensia.

"All the dicks are taken, Flowerensia. So it's just you and me now."

"Yeah, but don't get any strange ideas, Kimiko. I know you."

"Too late. There's a shit ton of things I'd like to do to you right now."

"What the hell? No. You can't."

"I'm *way* stronger than you, so I can do whatever the hell I want to you, sweetie. I *promise* you'll enjoy every moment."

"You're perverted, Kimiko. Gracious…"

"Cut the bullshit, Flowerensia. You know damn well if Courage were telling you nasty shit, you would've fainted by now."

"Damn it. True…"

Kimiko fondled Flowerensia's buttocks.

Then, she squeezed them.

Flowerensia was startled.

She grasped Kimiko's hand.

"Hands *above* the hips, Kimiko!"

Flowerensia placed Kimiko's hand on her waist.

Kimiko chuckled.

Next, Kimiko whispered seductively into Flowerensia's ear.

"I bet your cunt, tits, toes, and lips taste delicious…"

Kimiko gently blew on Flowerensia's ear.

Flowerensia shivered.

This girl's gonna be the death of me…

Kimiko snickered.

Everyone switched dance partners.

However, Courage was unfortunate to be paired with Helinara.

She purred.

"Well, well, well… look who I have in my hold once more…"

"Yeah… how amusing…"

"Our kiss wasn't amusing. It was beyond the sweetest thing we ever shared. I'd like to share my all with you whenever you're ready."

"Gracious…"

Helinara giggled.

"Feel free to grab a handful, dear. This ass is all yours."

"Shut up, Helinara."

"Maybe if you put *something* in my mouth, I'll "shut up". Punish this bad girl. Punish this bad o' Celestial Deer, my brave Celestial Bull."

"Ugh… I don't think I'd last a day in your universe…"

Helinara laughed.

Then, she kissed his cheek.

"Yes, you could. I know you'd break me. Just like you did to Asai. I bet her taste still lingers in your mouth. I believe Deathelena is another admirer. You can have any Mayethikayian female, let alone any female, that you want. Including me."

"You're right. However, I prefer my own class of women. We Mayethikayians offer so much to each other that all other species pale in comparison. We're the envy of the cosmos."

"And we will always be the pinnacle of all things, sweetheart. You're the toughest man in the universe."

Helinara placed her hand on his.

Then, she moved his hand toward her buttocks.

Once there, she placed mild pressure on his hand.

She moaned as she made him grasp her firm buttocks.

Courage attempted to remove his hand, but she did not allow him.

"Tsk-tsk-tsk, dear. I hope it's soft and firm to your liking."

"It is, now let go."

"Not yet."

Then, she slid his hand up her miniskirt.

Next, she slid their hand past the waistband of her purple underwear.

She made him grasp her bare buttocks.

She moaned once more.

However, Courage removed his hand from her underwear.

He placed his hand on her waist once more.

"We're supposed to be dancing, Helinara. Not borderline fucking."

"We can make love. And we eventually will. The offer's always open. I want to show you how much I appreciate you. I want my taste to linger in your mouth. From my face to my toes. Something I know you're very keen on. So sensual, yet passionate."

"You're obsessed."

"And I'll never let up. You're my only inspiration. I'll never forget you. Thank you. For everything."

Melharina and co. conversed at their table.

"If Courage can rap, your reign of the Velmelkia Rap Battles is over, Janeiholm," Gravulkim said.

"We'll see about that…" Janeiholm stated.

Janeiholm approached the stage.

He grabbed a microphone.

Then, he spoke.

"Hey, excuse me, everyone. I have an important announcement to make."

The Velmelkian Nation looked toward Janeiholm.

"Thank you, thank you for your undivided attention," Janeiholm said.

Kimiko giggled.

"First, I would like to congratulate my main man Courage for always whoopin' ass. Let's give him a round of applause."

The Velmelkian Nation cheered.

"Now, here's the bad news," Janeiholm continued. "I hereby challenge him to a rap battle. If he beats me, I'll acknowledge that he's the greatest in all of musicianship. If he loses, well… he has to do Helipak's Happy Dance!"

"Oh hell yeah!" Helinara exclaimed.

"While blindfolded!" Janeiholm added.

"Oh my, yes!" Helinara shouted.

"Hey, wait a minute!" Courage said. "Don't I get a say in this? And what the hell is… Helipak's… Happy Dance…?"

"Trust me, you don't wanna know…" Janeiholm stated. "It's the goofiest shit you'd ever see, let alone partake in."

"Hey, Cranky Jaguar!" Helinara called. "Shut your pie hole before I do it for you! The *hard* way! You better sleep with one eye open, asshole!"

"Okay, moving right along…" Janeiholm said. "So what's it gonna be, big man Courage? You up for the challenge? Whoever receives the loudest cheers is the winner. Since I'm the champ, I go first."

"Alright. I accept."

"Great! Grab a mic while I put on a beat."

Courage obtained a microphone from its stand.

Janeiholm played an upbeat tune from the DJ turntable.

This melody was the official tune for the Velmelkia Rap Battles.

It was called 'The Face Off'.

Then, Janeiholm and Courage stood before one another.

Janeiholm was smug.

Courage was calm.

"Whenever you're ready, you may begin, Janeiholm," Flowerensia stated.

"Got it, beautiful."

Janeiholm began.

"Listen, I hate to be the bearer of bad news,

"But it's time I give you the blues,

"See, you haven't a clue 'bout this groove,

"As it took you an eternity to finally make your debut!"

The Velmelkian Nation yelled in shock.

He proceeded.

"See, I been livin' it up while you were too busy chillin',

"You're not the only one who's bested these hardheaded villains,

"Though I respect your strength, it was already a given,

"'Cause I been bustin' heads and makin' bitches swimmin'!"

The Velmelkian Nation screamed.

Flowerensia paused the record.

She conjured a microphone.

"Alright, you're next, Courage!"

Flowerensia resumed the record.

"This should be good," Melharina said.

Then, Courage started.

"You talk a good game!

"But everyone knows you're a fucking lame!

"Your problem is that you have nothing to gain!

"With the way you act, how can anyone around you stay sane?

"Like, how can you keep crazy tame?"

Janeiholm and co., as well as the Velmelkian Nation, were amazed.

Most of them laughed at Janeiholm's detriment to Courage's insults.

Others praised Courage.

"So intense," Melharina stated.

"Very," Helinara and Asai blushed.

He continued.

"I'm the best in the game!

"You no longer make it rain!

"Because while you were too busy slacking, I was bringing the pain!

"You should sit in the corner until your stupidity wanes!"

Flowerensia paused the record.

She placed her hands over her mouth.

She wanted to laugh very much.

Yet, she refrained.

"Alright, everyone! Who do you favor? Our current Velmelkia Rap Battle Champion, Janeiholm?"

The Velmelkian Nation cheered.

"Or, do you favor his contender, Courage?"

The Velmelkian Nation shouted.

"Hmm… seems to be a tie…" Flowerensia noted. "My guess is that everyone wants more savagery?"

The Velmelkian Nation screeched in approval.

"Alright, that settles it!" Flowerensia said. "Final round! Winner takes all! Janeiholm, you know what to do!"

She resumed the record.

Janeiholm commenced.

"Wow, buddy. A little hot under the collar?

"Seems to me you're a little sour,

"Aw, don't be so dour,

"If you weren't the legend, I'd be makin' you my bitch by the hour!"

The Velmelkian Nation felt the sting of the barb.

He proceeded.

"By the way, you'd be bangin' Helipak if it weren't for me,

"You'd be makin' him scream like a bitch giving him that good "D",

"Are you blind? Or just in desperate need?

"Because anyone with keen vision could tell he's not what he seems!"

Helinara licked her lips at Courage.

Yet, she raised her middle finger at Janeiholm.

Regardless, Janeiholm continued.

"You say I'm a lame?

"Yeah, I'd rather be a lame than an overrated Star of Shame!

"I have nothin' to gain?

"Bullshit, I have no bane,

"Because while Sadon laid you on your back, I was makin' your sweetie
go sweetly... *insane*..."

Janeiholm pointed toward Asai.

She was composed.

"Bullshit, because if you were to touch me,

"I'd have you sucking your own candy... *cane*!"

Janeiholm was shocked.

Then, he scoffed.

"Calm down, dear. The adults are talkin',

"Hard to believe you're still walkin' after he got finish fuckin',

"Surprised? Yeah, we know you two were lickin' and-a suckin',

"No one gives their power freely by merely huggin'."

The Velmelkian Nation shouted in surprise.

Asai's ire escalated.

She rose from her chair.

"Oh pardon me. Last time I checked, it didn't take me an age to confess!

"Oh, but I wouldn't expect total manhood from someone less!

"I look at you as nothing more than a pest!

"If you're feeling strong, my friend, why don't I put you to the…"

Asai raised her hands.

She turned the back of her hands toward everyone.

The Glyph of Tauran'creima emerged on the back of her right hand.

And the Glyph of Auderesa appeared on the back of her left hand.

Both glyphs illuminated their respective color: green for Tauran'creima. And purple for Auderesa.

The Glyph of Tauran'creima on her neck also brightened.

Furthermore, the Glyph of Scorpreikia beamed purple and black on her forehead.

She grinned.

"Test!"

Everyone gasped.

Courage chuckled.

Janeiholm flinched.

And Flowerensia paused the record.

"Extraordinary! Alright, Courage! This is your chance to take the win!"

She resumed the record.

Then, Courage began.

"Had a lot to say? I know it's hard to escape obscurity!

"Of course you wouldn't know the essence of true purity!

"It's no surprise you have a severe case of immaturity!

"But unlike you, I'll always provide eternal security!"

Helinara giggled.

Too true, love…

Courage proceeded.

"It's a damn shame you let a woman own you!

"Even if you had a crew, you'd still be at the bottom of her shoes!

"Whaddaya gonna do? Heckle and say boo?

"Hmph, if I were in your shoes, I'd be ashamed, too!"

The Velmelkian Nation laughed.

"And yes! Sadon gave me a way to go!

"But unlike him, you're oh so low!

"Between me and him, you can't go toe-to-toe!

"This is big boy town! Not a preschool row!"

Some people gasped.

Others chuckled.

"I'll admit, Transidyus and Leiku handed me my ass!

"If I face them again, I know I'll surpass!

"Compared to them, you're absolute trash!

"Oh, and put this in a hashtag!

"#You'reGivingMeARash!"

Melharina snickered.

Then, the Tauran'creima Aura coursed through the Vesorai.

Next, the Tauran'creima Aura framed his being.

Janeiholm was shocked.

Everyone gasped.

A breeze blew around the Velmelkia Dance Hall.

Tauran'orsai Vecoraigus Courage continued.

"Overdrive!

"Quit wasting my time!

"Your pretty little rhymes ain't worth grime!

"You wanna know why I'm so benign?

"It's because I'm a total savage!

"If not controlled, I'd wreak complete havoc!

"I'd have you and all before me in a state of panic!

"If I wanted, I could own everyone on this entire planet!

"Have you forgotten who you're dealing with, goddamn it!"

Everyone screeched their praise.

Janeiholm became worried for his title.

"Lastly, I'm a Sacred Melhouna!

"The Sacred Star of the Cosmos!

"Tauran'creima, the Eternal Legend!

"You're nothing but a pussycat with no owner!

"Oh, and by the way, my horns aren't just for piercing!

"Kimiko will tell you the *entire* story!"

Kimiko blushed.

You nasty, powerful bastard…

Tauran'orsai Vecoraigus Courage proceeded.

"Live up to the legend, kid!

"I already have bounties on my head!

"My Sacred Staraidus is off the grid!

"And trust me, whatever you've experienced, I already did, kid!

"This rap battle is dead!"

Tauran'orsai Vecoraigus Courage dropped the microphone.

Then, a large Tauran'orsai Tauran'creima Apparition appeared behind Tauran'orsai Vecoraigus Courage.

Next, the Tauran'orsai Tauran'creima Apparition and Tauran'orsai Vecoraigus Courage released Tauran'creima's Bellow.

Planet Venusia shook.

When the quake ebbed, Flowerensia stopped the record.

"Wow! Such intensity! Alright! Who do you all like? Your current Velmelkia Rap Battle Champion?"

The Velmelkian Nation cheered.

"Alright! What about Courage?"

The Velmelkian Nation screeched.

"Well, there you have it! Courage is your new Velmelkia Rap Battle Champion!"

Janeiholm bowed his head out of respect.

Then, he approached Asai.

They gently collided one of their fists.

A sign of mutual respect.

You did good, girl.

Likewise.

Next, he conjured a silver cap with a gold speaker logo in the center.

This was the Velmelkia Rap Battle Championship Cap.

Janeiholm approached Tauran'orsai Vecoraigus Courage.

Janeiholm placed the cap backward on Tauran'orsai Vecoraigus Courage's head.

Tauran'orsai Vecoraigus Courage chuckled.

"Courage," Janeiholm said. "You're the greatest musician of all time. Thank you, man. For everything."

"Of course, Janeiholm. Anytime. But hey, since you lost, you have to do Helipak's Happy Dance with him. Uh… her."

"Hell no!" Janeiholm protested.

Helinara emerged a few feet from Janeiholm.

Her arms were folded.

Her expression was stern.

And she tapped her foot impatiently.

"Oh I beg to differ, my chocolate hunk. I'm *always* in the mood."

"It ain't happening, Fruity Deer. Deal with it. And that deal was if Courage lost. Not me."

"I'm gonna pay you back for all that shit you were talking. It's either the Happy Dance or a *nice, long, painful* session with me and my Melordias Claws."

"Hey, fuck you, Helipak. I ain't doing your stupid ass dance. Fuck outta here, man."

Helinara licked her lips.

"You're just making it *harder* on yourself, love…"

Helinara ran toward Janeiholm.

Janeiholm teleported out of the Velmelkia Dance Hall.

Helinara vanished as well.

They appeared above the clouds.

"I gotcha now!" Helinara said.

"Courage, help!"

Helinara chased Janeiholm through the clouds.

Flowerensia and co. and the Velmelkian Nation were at Lofty Plains at sunset.

Courage stood upon a white stage that had Swa'reikei Wreaths surrounding it.

Flowerensia stood beside Courage.

"We're gathered here this evening to further recognize the extraordinary nature that is Courage! May the light ever be one with him!"

Flowerensia conjured a Swa'reikei Wreath.

She stood before him.

She gently placed the Swa'reikei Wreath around his neck.

She blushed.

"May victory always be yours, Courage."

Then, she conjured a Swa'reikei Wreath Crown.

She placed it on his head.

"May your wisdom ever prosper, hero."

Courage chuckled.

"Don't worry. All bases are covered."

Flowerensia's blush deepened.

"O-of course, dear."

"And… thank you, Flowerensia. This means a lot."

"Courage… you'll always have my gratitude. Thank you. For everything."

"You're very welcome."

"Is… there anything you'd like to say to everyone?"

"Of course."

"The stage is yours, dear."

Flowerensia left the stage.

Everyone gazed at Courage with immense admiration.

"When I first arrived here, I was skeptical of what awaited me. I had no idea who I would encounter. Let alone what I would do.

"I no longer think landing in this kingdom was happenstance. I believe Flowerensia was right when she told me it was destined that I arrive here one day.

"Hell, I wouldn't be surprised if Tauran'creima knew about the tragedy that befell this kingdom at a critical time in history."

I did. Deathelena is a very nasty sort.

Yeah… But out of all the planets, why did you send me here?

I already answered your question. You know your purpose.

Do you have to be such a dick about it?

It takes one to know one, Courage.

…Damn it. Got me there.

"Well, ladies and gentleman. Tauran'creima just clarified everything."

The Velmelkian Nation laughed.

"Regardless, I'm glad I met Goddess Flowerensia, Ruler of planet Venusia and Velmelkia Kingdom!

"I'm also glad I met the following beings:

"Velcrimia Teretri'aga Celestia!

"Ulanahar Eidomularus Gekonia!

"Asai Auderesa Rionai!

"Feloreigro, Ruler of Rhol'heima!

"Celestial Spirit Serenity Addlebeen, Ruler of Zeinhailurein!

"Sadon Leodycreus Frendumar!

"Transidyus Fireiya Misohareila!

"Leiku Ole'donmori Gania!

"Melharina, Goddess of Light!

"Kimiko Rinaigora Lybena!

"Janeiholm Epi'phinahas Secremel!

"Helipak Wyen'deishia Zetesteen!

"And Gravulkim Doncil'doras Sydemyic!

"These people had a tremendous impact on my life. The same applies to most of you who welcomed me into this blessed kingdom.

"For that, I thank all of you!"

The Velmelkian Nation applauded.

Helinara nudged Gravulkim.

He looked at her.

She grinned.

Remember what I told you. See how sweet Courage is? Yes, he can be very scary, but he means well.

Yeah. I remember. You were right. It's very humbling to witness someone of his caliber recognize those not even on his level. It's beyond incredible.

Courage raised his hands when he wanted to continue speaking.

The Velmelkian Nation settled.

"And though many of you may disagree, I also learned from those who're committed to evil.

"These beings are:

"Elaimia Besolei, Lieutenant General of the Hychineirian Nation!

"Fesforia Ramonicos Meilorei!

"Goddess Deathelena, Ruler of planet Gwempteya and the Hychineirian and Relmi'shirian Nations!

"And Oblivionu'crei, the Cosmos Destroyer!"

The Velmelkian Nation murmured.

"Now, before you all protest me, I'm very open-minded. I can learn from almost anyone and any experience. That's why I'm grateful to everyone I just named. I accepted the Swa'reikei Wreath and the Swa'reikei Wreath Crown..."

He placed his hand upon the Velmelkia Championship belt secured around his waist.

"As well as the Velmelkia Championship because I know I can always do better. Here's a quote I'd like you all to ponder on.

"Whatever endeavor I undertake, I intend to create a masterpiece."

"I expect all of you to do the same. Thank you."

The Velmelkian Nation cheered.

Then, Courage raised his hands once more.

The Velmelkian Nation calmed.

"I have one more concern... Does anyone know when the next tournament is going to start?"

The Velmelkian Nation laughed.

Flowerensia and co. placed their hand over their face.

Courage laughed.

"What? I'm serious. I get bored easily."

"Courage," Flowerensia said. "You defeated Deathelena *three* times. You defeated *three* gods. You were about to extinct the Relmi'shirian and Hychineirian Nations. You defeated *all* of your friends...

"You dethroned Sadon and Janeiholm of their respective championship. And you defeated an intergalactic diabolical entity. How much fight do you *have*? My gracious..."

"Hey, it's not my fault. It's just who I am."

"Courage, come to Leidonia Kingdom on planet Ki'ordyna," Melharina stated. "That's my planet and kingdom. I'll hook you up. See if you can win the Leidonia Championship."

Courage became excited.

"What? Really? When does it start?"

"I'll see if I can get everything set for you in a month."

"A month? Goddamn it... Alright, I'll wait."

The Velmelkian Nation and Melharina and co. laughed hysterically.

You're something special indeed, Courage. You always have this Light Goddess laughing.

Courage chuckled.

Then, he placed his fist on his hip.

He turned toward the setting sun.

He was pensive.

New beginnings. I can't wait to witness what else awaits me.

The End

See you next time!
The next tale awaits!

CPSIA information can be obtained
at www.ICGtesting.com
Printed in the USA
LVHW110802130722
723390LV00003B/37